More Books by Daisy

Wingmen
Ready to Fall
Confessions of a Reformed Tom Cat
Wingmen
(a boxed set of Ready to Fall
& Confessions of a Reformed Tom Cat)
Anything but Love
Better Love
Small Town Scandal
Wingmen Babypalooza: A Christmas Babies Novella
The Last Wingman (Coming 2018)

Love with Altitude:
Next to You
Crazy Over You
Wild for You
Up to You (Coming June 2018)

Modern Love Stories:
We Were Here
Geoducks Are for Lovers
Wanderlust
Love, Laughter and a Happily Ever After

Tinfoil Heart

USA *TODAY* BESTSELLING AUTHOR

DAISY PRESCOTT

Jessie—
Believe in
the Impossible!
xo
Daisy Prescott

Cover Design: © By Hang Le

Editing: There for You Editing

Interior Design & Formatting: Type A Formatting

To RH, I still see the moon.

Prologue

"GO WEST."

I reread the note from my dead mother for the millionth time. Grease and dirt stain the edges of the single piece of notepad paper. Other than the messy scrawl of my mother's attempt at cursive writing, the page is blank. Two words. Six letters. Not enough to make an interesting anagram or a code to help me decipher a hidden meaning. Stew go. Got sew. Wet Gos, could be short for Wet Gosling. That one is my favorite, but I doubt Mom had Ryan on her mind when she wrote it.

The paper is from a notepad that hung on our fridge for years. Decorated with red chili peppers around the edges and "New Mexico" written along the top, it's hokey and unremarkable.

Maybe it's an old joke. Pioneers trudged west in the hope of a better life. Freedom and opportunity waited in the land of big sky. The great West of legends, full of promise only empty, uncharted land can have.

Or a nod to her favorite book, *The Great Gatsby,* where a group of Midwesterners get sucked into the glamor and razzle-dazzle of the big city. Spoiler alert, it doesn't end well for most of them. At least that's what I remember about what I read in high school.

Folding the paper along the dark lines, I tuck it back inside of my wallet before pulling out two twenty dollar bills to tip the men from the junk removal company.

"That's the last of it, miss," the bulkier of the men says, smearing droplets of sweat on his forehead with the thick hair on his forearm. "Glad we got it done before this heat gets worse."

Seems there's always a bulkier man and a taller man in these types of scenarios. Straight from a Hollywood casting office for a buddy movie.

His thinner, taller colleague shifts his weight from foot to foot, pretending not to stare at my breasts where the August humidity glues the thin cotton of my dress to my bra.

Without glancing down, I peel away the fabric and use it to create a light breeze over my damp skin. One of the joys of being short and curvy is taller men have a direct view of my cleavage unless I wear a crewneck, or even better, a turtleneck. Loose curls escape my ponytail and cling to my neck like sticky noodles to a wall. The thick, gray sky teases rain, a promise of a storm to break through the humidity.

Taller of the two licks his lips and blatantly shifts his personal junk around in his shorts using the palm of his hand. With a lazy smile, he asks, "You staying in town?"

He's familiar, but I don't know his name. Don't remember it from when they showed up an hour ago, and I won't bother to learn it now. There's no point in gathering more useless information like names of men I'll never see again.

I'm never coming back here.

"Well, thanks for taking everything." I wipe my hands on my skirt and try to put them in the dress's pockets, only remembering too late this dress doesn't have them.

What a waste of a nice blue floral summer dress. Every dress should have pockets. So should cardigans. This is why I buy mine in the men's section of thrift stores. Old man cardigans always have pockets for candy or rubber bands, or whatever old men need to carry in their sweater pockets. My own grandfather put butterscotch and star mints in his. At his funeral a few years ago, I snuck a couple pieces of each into his casket.

Full of rejects from the garage sale, the big truck drives away. I stand alone in the driveway. The desire to wave good-bye hits me in the center of my chest, and I realize it's not the stuff I'm going to miss, it's my life.

Behind me, my grandparents' house, the only home I've ever known, is an empty shell. Shadows of old frames and mirrors fill the walls, revealing the true colors of the Laura Ashley floral wallpaper my grandmother installed in the eighties. Sunlight faded carpet darkens where the sofa and Grandpa's favorite recliner once sat. Upstairs, the bathroom sink still drips, unaware no one is here to curse at the incessant tap, tap, tap against the pink porcelain.

Let the new owners deal with the unreliable plumbing.

The closing is tomorrow. A new family will move in and fill this house with their own memories. I hope they replace the carpet—it's seen some shit. Literally.

I'm alone.

Single.

No living family.

Can an adult be an orphan? Sure feels that way.

An orphan at twenty-seven. Too old for Daddy Warbucks to swoop in and adopt me into a life of wealth. No adorable mutt by my side to listen to my sad story.

I don't even have cats.

The last pet I had was a depressed goldfish. He could barely muster up the interest to do laps around his bowl. I could totally relate to him feeling trapped, living a monotonous existence without purpose or passion.

My entire life has been spent in this faded upstate town, long past its prime. Whatever good or interesting that could happen here, already has. Tethered here by my family and small town expectations, I've tried to make the most of growing up in a place where success is an echo and hope is a memory.

Now there's no reason to stay.

A strange sense of freedom expands my ribcage as I inhale the thick, humid air of the New York August day.

Now I can go anywhere. Adventure and the open road await.

Go west.

I stayed because of her.

Mom left once. Right out of high school. She packed up, impatient to put miles between her and this forgotten place. When she came home six months later, pregnant and married, her adventure became an example of why it's better to accept our place in the world than expose ourselves to unknown disappointments.

At least that's what the locals like to remind me.

The grass is never greener.

What about my father?

He followed her home and stayed. For a while.

Until he left in the middle of the night.

At first mom said he was away on a business trip.

Then the story changed to caring for a sick relative out of state.

Eventually, she told me the truth.

He'd been abducted.

By aliens.

One

Ten months later . . .

"HE'S HERE AGAIN. Table five," Wanda whispers conspiratorially, jabbing her pen in the air behind us.

Ignoring her, I finish filling a glass with Coke and set it on the tray next to the other two pops. I continue to ignore her and her pointing pen while I add ice to a fourth red plastic cup before squeezing the soda stream and repeating the process.

"Oh, look, a family just sat in my section. Guess you'll have to take over table five." She tucks her pen into her teased, brassy blond hair and grins at me. Today's lipstick is the frosted peach. Against her deeply tan skin, it reminds me of orange sherbet melting in the blaze of the New Mexico sun.

"I'm busy." I lift the tray and balance it on the open palm of my left hand.

Delaying the moment until I'll see him, I pretend I don't know where table five is located. I even take the long way around the small space to avoid putting him in my sight line.

After setting the drinks on the table, I smile at the tops of the men's heads as they stare down at their screens. They're regulars and I'm used to them finding their phones more interesting than the humans around them.

Going rogue, my traitor eyes search the sun-filled dining area for a familiar trucker cap squashing a cyclone of dark hair.

"Ready?" I ask, attempting to sound chipper and happy to be taking their breakfast order in a diner inside a convenience store where the faint scent of gasoline mixes with maple syrup.

Just west of this truck stop, the Pecos River snakes through a narrow channel full of shallow muddy water through flat scrubland. Color me unimpressed. Like most things in my life, the reality far underwhelms expectations. I know there are other more scenic sections of the mighty river, but my illusion is still destroyed.

In my head I always imagined the Pecos to be a majestic river winding through the high desert of New Mexico and the far edges of Texas. A deep blue line through the dusty rose and pale silver green banks like a painting.

I blame my dad.

His well-loved copy of Zane Grey's *West of the Pecos* sat in the bookcase like a mystical text. The brown lettering on the cream-colored spine barely visible from years of being cracked open for yet another read. My doodles from childhood decorate the title page. It's one of the few possessions I took with me from my old life.

After I scribble down four breakfast orders, I pick up the drinks tray and follow the same path back to the waitress station next to the kitchen.

Only then, from the safety of distance, do I allow myself to peek at the two-top table in the corner next to the window.

Table five.

First thing I notice is the boring, off-white coffee mug flipped right side up to indicate he'd like coffee. Next to the mug is a neat pyramid of three individual half and half containers. He's placed the thin paper napkin in his lap, betraying good manners despite his elbows on the table. The sugar canister remains untouched because he doesn't like his coffee sweet.

Once I've itemized everything on the table, I let my eyes wander to him. Today's trucker hat is from the Albuquerque Isotopes, a minor league baseball team. Below the rim, his dark brows are drawn together as he studies his phone. I'm too far away to see if his irises are gold or green, or some combination of both, today.

Straight nose, slightly too long for his face, but not sharp. High, wide cheekbones create harsh angles on his cheeks where most people are soft. They're offset by a ridiculous mustache he likes to chew on when he's thinking. Sometimes he brushes his finger over the absurd facial hair.

I wonder if the texture is like a rough bottle brush or soft like a makeup brush. Running my finger across my upper lip, I fantasize about what it would feel like against my skin.

This is my life now. Daydreaming about kissing some random man's mustache.

A man who regularly eats at a restaurant inside a gas station convenience store with a gravel parking lot.

A man who wears trucker hats indoors.

A man who has never spoken to me beyond ordering his food or thanking me for bringing said food or the check. Most of the time he doesn't even do the last two. I could be a robot for all he's noticed me.

He's still the most beautiful man I've ever seen.

Not that it matters.

I'm not looking to fall in love.

There isn't much of a dating market around here. Majority of our customers are passing here through on their way to somewhere more exciting. Most local men work in the local oil fields, at the border patrol academy, or for one of the big agro businesses. Those guys are the eligible bachelors of the bunch.

I'm leaving out the alien hunters, tinfoil hat wearing, UFO obsessed conspiracy lovers, aka my people. I didn't choose them, or this life, but it's mine now.

My body shudders at the memory of my last date with a guy who spent dinner telling me how the Kennedys are all aliens. By the end of the hour, he'd only convinced me to remain celibate.

Mr. Mustachioed drums his fingers on the table while staring at his phone's screen. I notice the absence of a wedding ring on his left ring finger, and note there's no tan line or permanent indentation either. Not currently or formerly married. Interesting. How does a handsome, apparently healthy specimen remain single around here? Probably his lack of personality.

I swing by the coffee station and pick up the fresh pot. At his table, I pour enough to fill his cup and still leave room for his pyramid of creamers.

"Ready to order?" I ask the top of his lime green hat.

Tilting his head back, his eyes flicker up from the screen. They're green today.

His gaze settles on my shoulder before focusing on the television mounted across the room. The long, dark lashes around his green eyes beat together as he blinks. Totally and completely unfair that men have naturally thick, pretty lashes.

"Uh, what's the special?" he asks, staring at the business channel streaming commodity prices along the bottom.

"Chile relleno with your choice of eggs. I think we still have some corned beef hash. And of course we have pecan pancakes." I don't bother to fake my usual friendly enthusiasm. It's Thursday. By now he should know the specials. Like the TV station, they never change.

"I'll have the pecan pancakes," he replies, equally as flat.

"Sure." I don't bother writing down his order.

Wanda's at the register and gives me a sly smile when I approach. "Saw you talking to him."

"He wanted to know the special. He wasn't flirting."

"Oh, I wouldn't know about that. Maybe he's shy and just wanted to hear your voice." She digs around in her hair for her pen.

"Not even you could mistake his obvious lack of interest as quiet pining." I enter table five's order in the computer.

Humming, she fluffs her hair. "The quiet ones are always the most interesting."

I know I don't want her answer, but I don't stop myself from asking, "Why? Because they don't speak and can't ruin the illusion of being a decent human?"

"I was thinking more about in the bedroom. I dated this man once. He barely spoke five words the entire night but the things he could do with his tongue made up for his silence."

Closing my eyes, I exhale a breath to find my patience for her stories. Wanda shares in an attempt to be friendly. Or at least that's the nicest excuse I can make for knowing way too much about her life, especially her sex life. Her stories are fascinating and she can make herself laugh over the simplest encounter.

The woman was born to interact with people. Probably why she makes a lot more in tips than I do. Plus, she's local. Grew up down the road in Artesia. Wanda knows everyone and I'm pretty sure has worked here longer than I've been alive.

I'll be forever grateful she took me under her wing and showed me around when I first arrived six months ago.

According to her, she knows people who know people who have proof about the infamous alien crash seventy years ago. I'm doubtful. Whenever I've asked her to introduce me to these people, it never happens. Instead, I've been introduced to more secondary connections who always know someone, but never the actual someone. Frustrated, I've given up asking her.

Now I'm another random waitress in a truck stop on a two-lane road in the middle of nowhere USA just east of the not-so-mighty Pecos River.

When I swing through the tables to refill coffee cups and drop off a couple of checks, table five is staring at the TV, furiously typing on his phone. I add coffee to his cup like an invisible ghost. His only acknowledgment is a frown when he lifts the cup and discovers its full.

He makes the same face when I drop off his pancakes and the syrup container. His brow lower as he examines his food that somehow magically appeared in front of him.

A few more regulars arrive, fresh from their early morning rounds of the oil fields. Outside, their white pickup trucks shine like a row of clouds against the bright morning sky. They greet each other, me, Wanda, and even Tony in the kitchen, as if they've entered the high school cafeteria.

Loud conversations drown out the droning of the business channel as the guys catch up on gossip.

Only Cranky in his green hat remains silent at his table in the corner.

He folds up his napkin and puts it on his plate, then rests his fork and knife on top. That's my cue to bring him the check. Knowing he won't want anything else, I already have it printed and tucked on a black plastic tray in my apron. I don't bother with the mint we're supposed to give customers with their bills. He won't eat it—always leaves them behind.

Silently, I slide the bill on his table and walk away.

He'll pay in cash and tip twenty-percent.

And never acknowledge my existence.

With a sigh, I plaster on my fake smile and greet my new table. "What'll it be, gentlemen?" I ask all friendly and smiley.

As they tell me their orders, I catch movement from the corner.

Mustache stands and pulls his wallet from the back pocket of his faded old Wranglers. He slips a couple of bills out of the worn black leather billfold, the kind my granddad used to carry, and sets them on the tray.

My eyes follow him as he saunters across the room to the double-glass doors leading to the parking lot.

Rather than push through the door with his hand, he turns and rests his back against the glass. For one brief moment our eyes meet across the room.

One second is all it takes for my breath to hitch and my heart to stumble in its rhythm.

Then I blink and the strangest thing happens.

He pauses, giving me a single, slow nod.

MY MIND IS still stuck on the single nod this morning. I've worked at the diner for six months and Mustache has been coming here daily for four of them. Sixteen weeks of breakfasts and sometimes lunches almost five days a week. We're talking at least sixty meals and not once has he ever smiled or nodded before.

He's obviously a weirdo.

A strange man.

A nut. And I'm a squirrel.

I'm obsessed with his silence.

At first, I tried to engage him same as I would any other customer. Chatting and smiling like a hired princess at a kiddie party. I would know. I've had that gig back home. With dark hair and pale skin, I can play at least three classic princesses and not have to wear a wig. I draw the line at clowns. I refuse to be a part of a traumatic childhood memory for some innocent kid.

This time of year there's not a huge market for princess cosplay in Roswell. The annual UFO festival officially begins next month, but the town is already abuzz with tourists because school's out and the great American summer road trip tradition has begun.

If it weren't for the aliens, there wouldn't be much reason for anyone to visit Roswell for anything more than gas, food, and lodging on the road to anywhere else. Whoever decided to make this town the official center for all things extraterrestrial and conspiratorial is a freaking marketing genius.

Even smarter than the guys who thought up the giant ball of twine or a palace made of corn to lure road warriors off the interstate to their towns. I have a lot of questions about those roadside attractions:

How big of a ball are we talking about? Don't birds and mice eat the corn cobs? That corn place has to have some major rodent problems.

These are the weird thoughts my mind focuses on.

Like I said before, I'm among my people here.

Sometimes we don't find our tribe, they choose us.

Growing up, I was told my father disappeared from my life not because he was a deadbeat loser but because an alien race of intergalactic travelers chose him of all people to kidnap as an example of the best humans have to offer. My mom believed this version of events with her whole heart.

It definitely makes for a better story than he ran out on his wife and nine-year-old daughter.

Especially in our small, forgotten town in the middle of nowhere upstate New York without a ball of twine or a corn-covered palace to keep it on the map.

His disappearance made the local paper. Then the national news got a hold of the story and we became semi-famous for a couple of weeks. Longer if you count the grocery store checkout where the *National Gossip* put its version of events in its front page headlines for months:

"Small Town America Under Attack by Aliens!"

"We ask the probing questions behind a rash of abductions in America's Heartland"

"Are Christians Being Kidnapped by Demons from Outer Space?"

"Roswell Aliens Return"

"Alien Abduction Diet: Lose 10lbs in a Day"

The articles were filled with interviews of "scientists" and "experts" who spun a fascinating narrative about people being ripped from their cozy beds and taken aboard spaceships where they were pricked, poked, prodded, and probed. Those lucky enough to return shared their nightmare encounters with the esteemed journalists of the *National Gossip* and other tabloids. According to my mom, some men, like my father, weren't so fortunate.

These experts came to the house and told my mother he was probably aboard a spaceship, comatose in a pod, speeding his way back to the home planet.

Trust me, I know how crazy this sounds.

Of course she wanted to believe her husband wasn't a loser scumbag who could leave her. As a kid I used to comfort my mom and reassure her he left because he was a selfish jerkface, not trapped as an alien medical experiment.

Why would the aliens choose him when they could have a noble prize winning physicist or mathematician? Someone useful to their cause?

From what I knew of the man who donated half my DNA, he wasn't exactly a blue ribbon winner. Other than his good looks. Mom shredded most of his photos, but kept a couple of him with me.

The weird color and fuzzy focus of the images make it difficult to see the details of his face. Tall, dark eyes when not red from a flash, and brown, short hair are what I remember most.

I was nine when he left.

I'm older now than Mom was when she became a single parent.

She always swore he was the funniest, most charming, smartest man she'd ever encountered. When they met, she thought he was perfect.

Evidently, she was wrong.

And had questionable taste in men.

Who leaves their little girl and wife behind with never a phone call or a letter?

Jerk face losers. Not perfect husbands and fathers.

Grandpa swore he was probably in the mob and went into witness protection. Or into the river in New York City with cement boots.

Sometimes when Mom wouldn't get out of bed for days, he'd get angry enough I worried that if Dad ever came back, Grandpa would kill him and bury him in the woods behind our house.

Maybe he already had.

At my high school graduation, I scanned the crowd for a man with dark hair and sunglasses who didn't seem to be sitting with anyone. I figured if my dad were in the witness protection program, letters and phone calls could be traced. I knew if he loved me enough he'd risk disguising himself to blend into a crowd.

I did the same thing when I graduated from the local state university. A much bigger crowd would provide better coverage. While the degrees were handed out name by name, I scanned the crowd for a dark haired loner in sunglasses, probably wearing a hat.

When my name was called, I smiled and waved at the audience, hoping to give him a sign I knew he was there without blowing his cover.

Because how could a perfect man disappear on his family?

Had to be the mob.
Or aliens.

Two

"CORNED BEEF HASH. Please." His deep voice rumbles when he speaks, like he's not used to saying so many words all at once. The pause between the order tells me please is an afterthought.

"Huh?" I ask, clearly struck dumb.

"If it's not sold out, I'd like the corned beef hash. With an egg over easy. Please." Still staring at his phone, he repeats his order, slowly and precisely.

"But you always get the pecan pancakes on Thursdays," I blurt, and then cover my mouth with the back of my hand.

Oops.

"I'll bring that right out," I mumble, then spin and speed toward the kitchen.

Only after I reach the coffee station, do I turn around. I fumble my pen when I catch him staring. Not at the TV and the boring business channel with the never ending loop of scrolling commodity prices. Not at his phone.

He's staring at me.

And then something even stranger happens.

His top lip lifts in amusement. Calling it a smile would be a stretch of the imagination, but it's a tiny seed that could grow into one with the right care and nurturing.

My eyes must be bugging out of my face and I realize my mouth hangs open in a fabulous impression of my depressed goldfish. Clamping my lips together, I turn to face the wall.

"I'm imagining things," I mutter, pressing my hands to my forehead.

"Why are you talking to the wall?" Wanda bumps my hip.

"I'm not."

"What's got you all flustered? The oil guys flirting with you again?" She twists her neck to scan the entire dining area.

I wave off the idea. "No, they're harmless."

"If they get handsy, tell me. Tony's not afraid to kick them out. They can find someplace else to eat around here."

Her pointless threat makes me laugh. "Only problem with that is there isn't anywhere else to eat around here. Not unless you drive all the way into town."

"Would serve them right to have to use more gas to get their morning coffee." She nods with a smug smile.

Wanda might put on the charms and smiles for the customers, but she holds a grudge against the oil workers. Not sure if it's a money issue or one of them broke her heart years ago, but she's always warned me to keep away from them.

The older ones aren't too terrible. Some of them tell sexist and racist jokes, but at least lower their voices when they do and I can pretend I didn't hear them. Unfortunately, that's the best option to preserve my tips. A lesson I learned when I first started and used to tell them off for being racist pigs. Sucks I have to put up with their bullshit, but I need this money.

The young, cocky ones who have the biggest trucks are more trouble. They think they're kings of the desert and should be fawned over by us lowly peasants. The newer the truck, the bigger the attitude. And probably the smallest dick.

Unlike most of the white company trucks, Grumpy drives

a gray rig covered in dust and bugs stuck to the radiator screen. Figures he's too lazy to wash it or take it to the car wash once in a while.

"Someone's staring at you," Wanda whispers close to my ear. Her strong floral perfume forms a bubble around us. "Is that why you're facing the wall?"

"No one is staring." Exasperated more with myself than her, I glance up at the ceiling.

"You won't see anything up there unless you're looking for faded ketchup stains and dust trails in the corners."

Sure enough, when I focus my eyes I land on a narrow thread of dust hanging off of the white ceiling tile above my head.

"Are you sure it's ketchup and not blood?" I ask, not really wanting to knowing if it isn't condiments gone wild. Most things in life are better if some of the nitty-gritty details are left out.

"Don't ask." Laughing, Wanda pokes my back with her pad. "Forget I ever mentioned blood stains on the ceiling.

"What?"

"Never you mind. No one shot anyone in here. Never happened, and if you look for a police report, you won't find one."

Sometimes I swear she makes stuff up to shock me. I give the ceiling another quick study. Surely if there was blood splatter, they'd spring for a couple new tiles. "That's got to be a violation of health codes."

"You'd be surprised by how many people never look up."

I stare at the ceiling. "I'm going to go with ketchup."

"What about ketchup?" Wanda gives me a wink that unsettles rather than reassures me. She gently reminds me, "Your tables are waiting."

Only two in my section are occupied. Table five and table six, which is currently home to a group of oil men. No one appears disgruntled or impatient. Although it's hard to tell without seeing their faces. That's because they're focused on their phones, necks angled down like swans.

How can black liquid be so interesting? Most of these guys are worker bees. The market goes up or drops, it doesn't affect their daily lives all that much. If one day a well suddenly runs dry or the refinery shuts down, I can see them getting their whiskers twisted. It's oil. It comes out of the ground and that's about as exciting as it gets around here.

I don't get it. When I first arrived, I tried to keep up with their shop talk, thinking it would be good to learn about the industry and be able to engage in small talk.

That lasted about a month. It's always the same, and more boring than a monotone voice online explaining mysterious lights in an Arizona night sky.

I can see why people become adrenaline junkies. We need something to break up the monotony of daily existence.

"Corned beef up," Tony says as he slides a plate under the heat lamps.

Walking to *his* table with his plate and the coffee carafe, uncertainty bubbles in my stomach. Will he speak to me again? Make eye contact? Now that he realizes his food and coffee are delivered by an actual sentient being, will things change?

"Anything else?" I ask the top of his head.

"Hot sauce if you have it. Please. Unless it's Tabasco, then skip it." He sets his phone down beside his half full coffee cup. "And a warm up, please."

Please count: four.

"Uh, sure," I mumble while filling his cup, leaving enough room at the top for his three creamers.

Lucy charm count: zero.

We usually keep green and red hot sauce on the tables, but his is missing. Maybe he stole them. Doubtful. I snag two bottles from an empty table and set them down across from his plate.

"Anything else?" I rest the bottom of the coffee pot on my palm. The heat starts to burn my hand and I jerk it back. The movement sends a small arc of scalding hot liquid right toward his bare arm. Cringing, I wait for contact, but luckily he shifts out of the way. Narrowly avoiding being burned, he glances to the left as the coffee falls to the floor.

Talk about lightning quick reflexes. I'd be covered in coffee if our places were switched. Grabbing a handful of paper napkins from the stainless tabletop dispenser, I wipe up coffee splatter from the table before crouching beside his chair and dabbing at the puddle. I'm eye level with his strong thighs encased in dark denim. This close I can see the individual dark hairs on his forearms and the small scar near his elbow. His scent wraps around me like a warm desert breeze full of sage and sandalwood. I wonder if it's soap or a cologne. He doesn't seem the aftershave kind of guy. Could be mustache oil or conditioner. Even up close, it's very well kept.

"I'm all set, thanks." His voice cracks through my thoughts.

"Oh, sorry. I'll clean this up. So sorry." I practically race across the restaurant and return the coffee pot to the warming plate.

"The man says a few polite words and I'm all up in his personal space like an over eager Yorkie." Shaking my head, I roll my eyes at myself.

"Talking to the wall again?" Wanda asks from behind me.

"Better than molesting costumers. I practically patted down someone's crotch after nearly scalding him with coffee."

"Did you?" Her face appears in front of me, eyes wide with shock, but mostly amusement. "'Bout time you made a move on the hottie."

"I don't think burning him near his favorite appendage is the way to win a man."

"Hell, I know I've threatened a few over the years. Excellent way to get their attention."

"Not the attention I want. Thank you." My hands shake as I pick up the water pitcher to check on my other customers.

After refilling some glasses and taking a few drink orders, I stop near table five to see if he's done eating. I don't get too close. Instead, I stalk him like a feral cat afraid of human contact.

As if sensing me, he lifts his gaze to where I stand.

I freeze, feeling pinned to the floor by his gaze.

"All done?" I ask, attempting to break the tension.

He nods, still staring. "Check would be good. Thanks."

Right. I haven't moved to take his plate. I dig in my apron for his check, and after pulling out everything from the pocket, realize that I never printed out the ticket.

"Be right back."

Wanda stands with her back to the counter, shaking her head and chuckling.

"Don't say whatever it is you're about to say," I warn her under my breath. "I don't know why you find this so amusing. Did you stop stealing your neighbor's HBO login again? You clearly need better entertainment if you're so amused by me."

"Cable's got nothing on you. I've never seen any two people more awkward than that little dance I witnessed."

With a deep exhale, I try to let it go. Engaging with her only feeds her amusement.

"Can you do me a favor?" I print my current tickets.

"Sure, hon." Wanda keeps her voice soft.

"Drop off these checks for me? I'm going to take my break now."

"No way," she replies, shaking her finger at me. "You're not due for another half hour. Pull up your skirts and march over there."

"You used to be my favorite person here," I tell her when she presses the tickets toward me.

"Still am." She steps away from me. "You can thank me later."
I flip off her back.

"Stop being rude and do your job, sweetheart," she says without turning around.

Instead of hiding in my car, I casually stroll over to table five with the check.

"All done?" I ask, reaching for his plate. It's a stupid question. The folded napkin and utensils on top tell me his finished. Unless he's going to eat his napkin, there's nothing edible left to consume.

"How come you never bring me a mint with my check?" Looking up, he makes eye contact. "All the other tables get a mint."

First, holy bananas are his eyes pretty today. Amber radiates through the green, a starburst through a swirling galaxy.

Second, he's been paying attention more than I think.

"You never take yours, so I stopped bringing them. You know, for environmental reasons." I throw in the last part to make it seem less petty.

He rolls his lips and chews on his mustache for a moment. "May I have a mint, please?"

That's it.

He doesn't question or comment. Simply accepts my answer.

"One mint, coming right up." I give him a thumbs-up for reasons unclear even to me. Maybe I'm welcoming him to the mint club.

Returning, I drop a handful of mints on the worn Formica of his table. "To make up for all the times you didn't get one."

His laughter surprises me. I wasn't sure if he could laugh at all. The sound coming out of his mouth is deep, rich, and kind of sweet, like a mocha. Irresistible.

AT FOUR A.M., I'm lying awake thinking about a man's laugh.

I can't sleep.

The AC hums to life, jogging through it's cooling cycle. Thick adobe walls keep the casita cool, but I like the white noise of the window air conditioner. Especially at night, when the quiet invites old memories to replay in my head.

Or in this case, new memories.

For months I've stared at Mr. Mustachioed while being comfortably ignored. I like the invisibility and anonymity of being a stranger in a new town.

Sure, the regulars know my name, but they don't really care who I am as long as I bring their food and listen to their chatter. A smile, a fake laugh, and a compliment is more than enough of me to give them.

He's different.

For the first time in months, I feel seen.

One glance, one moment of eye contact, and I'm no longer invisible.

I'm not sure how I feel about this.

Despite the air conditioner blowing cool air into my tiny bedroom, my skin is hot. Tossing off the thin cotton blanket, I starfish on my back for maximum cooling.

Instead, the soft breeze on my bare skin reminds me of the dream that woke me up almost an hour ago.

One conversation, if that's what we even had, and I'm dreaming about the tickle of soft facial hair brushing against my body. Specifically my thighs and stomach.

I woke up before the good part and now I'm restless, hot, and unsatisfied. Damn subconscious. Too long since I've had the real thing and now I can't even get the good stuff in a dream.

Rolling over, I press my pillow over my head and kick my legs in frustration.

Mustache and his stupid observational skills. He made a point of scooping up the pile of mints and taking them all with him. Suddenly he really cares about his post breakfast breath. Or he was making a point.

Either way, he left exactly twenty percent for a tip. Same as normal.

At least that hasn't changed.

I need those tips. Private investigators are expensive.

What I don't need for rent, car, food, and insurance mostly goes to paying an investigator.

The latest guy swears he's an expert in missing persons.

I've heard that before, but hope is a habit.

An expensive habit.

Knowing I won't be able to fall back asleep, I get up.

Might as well shower and dress for work.

And, of course, by work I mean seeing him.

The man I've been fantasizing about, the one who's spoken a few dozen words to me.

At this point, I'm sexually frustrated. I need to have an early morning session with my shower head so I don't explode if he smiles at me again. I might spontaneously orgasm if he touches me.

It occurs to me that my crush might be bordering on obsession.

I make a promise with myself that if I ever steal his used napkin or lick the fork he ate with, I'll check myself into a mental ward. Once I tell them about the alien abduction of my father, they'll lock me up.

It might be nice. Yes, I've thought about this before. Three meals a day, activities, someone who has to listen to me even if they're paid to do so. Sounds kind of lovely.

Right. I really need coffee if I'm considering how much better life would be if I were in a mental hospital.

This is why I'm going to die alone. If anyone had any idea of the crazy thoughts going through my head, especially when I'm tired and under-caffeinated, they'd put me away. Sometimes I freak myself out. Yikes.

Three

I'VE NEVER LIKED corned beef hash, but now I can't stop thinking about it. Not the actual meat but the low, masculine growl of the man who ordered it yesterday. Only he could possibly make chopped beef sound sexy. Heaven help me, I could develop a fetish based solely on him speaking random menu items.

We need to go back to the time when he didn't speak. Or kept his response to grunts and monosyllabic barks. I can handle those. Pretty sure I'm immune.

The sun isn't up yet when I pull into a parking spot behind the diner. If the front lot is filled with the shiny corporate trucks of oil workers and dust-covered SUVs of traveling families, the employee area is a mess of older vehicles whose better days were a decade ago. A tale of two parking lots reveals the difference between us and them.

Loud music pours out of the back door when I tug it open. Tony sings along to the Spanish lyrics at top volume while flipping a mountain of hash browns on the grill.

"You have a lovely singing voice, Tony. You should audition for one of those singing competitions on TV. You could be famous."

"You're late." He turns down the volume on the old school radio he keeps on a shelf near the range.

"I'm not." I double check the clock on the wall above our time cards. "Five-thirty on the nose."

"That's not early, so it must be late. Remember when you used to show up twenty minutes before your shift and sit in your car? What happened to that woman?"

"She realized she could get fifteen minutes more sleep and still make it to work on time."

"I like the other version better." He switches out his spatula for a spoon to stir a large pot full of bubbling, red sauce.

"Then you weren't paying attention. Those extra minutes of sleep make me a much nicer person. Add in coffee and some might even call me pleasant."

I dump my bag in my cubby before wrapping a black apron around my waist. The big boss man doesn't insist on a set uniform and doesn't require us to wear aprons, but I like them. I feel like Mr. Rogers putting on his cardigan. My apron sets the mood. I switch from real Lucy to Waitress Lucy. Easier to play a role of friendly server if I have the right costume.

"Wanda called and she's going to be late. Mind starting the coffee and getting the dining room ready?"

"Everything okay with her?" I ask, reaching for my favorite mug decorated with a flying pig and the words "I want to believe" above it.

"I didn't ask because I don't want to know the details. Next thing ya know, the three of us will be braiding each other's hair and gossiping about our love lives. If I want to do that, I'll watch telenovelas with my mother," he complains in a gruff tone.

I stare at his shaved head trying not to laugh.

"When you're finished laughing at me, bring me a cup of coffee when it's ready."

I've been dismissed and that's fine with me. There's no way I want to start sharing personal stuff with Tony the cook. Not that he's a bad guy, but I'm here in this middle of nowhere place because I like being anonymous. Not here to make friends.

Up front, I make a pot of regular coffee and one of decaf. Since Tony hasn't turned up his music again, I yell out to him, "You should get an espresso machine. Partner up with one of the local coffee roasters."

He responds by turning up the volume. I could learn a few things about non-verbal communication skills from the man. He's a master at the not subtle but silent message.

Keeping the lights off to deter any overly eager early bird customers, I move around the room to make sure we're ready to open at six. I give the tables a quick wipe with a clean rag and a few squirts from the mystery blend in the spray bottle.

The scent of brewing coffee drifts above the subtle smell of bleach from the rag. The coffeemaker sputters and puffs out steam as it finishes brewing.

"Yes," I whisper and do a small shimmy with joy over the idea of fresh coffee. I'm a firm believer in the expression about dancing like no one is watching, but only when no one is watching.

I swing my rag over my head in a wide circle to celebrate the impending jolt of caffeine.

Spinning around, I stumble when I see a figure standing in the entrance from the adjoining convenience store. I might've even let out a small scream of surprise but I'm not sure if the weird dinosaur squawking sound comes from me. It's not a sound I've ever made.

Then again, I've never had table five sneak up on me while I was dancing around with a rag like a sad solo production of the dance of the seven veils.

"Sorry. I smelled the coffee and assumed you were open."

"Your mustache is gone," I blurt out like I have the right answer on a game show.

He sweeps his index finger over the smooth skin of his upper lip. "Guess it is."

"Why?" I ask, temporarily forgetting we don't speak other than in restaurant lingo.

His brow pulls together. "Lost a bet."

"And had to shave it?" I don't know if I'm asking because the thought makes me sad or happy. Mustaches are weird. And often historically malevolent.

His finger returns to stroke the newly smooth skin, but he doesn't respond right away.

My skin prickles as he scrutinizes me, evaluating me. For the first time I feel like he actually sees me, not just a waitress who brings his breakfast.

He drops his hand and steels his shoulders. "What's your name?"

"Why?" My voice barely lifts above a whisper.

"I realize I don't know your name." Taking a few steps, he moves farther into the diner.

I swallow down the urge to be snarky. "Lucy."

"Nice to meet you, Lucy." He extends his hand. "I'm Boone."

I should tell him I've heard some of the other men greet him by name before, but I don't mention it. I don't want to ruin this moment. Telling each other our names feels important.

I hold out my hand and he grips it, warm palm and long fingers wrapping themselves around mine. Our eyes meet and I lose track of the seconds. With a squeeze, he releases my hand. I leave it extended, craving more contact.

"Is it too early for breakfast?" He shifts his weight from one foot to the other. "If it is, could I bother you for a cup of coffee in a to-go cup? The stuff they sell in the store is made of tar and the dregs of yesterday's leftover coffee."

With a glance at the clock on the wall, I confirm it's a few minutes to six.

"Have a seat." I point to his usual table.

"Mind if I sit at the counter?"

"Why would I?" As I walk over to the coffee station, I give him a genuine smile over my shoulder, even though I'm still embarrassed he witnessed my interpretive dance to the coffee gods. "You're the only one here and can sit wherever you want."

He slips onto a stool and gives it a small spin.

After pouring him a coffee, I slide a full mug over the counter to Tony in the kitchen.

"Let me switch on the TVs for you." Searching near the cash register for the remote, I finally locate it and hit the on button.

"Don't do it just for me."

I turn to face him. "But you guys always watch the business channel."

"Us guys?" A small twitch of his cheek tells me he's fighting a smile. "I usually sit alone. In case you hadn't noticed."

He's busted me.

"The regular breakfast and lunch crowd always watches the same boring blah blah blah about barrel prices and production demands."

He studies me, his finger once again stroking the smooth flesh above his lip. Damn it. I want to find out if it's smooth like his cheekbones or already rough like fine sandpaper as the hair grows back.

"You're in oil country, you know that, right?" he says sarcastically. "Around here, people live and breathe crude. Unless a hurricane is in the Gulf and heading toward the refineries or the local football team has a chance to go all the way to state, we don't care much for local gossip on TV."

"Way to be good citizens," I mumble before I stop myself from starting a speech on the environment and fossil fuels being behind climate change. When I started, Wanda warned me to keep my views to myself. Said no one wants to hear a waitress's opinion on anything but the coffee and the food.

"Sorry?" His eyes flash with amusement even though I've kind of insulted him.

"Nothing." I pick up the remote and turn on the business channel. Normally we mute the sound when it's busy in here since no one can hear it anyway. Because it's only him, I turn up the volume before grabbing a mug and three creamers.

"Did I say something to offend you?" he asks when I set his coffee down in front of him.

"Not at all. I stopped myself from saying something that might offend you. Tony doesn't like it when we speak our minds. 'Here to serve with a smile and keep your shit to yourself' is his motto. I'm thinking about making a cross-stitch for him."

Mustache laughs.

I'm going to need a new nickname for him. I guess I could start calling him Boone, since that's his name.

"I lost a bet and had to grow a mustache and keep it for three months."

It takes me a moment to figure out he's answering my question about his mustache. I pour coffee for myself and add a couple of creamers. "Sounds like a wager you should've avoided."

He smiles behind his cup. "I was overly confident about winning. Still think there was cheating involved, but I can't prove it."

If I thought he was handsome when he was silent and cranky, I was being naïve. When he smiles, he's a god amongst us mere mortals. Blinded by his good looks, I focus on stringing words together to keep him talking with me. "Sounds like a serious bet. What did the other guy get for winning?"

"She. I should've known better than to bet against a woman."
Girlfriend?

I'm not sure I want to know more. With a glance at the clock, I decide to unlock the front door. The sun is already up and streaming through the south-facing windows. "Be right back."

George, one of the older guys who always sits with a group, gets out of his white truck and strolls inside as soon as I flip the sign.

"Gonna be a scorcher," he greets me before sitting down at his regular table. He does a double-take when he spots Boone at the counter.

"Morning." Boone dips his chin.

"Didn't recognize you without the fuzzy mouth caterpillar. Sharyl let you off the hook early?"

Torn between wanting to know more about Boone and not wanting to have to know he has a girlfriend, I busy myself with bringing a set of flatware and a glass of ice water to George.

"Coffee this morning?" I ask.

"Better make it decaf. Been up since four and already finished a pot. And bring me a glass of tomato juice, no ice, please."

I swallow back a small gag. I can't stand tomato juice. Something about how it clings to the glass after you drink it reminds me of plasma. "Sure thing."

Boone openly watches me as I return to the counter. We keep single serve cans of tomato and grapefruit juice in a cooler, along with the mini cups of half and half. When I open the tomato juice, I turn my head so I don't have to smell it.

"Not a fan?" he asks, a mix of amusement and curiosity.

I wrinkle my nose. "What's the opposite of a fan?"

"Enemy? Adversary?" he offers as I pour the vile liquid into a small glass.

"Hater sounds about right." Shaking my head in disgust, I toss the can in the trash.

"What about Bloody Mary's?"

"Adding vodka would just be a waste of vodka."

"You feel very strongly about this. Have you ever tasted it?

Some people love it, especially on flights."

I stare at him in horror. "I don't fly, so that won't ever be a remote possibility of me changing my mind because I'm hurtling through thin air in an aluminum can at thirty thousand feet and suddenly want to drink a glass of liquid tomato. No thank you."

"Tomatoes are a fruit, you know. It's not that crazy to drink the juice."

I give him some major side eye before delivering the glass to George. This is the most Boone and I have ever said to each other since I began working here.

"Ready to order or are you going to wait for the rest of the crew?" I ask George, setting down the glass of tomato juice with a forced smile. While he pretends to study the menu, I sneak glances over at Boone. He catches me a few times and we lock eyes. Even his half smile might be my new favorite thing.

George clears his throat. "What's the special?"

I cast my attention to him. "Same as every Friday. Chicken fried steak, Christmas-style with hash browns."

"My heart doctor would kill me for eating that."

"I can bring you some oatmeal and a cup of fruit. Or a mini box of cereal with some skim milk and a side of dry wheat toast." I play my part of our routine.

"Well," he drawls out like he's considering the healthy options, "guess it's a good thing the good doctor is up in Albuquerque and won't know I had the chicken fried steak. Skip the red sauce and put some extra green chiles on the side for me."

If Wanda were here, she'd convince him to skip the gravy. I say he's a grown man. "Side o' gravy. Got it."

Passing Boone, I ask him if he's going to order, too.

"Huevos rancheros, please."

I'm tempted to ask him what happened to pecan pancakes, but who am I to judge a man for exploring new things.

After putting in their orders, I get lost in the morning rush. I barely have time to drop off Boone's order and fill his coffee. So much for chatting with him. Other than a few stolen glances from me, we don't interact until he asks for his check. I keep it professional and even give him a mint.

Figures he has a girlfriend.

Whoever Sharyl is probably wouldn't appreciate me flirting with her man.

Four

"SURE, IF YOU'RE gullible enough to believe the government." My date jabs his burger with his fork before slicing off a bit with a knife.

Ignoring that he's using cutlery to eat a burger with a bun, I decide to dive into the crazy pool with him. There's no way we're going on a second date, so might as well have some fun and learn new things. Which is the whole point of these dates. I'm not looking for love.

"What's the proof? Where's the hard evidence?" I ask before sipping my water. I never drink on first dates in case I need full sobriety to make a quick getaway.

Jared rattles off the names of several of the biggest alien conspiracy websites and YouTube famous names. Millions of people have read their theories and watched the videos. Yet after years of following them for answers about my dad, not one of them has convinced me aliens are real. UFOs are slightly more plausible.

"In today's world of smart phones and global tourism, is it possible aliens walk among us and not a single person has photographic evidence?" I ask, throwing down my favorite skeptic answer.

"No one's snapped a clear pic of Big Foot either. Yet people still believe," he argues back. "Sasquatch could be an alien life form.

A real life Wookie. Anything is possible."

I appreciate his optimistic embrace of *Star Wars* as proof. One of the reasons I keep hanging out with guys like him is their belief in the impossible. I may be a skeptic, but I can relate.

Alien abduction is the story my mom held onto as the years turned into decades and answers never came.

I guess she decided aliens were the better option, rather than imagining the love of her life swimming with the garbage and fishes in the foul water off Manhattan or married and happy with a new family under a new identity.

Strange that Dad could be abducted and no one else in the house woke up. The dogs didn't bark and the neighbors didn't notice. No late night security guard saw a spaceship take off over town.

Which is why, when I could've gone anywhere in the world, I came to Roswell.

After Mom died, my reason for staying put in New York did, too. She was the last of my family. My grandparents passed within months of each other several years earlier. I think his heart broke and he couldn't stand to exist without his love. Their story almost gives me hope true love is real, but I think they were luckier than the lottery odds most of us get when it comes to relationship.

"Aliens crashed in 1947, two years after the first atomic bombs are dropped in war. And about twenty-three months after the Trinity bomb was tested at White Sands. Coincidence we test an H-bomb and within a couple of years there's an alien crash not two hundred miles away?"

"Some people would say there are no coincidences." I try to make my voice sound deeply serious.

While my date talks about government cover-ups and NASA's true mission, I stare at his face. His full lips move rapidly as he hits his conspiracy theory stride. Smooth cheeks and a pale complexion remind me of veal cutlets, and I wonder if he lives in his mother's basement or ever ventures outside during daylight hours. I'm half tempted to ask him about his Vitamin D levels. I'm pretty sure he photoshopped facial hair in his profile pic. And maybe lied about his age.

Then again, I'm the one who said yes to a date with him. At a place that doesn't serve booze even. Why didn't I suggest we meet for coffee instead of a full meal? I'm betting he's the type to split the bill right down to the penny.

"As you can see, it's pretty obvious the shadow governments that truly rule the world don't want us to know about our origins or who is really in control."

"Girls run the world. Beyoncé reveals this truth in her song," I deadpan, hoping to discover a sense of humor in the man.

"I don't really follow pop music." He chugs some water and inhales before speaking again. "There would be chaos on a level the world has never seen before. Banks and governments might be able to hold on for a few months, if we're lucky. Once the paramilitary alien police forces arrive, order will be restored, but we'll all be slaves to our extra-terrestrial overlords."

It's like he didn't even hear me as he continues mansplaining his weird reality to me. I have no idea what he's talking about. "Sounds like a sci-fi movie plot. I think I saw something similar starring Dwayne Johnson and Benedict Cumberbatch. Pretty sure Benedict played the alien."

He blinks at me behind the smudged lenses of his glasses. From his frown and blank stare, I know my joke falls flat again. What is it with these guys and their lack of sense of humor? Why does the thought of alien overlords have to be so serious? When E.T. gets picked up at the end of the movie, those guys seem nice enough and he's clearly happy to see them. What if our new alien rulers like Reese's Pieces and cosplay? Would that be so terrible?

"Maybe our new alien rulers will be benevolent and bring

world peace to this planet. I've seen *Star Trek*, not everyone in deep space wants to kill us and destroy Earth."

He tips his head and gives me a look I might give a toddler with ketchup smeared all over her face, happily eating chicken nuggets without a care in the world. "I like your naïve optimism. And with your looks and body, you'd probably be selected as a mate for one of the Panaeons."

My laughter snorts out of me and I choke on the fry I was chewing on when I try to breathe.

He doesn't get up or ask if I'm okay as I wheeze and cough. After sipping some soda through my straw, I regain my ability to breathe and speak. Guess he does have a funny side after all. "You're hysterical. Are you one of those guys who writes sci-fi fanfic and posts it online? If not, you totally should."

He wads up his napkin. "I don't appreciate being made fun of for taking the time and energy to educate myself about the truths of the world instead of treating everything like a joke. This is serious. If you don't want to prepare yourself, then it's your loss. I have better things to do than try to inform the helplessly ignorant."

Given his angry tone, I suppress the smile fighting to break free.

Is this guy for real?

"So, that's a no on the fanfic?" I ask with a blank face.

With a huff, he stands and zips up his hoodie. "I didn't say that. It would all go over your head even if I told you my handle."

Oh, burn. I think.

"I think it's pretty obvious we're not a match, so let's not waste each other's time any longer. Have a nice life, Lucy. I hope you survive the invasion." He gives me a curt nod of his chin that feels oddly formal and then leaves.

"Well, that went worse than I imagined," I mutter to myself and stab a fry into some ketchup.

"Did your date just leave?" The waitress appears holding the check.

"Yep." I wipe my hands off on my napkin. "And he stuck me with the bill."

Her eyes fill with concern and I can feel her pity.

"Oh, don't feel sorry for me. I'm fine, trust me."

She twists her mouth the side. "If it makes you feel better, he does that a lot."

"Comes here on blind dates?" I pull my wallet out of my purse and hand her a couple of bills. Knowing I'm not the only woman to get duped into a date with him gives me some comfort.

"That, but I've never seen him pick up a check. Always manages to leave before I bring it over to the table. Sometimes I swear he sees me coming and bolts for the door. King of the dine and dash." Her white smile contrasts with her tan skin.

"You're kidding me. He's a serial date ditcher?" I'm stunned. Not by his character, but that he gets away with this on a regular basis.

"Sorry you were his latest victim. Did you meet him online?" I nod.

"I think he trolls newbies to town. I can't imagine he ever gets a second date with someone." She scrunches her nose in disgust.

"Figures. I'm definitely a magnet for the losers and weirdos. At this point, I should save myself the effort." I don't mention I tend to say yes to dates solely for research purposes. Not interested in potential love matches. A relationship would be a distraction. I'm not looking for a boyfriend.

"This town is full of weirdos. If you haven't noticed." Her wrinkled brow tells me I'm crazy if I haven't caught on to the above average ratio of weird to not-weird in this place. I'm not even saying normal because that's a loaded word. What's normal to one person is crazy to someone else. Like going on dates to research alien conspiracies.

"It's the aliens," I answer. "They're to blame for everything."

She blinks at me, waiting for me to indicate if I'm serious or joking.

"I'm kidding," I say with a laugh.

She audibly exhales. "Okay, phew. Thought you were one of them. You know, the true believers. Most people around here go along with the whole little green men thing because it brings tourists to this town. But it's a heavy price to pay when we have to listen to every whackadoo conspiracy theory and alien probing stories. So many probing stories."

Our shudders mirror each other. I'm grateful for my oil men customers. I'd rather have to listen to commodity prices over more stories involving spaceships and anal probing. People are weirdly obsessed with invasions of their own butts.

"If you ever want to hang out with some normal locals, there's a bar on the east side of town, away from the tourists. Cowboy Pete's. Live music on Friday and Saturdays. On Sundays they set up a couple of large grills in the parking lot and have a big cookout. Come by some time." She seems friendly enough and the invitation is genuine.

My weirdo radar doesn't ping and I could use a friend closer to my age than Wanda, who could be my mother. Or maybe biologically even my grandmother if she was a teen mom.

"Sounds fun. Thanks for the tip." I give her a friendly smile. "I'm Lucy."

"Shari." She flashes me a genuine smile. "Nice to meet you. Sorry to stick you with the whole bill."

I pull the check from her fingers. "Don't apologize. At least I got out of the house."

"Come by Pete's. I'll buy you a drink and we can share horror stories. Like the time my date showed up on a horse. With a spare horse for me to ride."

My mouth pops open. "No way. Was he a cowboy?"

Not that being a cowboy would be an excuse given it's 2018 and we have cars for transportation now. "Wait, was he an Amish cowboy?"

Her laugh is a short, quick bark. "Ha, that would've been better. He had a fascination with King Arthur and knights."

"Shut up." My laugh comes out a snort. "Was he taking you to a renaissance fair? Medieval jousting place where you eat turkey legs and drink out of fake pewter tankards?"

Pressing her lips together, she fights her own laughter. "No, the Sonic Drive-In south of downtown. For burgers."

Her words barely register because I'm laughing too hard to hear. "Why the horse? Can you even park a horse there?"

"Apparently." She wipes tears from the corner of her eyes.

"Stop. Hold on." I catch my breath. "You went with him? On the horse?"

"I did indeed. I figured it would make a good story someday. Hold on, I have pics." Pulling out her phone, she scrolls until she finds visual proof. "Here."

Sure enough, the picture shows her sitting on a horse in the Sonic parking lot. Her grin says everything.

"I can't believe you went. Did you ever see him again?"

"Like romantically? Hell no. But he still rides in local parades in full Charro costume. Last time I saw him, he was wearing a wedding ring."

"Wow." I wonder if they got married on horses.

"Wow," she echoes me. "I see it as proof positive there is someone out there for everyone."

"I like your optimism and I hope you're right. I tried to adopt a dog at the local shelter and was rejected."

"Ouch."

I bob my head. "My ego is still recovering."

A customer a couple tables over makes the international sign for the bill and I apologize for taking up her attention.

"Don't you dare leave me a tip." She points her finger at me.

"Fine, but if I see you at the bar, I'm buying you a drink."

"No way. You need free drinks for surviving the serial ditcher. And you should definitely show up some night. We're a good bunch and no one will bring up anal probing," she says the last part loudly over her shoulder as she walks over to the impatient customers.

I laugh when their eyes bug out.

Welcome to Roswell.

WANDA'S CAR'S GONE from our shared parking area when I arrive home. The three casitas that make up our complex face a central courtyard. Nothing fancy, but the small adobe buildings are still charming to my Yankee eyes. If the landlord called them tiny houses, he could probably make more money on short term rentals to hip travelers. I'm grateful he's probably never heard of this trend and still charges us peanuts. Otherwise, I'm not sure where else I could afford to rent without a roommate or two.

Not that I'm planning to stay here forever. I'm giving myself twelve months, and if I don't have answers at the end of the year, I'll move on. To where? Who knows. I have a second or third cousin someplace in California. The weird thing about not having family is I can go wherever I want. My roots are inside of me, not planted deep in any one soil. I'm a potted plant.

Jim, the retired Navy pilot who lives in the third casita, steps out of his front door. He's hooked up to oxygen but carries the tank in a little backpack on wheels.

"Evening." He stretches to reach the bottom of his flag as it glides down the pole. Every morning he raises it and then lowers it in the evening.

Observing him perform this ritual, I feel like I should do something like salute or hold my hand over my heart to honor his devotion. With a straight back, I choose the latter.

From the corner of his eye, he catches my pose and a smile breaks over his face. "Good to see today's youth still respects Old Glory. I'd lost hope for you."

I don't know if he means me in particular or the greater you of Millennials in general. Now I'm happy I didn't go so far as to stand at attention and salute.

"My grandfather served in Vietnam, and had a flag pole, too." Maybe this knowledge will give me some credibility in his eyes, although I'm not sure why Jim's opinion matters. I guess because he's the same generation as my grandpa.

He unclamps the cloth and it dips close to the ground. I leap forward to pick up the edge before it touches the dirt.

After telling me thanks, we silently begin to fold the flag together. I follow his lead, folding my sides like he does. I love how solemn he is and appreciate the quiet.

"Good job." He takes the folded triangle from me and tucks it under his arm. "There's hope for you yet."

Should I thank him? Should I be insulted? I could go either way.

"Don't get too optimistic there, Jim. I'll probably screw up something tomorrow." I touch his shoulder.

"Eh," he coughs out the word more than speaks it, "you seem like a decent kid. Your parents should be proud of you."

His words of praise cut deep.

"Unfortunately, that's impossible. My mom's dead and my dad left when I was little." I'm so used to explaining these facts, I remain emotionless.

He stares at me for a few seconds before saying, "That's too bad. If you make cookies this weekend, I prefer oatmeal raisin to chocolate chip."

Opening his screen door and stepping inside, he ends the conversation.

One time I dropped off a couple of chocolate chip cookies from work and ever since he acts like I'm holding out on him.

The guilt is real. I don't know how he does it. His grumpiness reminds me a little of my grandfather. Only Jim is alone. As far as I can tell, he doesn't have any family and only few friends. We're kindred spirits.

Even though I hate raisins in cookies, I'll pick up some and make a batch using my grandmother's recipe.

Jim's grumpy personality also reminds me of a certain oil worker.

He probably likes gross, shriveled, dried out grapes in his cookies, too.

With a sigh, I make the short trip to my front door.

Inside, I locate my laptop and bring it with me into my bedroom. After stripping off my date outfit, which is really just a clean pair of jeans and a top that doesn't smell like bacon from the diner, I take a quick shower to wash away the evening's bad mojo. Pink and warm from the hot water, I pull on my pajamas before crawling into bed.

"Let's see what's new in the world of aliens," I say to myself, clicking open my browser.

If the government is monitoring my internet searches, I first click on some celebrity gossip sites I have bookmarked. Throw them off the scent.

I avoid Facebook and other social media. No interest in seeing smiling, happy pictures of people I graduated high school or college with. Calling them friends would be a stretch. More like educational colleagues. Anyone I want to actually keep in touch with can text or email me their news.

Opening yet another tab, I scroll through a couple national newspapers' headlines.

An article about a secret government agency catches my attention.

"No fucking way," I whisper.

A former director at the Pentagon openly admitted that the government has been funding millions of dollars into researching extraterrestrial life and UFOs.

For years.

I wonder if Zed knows about this revelation.

Hitting print, my wireless printer in the living room whirs to life, spitting out paper copies of the articles. I'd forward the email to him, but the man doesn't believe in having a traceable online existence.

His entire house is probably lined in tinfoil.

Five

"HOWDY, LUCY," ZED shouts through the intercom, sounding chipper and upbeat.

I wave at the security camera, waiting for him to buzz me inside.

Zed's the current director of what he likes to call the Center. The full name is more than a giant mouthful: The Ufology and Universal Intelligent Life Center. Abbreviating it to TUaUILC doesn't roll off the tongue either. Clearly the people who devote their lives to studying these things never took a class on branding or marketing. In reality, they'd rather outsiders not know about the Center or their work.

Tucked above the old movie theater turned alien crash museum in downtown Roswell, the center is accessed through an unmarked door in the alley behind Main. A mural of spaceships and planets further disguises the entrance. Those in the know, know. And the rest of the world? I believe Zed's exact words were, "They can fuck off."

Or maybe that was his reply when I asked why the Center doesn't have a website or a phone. In fact, I'd bet they don't appear on the lease or a utility bill.

Wanda introduced me to Zed at a cookout when I first moved

in to my apartment. He made an impression on me when he ate a hot dog in two bites. That's something that'll stick with a person.

When I shared the whole sad story about my dad, I think he took pity on me. Or he genuinely likes me. Although I'm not sure Zed likes anyone, genuine or not.

After climbing the narrow staircase from the alley to the office, I exhale a wobbly breath. I'm not panting, but I'm more winded than I should be after a flight of stairs.

Without looking up from the desk top computer, he tells me, "You need to exercise more. Take up Jazzercise or whatever the ladies are doing these days."

"Zumba," I say.

"Don't know her."

Rolling my eyes, I sigh with exasperation. "First, that's a type of exercise. Second, you sound sexist when you talk about 'you ladies' like all women are the same. And third, speak for yourself. The only workout you get is climbing these stairs once a day and maybe lifting a file box once in a while."

"Someone's sensitive today." He taps away on his keyboard.

"Not just today. We've talked about this before. It's the twenty-first century. Times are changing." I repeat the same thing I always tell him when he slips into chauvinism.

"I'm too old to unlearn set patterns. Told you this before." Leaning back in his office chair, he rests his hands on the bald spot on top of his head. Today's T-shirt features a rainbow of aliens marching across Abbey Road over Zed's broad chest.

His long salt and pepper hair is pulled into a ponytail. I've never seen it down and wonder why he doesn't cut it if he's always wearing it up. I could ask, but I don't really want to know. Some questions don't need answers.

I set the plastic bag containing his lunch from the diner on his desk. "Turkey club, chips, and an extra dill pickle spear."

He pulls the bag closer. "You're the best intern we've ever had in the history of the Center."

"I think you mean I'm the only intern you've ever had." I smile down at him.

"Same, same." He greedily eyes the sandwich.

"Did you see the news about the secret government organization studying UFOs and alien life?" I ask, excited to discuss the mainstream news I discovered over the weekend. "I don't know if you follow the *New York Times* or where you can get a copy around here, so I printed out the article for you."

When I hold out the papers to him, he waves them off. "I heard something about this through my channels. Set it on the desk and I'll get to it later."

His disinterest seems odd. Maybe he didn't understand me. "Don't you want to discuss this revelation? Isn't the Department of Defense having a UFO division huge news?"

"Old news is more like it. You think those Hollywood creators of the *X-Files* came up with the idea out of thin air? We've all known the government is behind the cover-ups, so that puts them smack in the crosshairs of all things extraterrestrial, including identifying and suppressing information about UFOs. If they have a budget of millions, you better believe that money is a hush fund to prevent the truth from getting out."

My eyelids peel back farther and farther as he speaks until I can feel my eyeballs bugging out. "Hush money?"

"To keep people quiet."

I almost say my family didn't get any hush money, but I can't be sure. My grandparents were the kind who kept bundles of cash in their mattress.

Taking a bite of his sandwich, Zed chews and swallows. "Listen, I have clippings and photos for you to scan. Brought a couple of boxes over from the warehouse."

"Wouldn't it be easier for me to work out at the warehouse than you hauling boxes here?" I steal one of his chips.

He sits up abruptly. "You don't have the security clearance for the archives."

Meaning I haven't earned his full trust yet. "Suit yourself."

Truth is, my internal doubter suspects the so-called warehouse is his garage. Or his parents' garage.

"Hand over your cell phone." He wiggles his fingers. "Can't be too careful."

"Afraid I'm going to take pictures of sensitive materials?" If they pertained to my father, I would totally be tempted.

"No. Big Brother is always listening on those things. Tracking everywhere you go, everything you click, and each boring conversation you have."

"Paranoid much?" I open my phone's home screen and switch it to airplane mode to show him.

"Not good enough. Power off. In fact, next time, leave it at home. They can track your GPS if you have location settings turned on, which I'm guessing you do."

"It's better than getting lost all the time. Maps are helpful." My tone is defensive, but I turn the phone off. I can live without being connected for an hour or two.

"Buy a paper map. This town isn't that big. If you head in any direction for longer than ten minutes, you'll be out of town and can turn around to find your way back. Main Street runs north and south. Here's a hint, pay attention to the sun's movements across the sky. It's always going to set in the west."

"For fuck's sake," I exhale more than speak the words. Raising my voice so he can hear me, I chastise him. "You've already given me this lecture. I get it. Secret organization. Be careful. Tell no one. Deny all knowledge."

"At least you've paid attention to my words. I couldn't tell since you can't seem to remember something as simple as not bringing your cell phone with you." He's tone is flat and full of sarcasm.

"How about I leave it in the car? I parked a couple of blocks away, as instructed," I add sarcastically.

"Sounds good. You should still turn it off."

"You must have a computer and internet at home, right? How else do you keep up with mainstream news and discoveries?"

He stares at me over his big glasses like I'm crazy for asking such a question.

"I use the computer at the public library and delete the browsing history every two minutes. That way if someone is tapped in and tracking me—"

"Okay, stop. I get it." I hold up my hands in surrender.

"Do you?" he mocks me.

"Assume someone is always watching," I repeat his warning in the same flat voice he uses.

"You think you're anonymous because you don't use your daddy's last name, but the people who keep track aren't easily fooled." He shoves his glasses back up to the bridge of his nose.

"Somedays I regret telling you about my dad." I keep my focus on the top of the file box.

"You wouldn't be here now, with the access you have if you hadn't. You may call me paranoid, but I'm one of the good guys in all this. My only mission is to find and protect the truth. Whether you like it or not, or help or not, my life's work doesn't change."

I exhale out all the defensive energy squeezing my chest.

"Thanks, Zed. It's a new world to me and I'm still processing this reality." I find my car keys in my bag. "I'll be right back."

With a nod, he pulls the bag open and reaches for the plastic container inside. "You're not alone anymore. There's a whole community of people who know what you've been through because they've also experienced it too."

I will not cry in front of Zed. I mumble thanks, then dash back down the stairs with my phone and keys. Yes, I think he's paranoid but I don't want to piss him off before I find answers.

Returning a few minutes later, I hold up my hand as I pant, "Don't say anything. I jogged to the car and up the stairs."

He nods and thankfully remains silent.

"Enjoy your lunch." I pick up the file box and carry it through a door to another small room not much larger than a walk-in closet in a mansion. Overhead fluorescent lights flicker to life, revealing the long work table, a couple of ancient microfiches machines, and a scanner on a counter along one wall. Newspaper clippings and tabloid articles spill out of overstuffed binders. A large white board occupies the short wall opposite the door and a bookshelf fills the other.

Part of my "internship" at the Center is to organize and digitize all the paper. Zed's worried about a fire, arson in particular if "they" find out what he has. Of course when I ask him who "they" are, he won't say. Too worried about being overheard.

Nor can I upload anything online. I thought Zed's head was going to explode when I suggested cloud storage on my first day.

Digitizing to a thumb drive is about as far as Zed will go. Even then he's super paranoid about copies getting made or distributed.

My job is to scan the files into folders on an ancient Dell desktop. He handles the transfer to thumb drive. For all I know the drives end up buried in coffee cans in his mother's garden. Isn't that where serial killers and conspiracy nuts always hide the evidence?

Before moving to Roswell, I exhausted normal channels for locating a missing person. I conducted online searches on my own and eventually I hired a private investigator to try to find my father. I was in high school and saved up all my money from babysitting and allowance to hire a guy I found online.

I checked references, got referrals, read reviews, and even asked the local police station for recommendations. And after paying the sum of my entire life's savings, I still don't have answers.

My first investigator found out nothing we didn't already know. Name, birthdate, social security number, marriage license, my birth certificate, the limited financial records of the joint bank account with my mother and a shared credit card.

No student loans or secret credit lines.

School records corroborate the stories my mom knew about him moving around a lot as a kid before going to university in Albuquerque where he met my mom.

That's it. All information ceased after July third nineteen ninety-eight. The private investigator found no paper trail or evidence of dear old Dad after that date.

Poof. Disappeared into thin air. He left his wallet, car, and all of his clothes behind.

If all these other people were returned after their abductions, why wasn't my father? Why did he disappear forever?

As a cynical teenager, I fully believed he'd run off and dumped his wife and kid for a new life. Maybe he was the kind of man who couldn't be domesticated and found a woman who didn't have a kid to tie him down.

I knew other kids whose parents got divorced and the dad left town for a new life. They maybe got to see him on weekends or during summer break. Birthday and Christmas presents showed up in the mail. Or they received an apologetic phone call with a half-hearted excuse when they didn't get anything.

I was jealous of those kids. Even as they complained about how much their dads sucked, at least they had some contact.

Flipping through a new pile of tabloid articles, I read more stories about abductions. A woman in Iowa recalls waking up as she levitated above her bed in a glow of green light. A man in Tennessee says he heard the little green men speaking in a strange language but wasn't afraid. The guy who woke up with his pajamas inside out told the reporter from the *International News Gazette* he found strange marks on the back of his neck, but the chronic asthma he'd had since childhood disappeared for good.

"Maybe because he came back as a clone of himself." I flip the page. "That would make sense."

Beside the file box, the scanner hums as it waits for a new page to scan. I remove the article about the mysteriously absent asthma and replace it with a wrinkled piece of paper about crop circles.

When I lay it down, a pattern on the back of the page catches my attention. Hand drawn in the margins of the article is a vaguely familiar design.

Without thinking, I hit scan and the bright light flashes in my eyes.

"Damnit," I swear and put my hand over my face before closing the top and pressing scan again.

Bright orange dots fill my vision when I blink, mirroring the pattern on the page. It's familiar but not a symbol I know the meaning of.

When the scan finishes, I flip over the page and read about the sudden appearance of strange crop circles. This is a whole other level of conspiracy theories I try not to get sucked into. Seems entirely random and yet plausible that farmers or bored teenagers could be behind the appearance of patterns in fields.

The question is why bother?

Fame? Notoriety? A desperate plea for attention? All makes sense. Living in the middle of nowhere can be pretty boring.

Once I finish scanning the articles in the box, I reorganize the clippings into a binder so they're not shoved together and wrinkled. My attention catches again on the symbol in the margin and I decide to copy it. The copier sits behind his desk and I have to ask his permission to use it. So that option is out.

Of course I could steal the clipping itself, but Zed would probably split a blood vessel in his eye if he found out.

I need to stay on Zed's good side. He's my last hope of finding out more about my father's disappearance. After years and thousands of dollars on private investigators and psychics, pulling declassified documents, researching John Does in hospitals, culling through criminal records and mug shots, and the sleepless nights reading and listening to ufologist accounts, I need to get answers or walk away. Either be convinced aliens are real or give into my inner cynic who doubts everything.

Zed's the closest thing I've come to a true believer. Who knows who else he works with or the extent of what he knows. I believe he's capable of helping me find the truth while not exposing me to more public scrutiny. If he's paranoid enough about secret government agencies and shadow international cabals, I doubt he operates as a lone wolf. I'd bet he has people willing to do whatever it takes to protect the Center, including making a single woman with no family disappear without a trace. Poof.

Feeling uncomfortable enough with the thought of Zed's legions, I decide to draw the symbol on my skin. First I think forearm, but I'm wearing short sleeves. Instead, I decide to copy it on my chest. Given my complete lack of social life and the zero possibility of anyone seeing my naked boob in the near future, it's probably the safest place.

Using the sharpie I typically label files with, I carefully copy the symbol's outline onto the top of my left breast. It's simple enough. A circle inside a larger circle, with intersecting lines that form a cross and then a diagonal line that rises from left to right through the cross. Each of the straight lines extend past the outer circle.

It's not complex and I could probably recall it without seeing it again, but something urges me to draw it.

After I finish, I cap the marker and readjust my shirt.

"Almost done in here for the day?" Zed's voice from the doorway makes me jump. "Didn't scare you, did I?"

I press my right hand over my heart, feeling the quick thump of panic under my ribcage.

"Not at all." I have to clear my throat to continue. "I was in the zone of scanning and organizing. Finished the whole box."

He opens a binder and flips through the clear plastic sleeves. I swear he pauses for a second longer on the one article about the crop circles.

"Do you believe those are made by UFOs?" I ask, keeping my voice casual.

"Until I have proof otherwise, no reason to assume they weren't made by alien craft. Of course, some of these have been proven to be hoaxes made by a bunch of meddling kids."

His serious tone in contrast to his almost exact quote of every villain on *Scooby Doo* cracks me up. "If it weren't for those meddling kids."

He misses my joke. Or chooses to ignore it. "The vast majority of these circles and geoglyphs, including the ancient Nazca earth drawings in Peru, do not have simple explanations. Their patterns can only be seen from the high above, yet the Nazca lines predate human air travel by thousands of years."

Despite really not wanting to be drawn into this particular pool of conspiracy theories, I'm curious about his take. "What made them?"

"The circles could be from a small craft landing or hovering over the area. Could be vibrational coming from underground as a signal or marker. A simple science experiment shows how sound frequencies and vibrations can move dirt. Why not larger matter? As for as the Peruvian geoglyphs, rocks were intentionally placed in the pattern. Why?"

Sure. Why not? I have to give Zed credit for his ability to be open to all possibilities for the weird in the world.

He continues speaking, "Decades ago, a sinkhole opened up north of Roswell. One minute it was flat desert, the next there was a big circular hole. No big deal, right? Sinkholes happen all over the world on a daily basis."

I nod enthusiastically to encourage him.

"Thing is, most of them aren't a geometrically perfect circle. And this one intersected a bunch of dirt roads." He flips the page in the binder and lands on the article with the hand drawn symbol in the margin. "Kind of looked like this, but without the inner circle."

He pauses and releases a small, humorless chuckle. "Almost like a lopsided drawing of the sun done by a little kid."

At his overly casual laugh, a shiver of cold draws out goose bumps on my skin.

Shrugging, he pushes his glasses back into position on the bridge of his nose. "Probably a weird coincidence. Especially given this article is from the 1950s. You could easily dismiss it as random correlation. Most people would."

"But not you." I stare at the symbol again as I itch to get out of here to look up the sinkhole pictures online to confirm his story.

"Not me." He steps over to the shelves. "Let me find another picture, since I bet you're dying to doubt me."

While he has his back turned, I press my hand over my heart again. Even knowing he can't see through the cotton of my shirt, I feel like somehow he knows. I'll wash it off as soon as I get home.

"Ah, here it is. Filed under natural phenomenon," he says, happily. "Not quite the same, but close enough."

Staring at the picture he holds in front of me, I read the caption, "Sinkhole appears above a brine well on Carlsbad property owned by SFT, Inc, a local land holding company."

"Seems their land is prone to salt caverns and sinkholes." He closes the binder and replaces it on the shelf.

I make a mental note to research salt caverns on my own time.

"Our mission isn't focused on only what's out there in space. Would be pretty foolish to assume no one has visited this planet. Or colonized it."

We've had this conversation before and I'm still not buying his version. "Are you saying the aliens don't just visit?"

"The better question is why not? Seems a decent place."

"Wouldn't we know if there were little green men roaming around all the time? I highly doubt that our atmosphere would be compatible to Martians or invaders from Pluto."

"Open your mind, Lucy. Life takes many forms. Look at the biodiversity on Earth."

"Are you saying some of the living beings here aren't from here?" Why do I keep asking?

"Have you ever seen a giant squid?" He laughs. "What about lemurs with their big glowing eyes? Kind of look like the classic alien faces. Ever notice that coincidence?"

"Right. Sweet lemurs are aliens from another planet." Even though a spaceship piloted by lemurs is an adorable visual, I've had enough crazy for today. "On that thought, I'm going to call it a day." I pack up my work and leave it neatly stacked so I know where to start when I return.

"I hope I didn't scare you away," he says, sounding contrite. "If we can't laugh at the absurdity of this life, we'll never make it out of here alive."

"No one makes it out alive."

"You can't say that. Maybe we shed these floppy human forms when we elevate to the next level. Or return to our mother planets."

"Now you're sounding like a Scientologist."

He stares at me.

"Stop staring. It's a cult. You need to cut back on your caffeine consumption, Zed." He follows me out of the room after I shut off the scanner and mark today's date on the box.

"Why is being dead and lifeless in the ground more realistic than our spirits returning to where we came from? Isn't that the same idea of Heaven? We ascend into the clouds, into the sky and beyond. Where do the all the gods live?" He points at the ceiling. "Up there."

This conversation has swung a wide left turn into metaphysical territory. While I am curious about Zed's theory, I also have to pee. The debate between Heaven and home planets is going to have to wait until another afternoon.

"You can share your thoughts on the afterlife next time. I'll be back again on Tuesday. As for the giant squid, if they stay deep in the ocean, I can pretend they don't exist. Aliens or not."

He sits down in his chair so hard it spins. Chuckling, he says, "This is why most people stick to the idea of little green men with big eyes. Easier to go about our lives if we assume the other is so outrageously strange, we can dismiss the possibility. Takes bravery to question everything."

"Even sinkholes," I reply.

"Everything." He pulls his chair closer to his desk. "Now go have fun this weekend."

"Right. Like I won't be having nightmares about giant squid."

Outside, I shut the door behind me and make sure it clicks closed. The alley is empty as usual but I hurry to the street and the comfort of traffic. I feel like I'm being watched.

"Bye, Lucy." Zed's disembodied voice carries through the intercom.

I wave at the camera.

Once I'm on the sidewalk and surrounded by oblivious tourists, I shake off the creepy feeling leftover from my conversation with Zed. I think his paranoia is contagious. I'm struck by how he narrowed in on the symbol I copied. Like he knew I'd drawn it on my skin. Next time I'm there, I'll have to check for more cameras.

I need to be around normal people, or at least people who don't talk about conspiracy theories and aliens.

It's Friday and I think I know the perfect place to forget the weirdness of this afternoon.

Six

ROSWELL ISN'T A big place. Mostly one story buildings and vintage storefronts dominate Main Street, giving the town a feeling of being trapped in its prime last century. North of town is newer, with chain restaurants and hotels close to the military school. Suburbs trickle out to meet the desert in the west and south.

Warehouses, empty lots surrounded by chainlink fences, and a few silos hug the railroad tracks on the east side of downtown. It's not a place I've hung out before. Or even driven through. It's not exactly a tourist friendly area.

Housed in a red brick warehouse building not far from the tracks, Cowboy Pete's doesn't look like a western bar from the outside. A large, faded mural decorates the side facing the parking lot. With the sun behind the building, it's difficult to make out the peeling lettering, but a smiling blond cowboy tipping his hat gives me a clue to the origins of the bar's name.

Inside, the decor is surprisingly modern, with lots of exposed brick, old wood beams and metalwork. Enormous windows face into the sun, casting half of the space in a warm glow and the rest in deep shadow.

Not a single alien in sight. No campy spaceships either. This is exactly what I need.

Most of the tables and booths are filled, but I spot a seat at the bar. I'm so excited to find a place, I don't take the time to study the other patrons.

Scanning the drink and snack menu in front of me, I bounce a little with happiness. I might even drool over the food options when I read the descriptions of their barbecue.

After deciding what I want, I catch the bartender's attention. He's around my age, with full sleeves of tattoos on both arms and a septum piercing. Okay, so maybe he's not normal in the eyes of most, but I've found my people.

He gives me a friendly smile. "How's it goin'? Know what you want?"

"I want everything, but I'll start with the brisket sliders and an order of the fried pickles."

"Excellent choices. Anything to drink?" His smile feels genuine and friendly.

"Whatever beer you recommend," I tell him, letting myself return his smile.

"Are you a fan of hops?" Picking up a pint glass, he pauses for my answer.

"I'm feeling very hoppy today." I smirk at my own pun. Because honestly, puns are really for the one who makes them and no one else.

"New Star IPA coming up." He pulls a handle and fills my glass with a golden ale. "Haven't seen you here before? Passing through?"

"In the long term, yes, but I've been living south of here for a few months. I had no idea this place existed until Shari told me."

"Dark hair and a smile that could make a troll happy?" he asks, setting my pint down on a round coaster bearing the same cowboy image as the mural outside.

"That's her."

"She should get a commission for promoting us."

After taking a sip of the IPA, I moan with pleasure. "If your food is as good as this beer, you shouldn't have to worry about attracting customers. Plus, the place is packed for a Friday afternoon."

"We do have some loyal regulars. Glad you enjoy the beer. Let me put your order in so you don't have to wait forever." He knocks his fist on the wood bar in front of me before walking to the other end.

Why don't I work in a place like this? I bet the tips are better and the people are definitely cooler. Thinking this, I feel guilty for ditching Tony and Wanda. They were there for me when I knew no one, had no money and no place to live. I owe them some loyalty.

On the other hand, this girl has bills to pay.

Happily sipping my drink, I twist on my stool to check out the crowd.

When I spot a familiar messy head of hair, I miss my mouth and spill beer on my white T-shirt.

Dabbing at it, I make sure I'm not starring in a one woman wet T-shirt contest. There's only a large wet spot over my left boob and it doesn't show my bra.

BOONE'S HERE AT Cowboy Pete's.

Of course I know he exists outside of the diner. He must have some place he calls home and I'm guessing a job in the oil industry. Yet somehow I've never thought of him having a social life with friends. Apparently he's the kind of guy who's a regular at the coolest place in town where everyone knows him. And has a beautiful girlfriend.

He's all smiles and hellos until he catches me sitting at the bar. For a moment he stares at me, then the warmth leaves his eyes and his brows knit together. Seeing me in his space isn't a happy little coincidence. Not by his expression.

Straightening my back, I brace for him to do one of two things: either he'll ignore me completely or acknowledge my existence but pretend he doesn't know me.

Not that he does know me. I'm his breakfast waitress. We're not exactly friends or work colleagues even.

"Hi," Shari greets me warmly with an open half hug. "I'm so happy to see you again. Boone, this is Lucy. I told you about her."

"What is she doing here?" Boone directs his question at Shari. He glances at my chest, but doesn't meet my eyes. Feeling awkward about the beer stain, I pull at my shirt.

"Why are you being a weirdo? Ask Lucy yourself." Pointing at me, she continues, "She can hear and speak perfectly fine. Although with what a jerk you're being, she's probably better off ignoring you."

He scratches behind his ear and looks across the room. I don't know if he's waiting for one of us to explain my shocking appearance at a local bar, or if he's counting to ten so he can act like he doesn't hate me.

Shari jabs him in the shoulder with her index finger. "And for the record, I invited her."

"How do you know Sharyl?" he asks, finally looking at me and not snarling out the words.

"Oh no. He's extra cranky if he's using my full name." Shari, I mean Sharyl, rolls her eyes. "My friends call me Shari."

This is the woman George asked about at the diner. The one who made him grow out a mustache over a lost bet. Figures he'd be with someone as gorgeous. Do I admit my humiliating date and Shari's rescue? Add lonely to my stalker moniker?

"She came in the Burger Joint. We hit it off," she explains for me. It's all true.

Boone stares at her and then switches his attention to me. The intensity of his focus makes me want to curl up like a little potato bug. I resist the urge to shrink myself and instead roll my shoulders back. He doesn't own the place, so why does he care if I hang out here? It's not the only bar in town.

"Are you following me?" His eyes challenge mine. I can't tell if he's joking or serious.

"You're so full of yourself, Boone. Not every woman is obsessed with you. Some have brains and taste." Shari laughs as she puts him in his place before I can answer for myself.

Third option: he accuses me of being a stalker in front of his girlfriend. Wasn't expecting that to be the winner.

"Some people find me likable." I jut out my chin like a bratty kid.

For a quick second he narrows his eyes at me, opens his mouth as if to snark back, and then changes his mind. "You two have fun."

"We're supposed to have dinner," Shari says, halting his getaway with a hand to his bicep.

"I've already ordered food, so don't let me stop you." I don't want to ruin their plans, which by his attitude, I clearly have.

"You don't have to eat alone." She touches my arm, making a connection between the three of us. The static in the air shocks me like a rubber-band snapped against my bare skin.

I jerk back at the same time Boone does.

"Jesus, Shari. Watch it with the static electricity." He rubs his bicep.

"Oops, sorry." She shakes out her wrists. "Wasn't thinking."

"Dry air," I offer as explanation.

Two pairs of eyes stare at me.

"Static electricity is more common in dry air," I explain the obvious reason for Shari shocking both of us.

"Opposites attract," she adds while Boone focuses on something behind me. "Right, Boone?"

"Sure," he mutters, clearly not paying attention to her question.

A brunette with long braids interrupts us by touching Shari's shoulder. No static shock this time. "Your table's ready."

"Can you squeeze in a third?" Shari asks. "Our friend is going to join us."

Boone's attention shifts to her. "Take the table. I'll steal Lucy's barstool."

The hostess waits for us to make up our minds.

I'm saved from splitting up their date when the bartender drops off my food. "Please, keep your plans. I'm fine sitting here."

Shari blatantly elbows Boone.

"Another time maybe," he speaks to me, but his answer is obviously prompted by her elbow jammed in his ribs.

"Sure, no pressure." Resuming my seat, I give them a cheesy smile. "Honestly, I'm used to eating alone."

My statement hangs between us in an invisible speech bubble.

An imaginary sad trombone plays in my head.

Shari leans around me and calls over to the bartender. "Rafi, can you bring Lucy's food over to our table instead? Thanks!"

He nods and collects the plates. "Lead the way."

Silently I'm protesting "no, no, no," but I slap a smile on my face and try to make the best of it.

Yay, new friend. And Boone.

Shari keeps the conversation going, mostly by talking about herself and local gossip. I don't know if this is typical, but I'm grateful for her social skills. If it were up to Boone and me, we'd be playing the staring game in silence.

They make a good couple.

It's strange to see him outside of the diner. Apparently, he feels the same. Or his silence in the mornings is his baseline. The strong, silent type. Who occasionally has odd facial hair.

And still manages to be too handsome for his own good.

And mine.

Boone orders a Mexican Coke and drinks it from the bottle. Shari sips from a root beer.

I'm the only one drinking alcohol.

"So how long have you two been dating?" I ask, attempting to make conversation.

He chokes on his Coke, turning red as he coughs.

With a loud cackle, Shari slaps him on the back. "Ew, gross, no. He's my older brother."

Just when I think the evening can't get more awkward.

Sister betting him to grow the fuzzy caterpillar makes complete sense.

Boone mostly ignores me during the meal and makes an excuse to leave as soon as he finishes eating.

"Sorry about my brother. He's shy," Shari apologizes as soon as he's gone.

"You don't have to make excuses for him."

"I'm not. He's always been quiet and a lot of people think he's full of himself because he's objectively good-looking. Don't let the outside packaging fool you. He's a good guy." Her earnest need to share this with me doesn't make up for his rudeness, but it does make me like her more.

"I'll have to take your word for it," I offer. She doesn't have to explain his actions to me.

Is she saying I should date her brother? Or that he'd be interested in me? If anything, he seems to tolerate me for my newness.

"If you don't already have plans, we should meet up at the alien festival. It's the week after next. Over the top cheesy, but there's decent live music and yummy street food. Costumes are optional."

Her enthusiasm is contagious and I'm definitely curious to check out the festival.

"I'd love to join you," I happily agree, not even thinking about whether or not Boone will be there, too.

Not at all.

Seven

MONDAY AT THE diner is the same as every other morning. The oil workers come in, stare at their phones, order food, watch the commodities ticker, eat, and leave. A couple in matching Roswell alien hats sit at table five, Boone's table. He hasn't shown up yet. After his cold behavior at Pete's on Friday, maybe he's decided to get his breakfast somewhere else.

I'm busing a table when a familiar dirty, gray truck pulls into a spot right in front of the windows.

Boone strolls in, glances over at his regular table, then takes a seat at the counter like he did last week.

No baseball cap or trucker hat today. He removes his sunglasses and sets them next to the placemat along with his phone. Screen down. And he doesn't stare at the television. What's even more unsettling is he's staring at me, tracking me as I move through the tables.

"Morning, Lucy," he says when I stop in front of him to fill his cup.

"Boone." I'm not sure where we stand.

"What are the specials?" He meets my eyes with a small curve of his lips.

"It's Monday. Blueberry pancakes, smothered breakfast burrito, or biscuits and gravy." I set the coffee pot back on its warmer and pick up the pitcher of water. "Or you could just have pecan pancakes like you normally do."

"Trying to break out of my routine. Be open to new things." His smile spreads as he fiddles with his knife.

"Don't go too crazy." I don't return his happy expression.

"May I have the blueberry pancakes, please?" He glances down and then meets my eyes. "With a side of apology for my behavior on Friday."

"Sure." I'm half turned to give his order to Tony when the second part of his sentence clicks in my brain. I set down the water pitcher next to his coffee. "Excuse me?"

"Blueberry pancakes, please?" He taps his finger on the knife like he's nervous.

"Got that part." Staring at Boone, I ignore a man making a check sign across the room.

Focusing on his hands, he inhales and blows out his cheeks like apologizing isn't something he does often. "I'm sorry for being rude to you at Pete's. I thought Shari was meddling and let my annoyance at her spill over to you."

"You accused me of stalking you." My eyebrows draw together in confusion.

"It was a shock to see you away from the diner. And with Shari," he says, meeting my eyes.

Over his shoulder, the impatient customer snaps his fingers. Snapping is one of my biggest pet peeves.

Searching in my apron, I find the check for the rude man. "Be right back."

I put in Boone's order, drop off the check, and clear a table while processing Boone's apology.

Whenever I glance over at him, he's watching me, cautious optimism in his eyes.

"Can I get some water?" a woman at table six asks me when I walk by.

"Sure thing."

Only the water pitcher isn't in its spot when I go to grab it. Wanda's standing with a group of regulars and has one of the waters, but we should have two. Confused, I stare at the tray where it should be.

"Looking for this?" Boone asks, pointing to the pitcher in front of him.

"Thanks," I tell him, and quickly walk away.

Boone sitting at the counter, being nice, and apologizing is throwing me off my routine. He's table five. Grumpy, silent, handsome lover of pecans. Not the man who's occupying a stool and ordering blueberry pancakes. And asking for forgiveness.

Tony calls out his order and I'm forced to face Boone again.

"Pancakes." I set down the plate and a bottle of syrup. My eyes flick to his. "And apology accepted."

His face crinkles with a genuine smile that makes his green eyes sparkle. "Really? You're not going to write me off for being a jerk?"

"You sound like you're surprised. Maybe I should change my mind." I lift my eyebrows, challenging him to tell me I'm making a mistake.

He touches my wrist, sending sparks of warmth up my arm. "No, please don't. I'm not always an asshole."

"Part-time asshole? Or do you have a timeshare on being a jerk?" I ask, not quite ready to let his behavior go even though I've accepted his apology.

"More of a lease option." He grins at me.

Tony slaps the bell in the window, announcing orders are waiting.

"Good to know. I have customers." I step back and he drops

his hand. Walking away, I can still feel the sensation of his palm on my skin.

Wanda and I meet up at the drink station. With our backs to the room, she bumps her hip against mine.

"Now that was flirting and don't you try to deny it." She winks at me.

Ignoring her shimmy, I fight my smile as I fill an order.

"He's a handsome one. Although I think he's better looking with the mustache. Reminds me of a lover I had in the eighties who looked just like Tom Selleck. Hubba hubba." A smudge of pink frosted lipstick shows on her teeth when she laughs.

"You have a little lipstick." I pretend to rub my finger over my teeth.

"Oops. No wonder those young oil guys were staring at my mouth. I thought they were flirting with me."

Apparently, everything is flirting to Wanda.

Boone's doodling on a napkin when I walk by with the coffee pot. For a brief second, I fantasize he's writing his phone number for me. After his cold behavior at Pete's, he's done a one-eighty this morning. I'm not sure where we stand, but I think Wanda's been right about the flirting.

Glancing down at his hand, I bobble the pot of coffee I'm holding. I feel it slip from my grasp and attempt to catch it with my other hand. This only causes me to slam the bottom and change the trajectory of the liquid from down to up, and out.

With my eyes closed, I cringe and wait for the inevitable splash on Boone. Except the yelp of pain I expect from him comes out as deep laughter.

Slowly peeling open one eyelid, I squint at him in dread. Mentally I'm prepared for his back to be doused in coffee. Instead, he's spun his stool sideways, his large hands gripping the side of the coffee pot. There's not a splash or a drop of liquid on him, the counter, or the floor.

"How's that possible?" I ask the coffee pot.

"What?" he asks, a grin shining on his too handsome face.

"I felt the pot drop and was sure it would splash all over you."

"Must've caught it in time." He sets the pen down and continues to smile at me.

"You were facing the other way. I—" I have no words. Staring at his doodle, I nearly drop the pot again.

"Maybe you should set that down." He lifts the pot out of my reach, refills his cup, and places the coffee on the counter. "You feeling okay?"

"What is that?" I find my voice and point to the group of symbols he's doodled on the napkin.

As if seeing it for the first time, his eyes widen and he sweeps up the paper before folding it. "Nothing. Random Minkowski diagrams."

Opening his wallet, he tucks the napkin inside and pulls out cash. Holding it out to me, he waves it to get my attention. "Here you go."

I'm still staring at the spot on the counter where Boone was doodling the same symbol I drew on my boob. I have no idea who Minkowski is, but I make a note to look up the name when I get home.

There's no way he saw it through my shirt at Pete's. Gotta be a coincidence. Has to be. I glance down at my chest to double-check the drawing is gone. No trace of black ink peeks out from my V-neck.

It's not a complicated design. Kind of like a ship's wheel, only missing a couple of lines. I'm sure a lot of people draw circles and spokes coming out of them. Like a kid's drawing of a sun with an extra circle.

"Earth to Lucy." His voice sounds far away.

Blinking a few times, I bring myself back to the present. "Sorry. Uh, thanks for the tip."

Accepting the bills, I stuff them into my apron. I don't bother checking the amount. Because like every other time, he'll have tipped twenty percent.

"Gotta get to work." He pauses. "You sure you're okay?"

I nod, still lost in figuring out if it's the same pattern.

"I, uh . . ." He stops speaking.

Glancing up at him, I find he's staring at me, concern all over his face.

"Maybe we can hang out some time? Other than here."

His eyes are more green than amber today. As I focus on his eyes, his pupils widen and I swear the color of his irises shifts more to green. Must be the fluorescent lights in here mixing with the sunlight.

"Sure?" My voice turns my answer into a question.

Tony's voice yelling, "Order up," snaps me out of my brain haze.

"No rest for the weary." I pick up the coffee pot and head toward the kitchen.

"See you tomorrow, Lucy."

Something about hearing my name formed by his lips ignites a blush on my cheeks.

"You too, Boone."

He flashes his too beautiful smile at me right before he walks out the door.

I'm in trouble.

Falling for him is not part of my plan.

WHEN MOM DIED, she left me alone in a house filled with ghosts and a mortgage we took out to cover her medical care. No way I could pay for student loans and a house on a retail job. Selling became my only option.

Turns out the real estate market in a forgotten town isn't hot. Took me almost a year to sell the house with three price drops. When the realtor finally presented me with the lowball offer that wouldn't require me to declare bankruptcy, I took it. First thing, I paid off all the remaining debts. Her small life insurance went toward my student loans.

Essentially, I'm broke again, but out of debt.

I guess that's a silver lining.

With just enough to make a rainy day fund, I packed up and drove out of town in my dumpy old car stuffed to the roof with the few possessions I wanted to keep.

Among them, Dad's beloved copy of the Zane Grey book. I can picture it sitting on my bookshelf in my apartment.

After finishing my shift, I drive home, thinking about the symbol and possible reasons why Boone would doodle it.

Dropping my bag on the kitchen counter, I head straight for the worn binding of *West of the Pecos* in the bookcase.

I slip the book off the shelf and curl up in the corner of my old red velvet love seat I bought at a garage sale when I first moved here.

Apologies to Mr. Grey, but I'm not interested in reading his western tale. I'm looking for my old doodles. The ones I drew in Dad's collection to make the books pretty when I was four or five and thought all books were coloring books.

Resting my palm on the cover the way someone who is about to swear an oath on the Bible would, I calm my breathing. The colorful dust jacket is long gone and the binding is loose enough the book wobbles in my hand as I hold it.

It's impossible that Boone was drawing the same pattern I used to doodle.

Has to be.

Flipping the pages, I spot my messy pen drawings. Most are of people, probably portraits of my family. A few oddly shaped animals float above them.

There, in the middle of the title page, is a messier version of the symbol from the Center. A child's version of what Boone drew on his check.

With shaking hands and a twisting feeling in my stomach, I close the book before I drop it.

It must be a common scientific symbol I'm not aware of. When I got home from the Center last week, I snapped a pic of the drawing on my chest. I can upload the pic and do a reverse image search on Google.

The first result is the radioactive symbol with its familiar three triangles in a circle.

Close, but not quite right.

A captain's ship wheel also shows up in the results, but it has too many lines.

A shooting target has too few.

The closest to my drawing is a radar symbol.

Radioactive captain's wheel radar target.

That doesn't make sense.

While I'm searching, I enter "earth symbol" and click on the first link, which takes me to a Wikipedia page.

The graphic is a cross inside a circle. Next to it is a circle with a cross on the top, like an upside down symbol for a woman.

The circle encompassing the cross definitely matches the mystery icon.

Still doesn't explain why this combination is something I drew as a kid, someone added in the margin of an article about crop circles, and Boone doodled.

I can't make the connection.

Next I enter Minkowski in the search bar and find an article with an illustration of his spacetime diagram. It's similar, but doesn't have the circles. I try to understand his idea of four dimensions, but my brain glitches when I get to the formulas.

Strange thing to doodle on a napkin while eating pancakes.

Trusting my gut, I slip *West of the Pecos* between the family Bibles on the lowest shelf—more tucked away and out of sight than it was before.

Eight

FRIDAY IS HOTTER than Satan's balls. Even parked in the shade behind the diner, my car is about eleventy billion degrees inside. The silver sunshade thing that Wanda bought me has kept the plastic on the dash from melting into a puddle, but hasn't prevented my little Honda from turning into a dry sauna that smells vaguely of french fries. It's possible that while I was working someone broke into my car and used it as an air fryer.

Leaning into the car without committing to sitting on the molten fabric seat, I slip the key into the ignition and turn it so I can lower the windows and blast the air conditioner. It should be cool enough to drive in about an hour.

After mere seconds inside of the car-shaped oven, sweat drips down my face and I have boob sweat.

Why does anyone live in this desert?

'At least it's a dry heat' is lying propaganda. Arid or humid, hot is hot.

Heat rises from the asphalt and from the open door of my car, creating shimmering waves in the midday sun.

I could go home, take a cold shower, and plant myself in front of the window air conditioner. *Not today, Satan.*

Instead, I swing by the apartment, wave at Jim through his

screen door, change, and quickly pack a bag for the lake.

Driving east of Roswell, the landscape gently swells and drops in hills and arroyos covered in scrubby bushes. In case I forget I'm in the southwest, a few tumbleweeds cling to barbed wire cattle fencing running alongside the narrow two-lane road.

At the sign for Bottomless Lakes, I turn and follow the winding asphalt through more scrub and a few occupied campsites. Obviously these happy campers don't care about sleeping among rattlesnakes and scorpions. I'd have to be paid a lot of money to sleep in the desert. I'd accept a slightly lesser amount to sleep outside in someone's backyard.

The parking lot by the largest lake holds about a dozen parked cars. On the weekends, hundred of people will cram themselves on the manmade beach. That's why I avoid coming here on Saturdays or Sundays even though I have the days off work.

The name Bottomless Lakes is a lie, but these turquoise pools are deep enough to have fooled the first cowboys who tried to measure their depth with lengths of rope.

If I think about lakes without bottoms, my mind goes straight to the Loch Ness monster or giant alligator-like creatures in the Great Lakes.

Who knows what lives in the depths?

For that reason alone, I'd be justified in keeping to the public pools.

But those are filled with kids—screaming, splashing, peeing in the water, kids.

No, thank you.

I'll take my chances.

Plus, geologists proved that these lakes are really deep, but not bottomless. More like limestone cenotes, or sinkholes, that filled with fresh water over time.

Parking my chair and towel on the sand, I carry my pink,

donut-shaped floatie to the water's edge. At first touch, the chill of the water sends goosebumps along my heated skin. My body is stuck in a moment of contrast between hot and cold, wet and dry.

When the water hits my knees, I half-dive, half-belly flop into the lake. As cool relief washes over me, I exhale and flip onto my back for a few seconds before submerging my whole body again. Surfacing, I exhale and revel in how quickly the overheated, sticky feeling of the day washes away.

Swimming the breast stroke, I head straight for the far side.

I plan to swim a few laps, then come back for the inflatable and float for a while.

A few yards ahead of me lies a row of buoys, marking the edge of the designated swim area. During the week, there isn't a lifeguard on duty. Visitors are supposed to honor the random border between safety and danger.

I dunk my head into the cool water and glide beneath the boundary line.

'Cause I'm a rebel.

With steady strokes, I swim out to the middle of the lake. This is where the freshwater shark or lake monster would be enticed by my fluttering legs to leave the safety of its underwater den, speed toward the surface, and either chomp me to bits or swallow me whole. At some later point, someone might notice the unattended donut or a ranger might discover my car parked alone in the lot as dusk approaches and the park closes.

By then it will be too late for me.

Treading water, I wait for the attack to come. When it doesn't, I decide to swim back to shore.

After taunting death for another two laps, I scoop up my donut and float in the safety of the designated swim area.

With my head dipped over the edge of the floatie, my hair skims the surface behind me while my butt and feet hang out in the water. Sunshine warms my face and chest, arms, and the tops of my thighs. The heat dries the droplets of water on my skin.

Yawning, I close my eyes against the bright glare of sunlight reflecting on the lake's surface.

In the background, I hear a few kids splashing in the water near the shore. A hawk whistles overhead, probably contemplating if he can carry off one of the smaller toddlers.

Eyes closed, I drift around the swim area, buffeted by a faint breeze that pulls small waves along the lake's surface.

All week I've watched Boone for more napkin doodling. He's been sitting at the counter and we chat while he eats breakfast. No more doodles, but definitely more flirting.

I still can't find a source for the drawing in my dad's book. Nothing on the internet matches exactly and my brain hurts from reading too many articles involving physics.

When I feel my donut bump against a buoy, I spin myself and kick my legs to propel myself away.

The sound of kids splashing and yelling fades. I yawn again, feeling sleep tugging at me in the warmth of the sun.

Safe in my pink donut, I give in to the sleepiness. A short nap is the best idea I've had since deciding to come swimming.

Nine

"LUCY!"

In my half-dream state, I hear someone calling my name. Whoever it is has also stolen my covers. Cold air brushes my skin and this makes me unhappy.

I stretch my arms out to the side to locate the blanket, but come up short. With a huff, I roll over to my side to reclaim a corner of the blanket.

"Lucy!"

My bed wobbles and dips before transforming into a waterbed. With a leak.

"What the hell?" I inhale a mouthful of water, coughing and sputtering as my arms flail through the air. Opening my eyes, I realize I'm still at the lake. Or more aptly, I'm in the lake, floundering like a cat thrown in a bathtub.

"Lucy!" Someone calls my name.

With a grip on my donut, I spin myself around to find the source of whoever is calling me.

That's when I notice the black wall of a thunderstorm to the west. Wind kicks up bigger waves on the water, creating small whitecaps.

I also notice I'm the only one in the lake. Everyone else has left. Not only that, I'm in the middle, far from the safe area of the buoys. Scanning the shore, I spot a familiar tall figure waving his arms and shouting.

My own personal lifeguard.

Boone.

What's he doing here?

Thunder rolls in the distance.

My grandfather's warning comes to mind: if you can hear thunder, you're at risk for getting struck by lightning.

And I'm floating in water, a perfect conductor of electricity.

I must not be moving quickly enough because Boone reaches over his shoulder and pulls off his T-shirt while toeing off his sneakers. Watching him, I hold the donut in front of me and kick my way closer to shore and the safety of the covered pavilion.

When he drops his shorts and kicks them off, I stop paddling.

"What are you doing? There's a storm coming!" I yell at him. Now's not the time for a swim.

Ignoring me, he runs into the water and then dives as soon as it's deep enough. With strong strokes, he swims toward me.

I'm too stunned to move.

Lightning splits the dark sky miles away and the sound reaches us a few seconds later.

"Lose the donut," he tells me from a few yards away.

Kicking my way toward him, I ignore his command.

"Stop being stubborn. Unless you want to experience what it feels like to be electrocuted by lightning."

He makes a good point. With a sad sigh, I release the donut. The wind picks it up and skitters it across the lake, into a group of reeds near the cliffs.

"Can you swim?"

"I'm not an idiot," I yell back at him.

"Then swim faster." He's directly in front of me now,

encouraging me.

Thunder crackles and then booms over our heads.

We're still a few yards from shore when Boone stands. I try to touch the bottom, but can't. Doesn't matter because he scoops me into his arms. By instinct, I loop my arms around his shoulders and hold on as he jogs out of the water.

A flash of light brightens the black sky and I can smell ozone right before rain pelts the sand like invisible bullets.

"Hurry." I tighten my grip.

In seconds, we're beneath the roof of the pavilion.

The hairs on my arm stand on end as electricity crackles through the air. Strange buzzing surrounds us a second before a line of lightning splits into a spiderweb that crawls above the lake, grounding itself in the rose-colored cliff. Simultaneously thunder booms overhead, so loud my ears ring.

And still Boone holds me in his arms.

The storm's directly above us now. Pounding rain slams noisily into the roof. Clouds swirl overhead. Raindrops and wind churn the lake's surface and the water appears to boil. Wind pushes rain through the lattice work of the covered picnic pavilion.

And Boone doesn't put me down.

Without my phone I have no idea what time it is or how long we've been trapped by the storm. He's been holding me for minutes; I must be getting heavy, but his arms never shake.

Not that I'm complaining. Warmth spreads through me from where our skin touches. My left arm rests across his shoulders, leaving my bikini-covered boob pressed against his naked chest. His right arm wraps around my back and his left is tucked underneath my knees, his hand resting on my bare thigh.

The way he holds me is intimate and way outside my comfort zone. Skin touching anywhere but our hands is above our friendship level, if anyone could pretend our few random conversations make us more than acquaintances.

His hand grips and then relaxes on my thigh. I feel more than see him gazing at me.

If I turn my head, our faces will be inches apart.

"Are you okay?" he asks, his breath warming my temple.

"You can put me down now," I whisper, not looking at him. "Your arms must be getting tired."

"They're not. Body heat will prevent us from getting hypothermia." I can feel the vibrations from his laughter against my skin. His back muscles tighten and release beneath my hand.

"It was a thousand degrees an hour ago. I think we'll be okay." I don't know why I'm trying to convince him to release me. I must be an idiot. This is the most skin-on-skin contact I've had in forever. Sadly, it's not sexual. After our encounter at Cowboy Pete's, I don't think he even likes me.

His hold on my thighs loosens and my legs tip down. My feet still don't touch the ground.

"Are you going to let go?" His right hand squeezes my side above my bikini bottom as his quiet laughter rumbles in his chest again.

"Right." Embarrassed, I unclasp my arms and slide down until my toes hit earth. I notice his hand still rests on my waist, warmth burning an imprint of his palm on my skin.

"Sure you're okay?" With our normal foot of height difference restored, he has to duck his head to meet my eyes.

"I think so." My brain is stuck between sleep and panic. Everything feels surreal and intense right now. A sunburn tingles on my pink skin. "I can't believe I fell asleep in the lake."

Standing next to him, I glance down at the wet ground. He's in his black boxer briefs. They're soaked through and clinging to his thighs. I should suggest he peel them off. He must be uncomfortable wearing wet underwear. Then he'd be naked. And we could have crazy thunderstorm sex. No one's around to catch us.

I won't let my eyes scan any higher for fear I might combust from embarrassment if I get caught sneaking a peek.

I might be wearing a bikini, but more of me is covered with the high-waisted bottoms and vintage-style bra top. Of course my nipples are standing at attention from the cold rain. Or maybe from Boone's hands on my body.

"So much for keeping my clothes dry." He points to the soggy pile of fabric on the sand.

"Mine too." I spot my towel and bag farther down the beach. "Chair's gone, too."

The pink donut bobs in the reeds, barely visible through the monsoon. Once the storm passes, I'll swim out to rescue it and locate the missing chair.

Lightning flashes to the east and thunder follows, a low, growling rumble rather than the sharp cracks from a few minutes ago. Above us the din of rain hitting the roof softens.

"Storm's moving away. We should be in the clear soon." Boone runs a hand through his dripping hair; his bicep coils and muscles stretch over his ribs. His beauty doesn't stop with his face.

I resist the urge to twist a ringlet around my finger or run my fingertips over his muscles. Barely.

We're standing inappropriately close for two strangers who are practically naked.

Out of nowhere, he asks, "Did you really think Shari was my girlfriend?"

"How was I supposed to know she was your sister? I didn't notice the family resemblance until after I opened my mouth and swallowed my foot. At least Shari found it hysterical."

"I almost choked to death." Water droplets hit my shoulder when he shakes his head while laughing.

"I know CPR. I would've saved you." I give him a shy smile.

"Good to know you're an expert in mouth-to-mouth." He lowers his voice to a deep rumble.

I snort. I wonder if Boone's ever had to use a line to get a woman to talk to him. They probably throw themselves at him like salmon climbing a fish ladder.

"Let's pretend I didn't say that. While standing in my underwear." He covers his face with both hands and rubs, as if trying to erase himself from existence.

I chuckle, completely empathizing with how he's feeling. "I'm usually the one who can make a situation awkward with a single sentence."

Spreading his fingers, he peeks at me through them. "Tell me once when you did that in your underwear."

He's got me there. "You win."

"Fantastic. What's the expression? No good deed goes unpunished?" he grumbles.

"Speaking of, what are you doing out here at the lakes? Just driving by right before a storm and happened to see me asleep on my floatie?" I ask, because my mind is now focused on his mouth and I need a distraction. I decide to throw his words from Cowboy Pete's back at him. "Coincidence?"

He moves his hands to the back of his head and stares at the roof above us. "Had the same idea you did. Swim on a hot afternoon."

I'm not sure I believe him, and am about to question him further when a loud clap of thunder snaps the air at the same time a flash of lightning zig-zags across the sky. The electricity in the air lifts the hairs on my arms. Scared by how close the strike is to us, I jump. "Shit, that was close. I wasn't planning to die today."

Chuckling, Boone wraps his arms around me before pulling me against his chest.

"You're safe. I've got you," he whispers, reassuring me.

If his mouth-to-mouth comment was the world's cheesiest attempt at flirting, he unknowingly has spoken words that hit the most tender part of my heart.

Thunder rolls farther away but I still cling to his forearms.

His hands flex at my waist before he wraps them around my back.

Lightning brightens the dim light right before Boone crushes his mouth to mine.

I gasp, my fingers pressing into his warm skin. Shocked he's kissing me, I hesitate.

He groans and begins to lean away, his hands resting gently on my waist like we're at a school dance and got busted by a chaperone.

If he thinks I'm rejecting him, he couldn't be more wrong.

Looping my arms around his neck, I tug him close again, pressing my lips to his. Thankfully he responds by tightening his grip on my hips. His mouth is commanding, ravenous. When he sweeps his tongue against mine, heat blooms across my skin. The contrast between the warmth of his mouth on mine and the cold rain blowing against us sends a shiver along my spine. Like standing in the cold water with the sun burning my back, my body is a giant contradiction.

I've never been kissed like this before. His slight shadow of a beard scrapes against my sunburned skin, sending a mix of pleasure and pain through my body right to my core.

I feel safe and fearless. Emboldened.

I think about stripping off his clothes and having my way with him on the beach.

Then I remember he's not wearing clothes, boxers only.

His palm cups my breast through my wet bathing suit, brushing over the peak of my nipple. I squirm, breathless, rubbing my hips against his. My movement draws a moan from him when I come in contact with his hard length.

I lose all sense of time while my hands explore his upper body. Sweeping them over the hard curves of the muscles on his shoulders and chest, I struggle to believe I'm not still dreaming.

A few days ago I didn't think he could stand me and now he's claiming my mouth during a storm.

He trails kisses from the corner of my mouth along my jaw. His voice is a warm rasp against my ear, "Lucy."

When he lifts his head, I kiss a line up his throat. "Yes?"

"Storm's passed."

I sense the sunlight before I open my eyes. Water drips from the roof, splashing into puddles around our feet.

The sky is split in two. Sunlight and blue sky contrast against the black clouds of the thunderstorm as it moves off to the east.

I press my hands on his warm chest, noticing a thin line of chest hair between his pecs. I focus my eyes there when I say, "We should go.

"We should." He doesn't release me.

"You should probably let me go, unless you plan to walk us over to your clothes like this." When I wiggle against him, pretending to try to escape, his erection bumps against my stomach. "Oh."

He rests his chin on top of my head. "Oh is right. Give me a minute so I don't get arrested for indecent exposure."

I still haven't glanced down, but I can feel how long and hard he is.

When he finally steps back, I sneak a peek.

He's no longer hard, but still completely indecent.

He tips my chin up with his knuckle. "Ready?"

"So ready," I mumble under my breath.

I've never experienced storms like the ones in New Mexico before. On the high desert, lines of rain can be seen from miles away. One side of the road is dry, the other covered in puddles.

Before and after.

My lips still hum from Boone's kiss.

For months I wondered what it would be like to kiss him. Before today, it felt like a fantasy.

After this afternoon, I'll always remember the feel of kissing him during a storm.

IN THE BRIGHT sunlight, I'm once again shy and awkward around Boone.

He returns to his quiet self, but I catch him staring at me.

We gather our drenched clothes and wring them out, laying them on the sand to catch the heat from the sun. My bag is soaked, but it kept my towel mostly dry during the storm. I offer it to Boone. No longer dripping wet, he pulls on his shorts but not his T-shirt.

I swim across the lake to recover my pink donut while he scours the shore for my beach chair. Successful in locating both, we meet back at the main beach.

My dress is still damp and I skip wearing it, opting instead for wrapping my towel around my waist.

A few families return to the beach from wherever they rode out the storm. If they had more sense than us, they would've hunkered down in the bathrooms.

Safer, but not as romantic. More private than the pavilion, though. My mind drifts back to our kiss.

"Earth to Lucy?" Boone asks, still holding my chair. "Where'd you go?"

I blink at him, lost in thoughts of us making out.

"I need to head out. I have an appointment in downtown," he says.

"Sure. I'm going to leave, too." I lift my bag over my shoulder and loop the donut around my elbow.

"Can I walk you to your car? I'll carry your stuff." He's sweet and awkward and it reminds me of a boy who once carried my backpack in junior high.

I nod, unsure of where this is going.

On our way to the parking lot, I jump over puddles Boone steps around. We're quiet and I find the silence comfortable.

At my car, I toss the chair and floatie in the backseat, then set my bag beside them. The rain has washed the dust from my old Honda, making it look less neglected and old. Boone leans against the side, waiting for me to finish.

"I'm busy this weekend, but I'll see you on Monday." He trails the back of his hand down my arm.

My skin pebbles in the wake of his touch.

"It's a date. For breakfast." I smile up at him.

"I like the sound of that." Leaning down, he lightly touches his lips to mine. Once. Twice. Then he steps forward, switching our places so I'm pressed with my back to the car and he's caged me between his arms. "We should do it every day."

"I'm not sure about doing it every day. Maybe five times a week?" I give him a soft, open kiss.

He moans and kisses me deeper.

When we come up for air, I add, "I meant Monday through Friday at the diner."

"Good point." He chuckles. "We're doing this all backward. I need to take you out on a date."

"I've already seen you in your skivvies." My eyes drift down his bare chest.

"I'm going to plan a date." He nods as if he's confirming his own idea. "Are you free next weekend?"

"It's the Alien Festival."

"Right. Not that. I don't want any little green men competing for your attention." He kisses the corner of my mouth.

A giant RV drives by and honks. The gray-haired man in mirrored RayBans driving it leans out the window and yells, "This is a family place. Get a room!"

Boone's shoulders shake with laughter. "Easy enough to say for a man driving his home around town."

My giggles join his. "He's probably a pervert."

"Or a genius." His eyes crinkle in the corners before he gives me another quick kiss on the lips. "I'm going to be late. I wish I could stay."

He didn't suggest getting together this weekend and I'm being cool, so I give him a gentle shove and say, "See you Monday."

He grumbles, but releases me. "No more naps in lakes."

"Promise."

Ten

ALONG WITH decorating the town with little green men, the annual Alien Festival brings hundreds of experts and believers to town for a convention of panels, discussions, and presentations of the latest theories about the who, what, how, why, and when of extraterrestrial travelers on Earth.

Taking time off of work, I spend four days in windowless ballrooms, listening and writing notes, hoping for some sort of proof. When I registered, I listed myself as Lucy Wesley Halliday, from Pine Bluff, New York—optimistic someone might make the connection between the name and my hometown. For a brief window of time, the story of my dad's abduction was national news. If anyone out there might have information or clues, they're also the type to attend a convention about UFOs and aliens.

I sit through panel after panel, making small talk in between sessions. I introduce myself over and over again. I hear way more than anyone ever should about probing.

No one says anything that convinces me my father was kidnapped by aliens.

I'll never get these hours of my life back.

During one particularly New Age seminar, we follow a meditation to travel through time and space on a higher astral plane, seeking out our past or future selves.

I fall asleep within minutes and don't remember meeting any other versions of myself.

Sadly, I leave at the end of the second day no wiser.

On the upside, I got in a decent nap before tonight's festivities.

I'm meeting Boone and Shari in an hour at the main stage where local bands will perform before the parade of aliens after dark.

I haven't seen Boone since the beginning of the week. Sadly, we didn't make out in the cooler. He did give me a quick peck when he left, setting my cheeks aflame and Wanda all atwitter.

ALIEN AUTOPSIES PLAYS on the raised stage in the middle of the park in front of City Hall. The enthusiastic crowd bounces and dances along to the upbeat rock-pop music. Surrounded by little green men in every incarnation from two dimensional to three dimensional, the concert is the perfect mix of Coachella and Roswell.

The band is dressed in a combination of spacemen and aliens. How the drummer can breathe or see with the alien mask fascinates me, let alone hold his sticks with the long fingered green hands, is a miracle. That's talent right there. In his mirrored helmet, the bass player captures my attention. Without a face to ruin the fantasy, I focus on his long, nimble fingers, broad shoulders, and the way he tilts his hips forward when he really gets into jamming. Not sure what it says about me that I prefer my rocker fantasy to be faceless, but I'm not questioning it right now.

I'm so far out of my element being here alone. My norm is to stay at home on a Saturday night, reading or watching crazies on YouTube talk about UFOs. Just another single girl in Roswell.

It's hard to say which is the more desperate evening: home

alone or subject to being picked up at an alien festival.

Jury's still out.

Several men have approached me, offering sloshing cups of beer or similar, half-assed pick-up lines. Maybe they were given the same playbook.

"Is your name Sunshine?" asks the guy in the green, over-sized alien eye sunglasses. "It should be because you made my day brighter."

"Can I call you Sunny?" a man in a head-to-toe green body suit asks. "'Cause you're the hottest body here."

Those were the two that made me snort. The others I want to bleach my brain to forget.

Yes, Uranus is funny.

No, it shouldn't be used as a pick-up line.

Ever.

I texted Boone when I parked, but haven't located either him or Shari yet.

The floor show distracts me from my social anxiety. Crowds, especially ones where people are in costumes, freak me out.

I'm trying to step outside of my comfort zone.

Normally, I'd wear a T-shirt and jeans when going out, but tonight I'm in a dress with thin straps and an off the shoulder sleeve. Still wearing my favorite new cowboy boots, though. They have extra pointy toes in case I need to use them as a weapon of self-defense.

On stage, the guys jam out, riffing off of each other before the guitar player takes a solo. The bassist prowls to the edge of the stage, where a group of teenagers squeal and stretch their arms toward him.

He bobs his head and gives one lucky girl a high five. She makes the universal gesture for never washing this hand again by holding it close to her chest and screaming while her friends form a jumping circle around her. The boldest girl takes the blessed appendage and rubs it on her own face.

An involuntary shudder passes through me at the thought. Who knows where that hand has been or what it's touched? Or when the last time it was washed with soap and water.

Before working at the restaurant, I lived in a happy delusion that people wash their hands, that we all share a common decency when it comes to touching our nether bits and being out in public. Sure, you do your own thing in the comfort of your own home, but out in society? Come on. We've all seen enough zombie apocalypse movies to know that one super strain of flu is all it's going to take before we're screwed.

The crowd screams and claps as the gentleman of Alien Autopsies bow and begin making their way off stage. Next to me, a couple in shiny silver disco space costumes yell for an encore. He has an impressively loud whistle using two fingers in his mouth.

I hope he's washed them recently.

Given how crazy amped this group has been the entire show, I think we can all assume an encore is a foregone conclusion. Apparently, I'm the only one who feels this way when a roadie comes out and removes the mic stand and my fellow music lovers begin booing.

Where is their faith? Have none of them been to a concert before?

The drummer returns and settles in behind his drum kit. Gone is the green alien mask. My view of his face is obscured by people and instruments, but the revelation of his normal self has my heart beating quicker as I wait for the bassist to return.

I need to see if the face is as hot as the hands.

When he steps back stage, the mirrored helmet is absent. My hopes for a clear view crash and burn when I see the huge, round sunglasses covering most of his face. What's not hidden behind neon green plastic and dark lenses is too generic to be recognizable. Sweat dampens his dark hair, which is shoved off of his face in a slick pompadour Adam Lambert would love.

Only when they finish the encore and the bass player smiles at something the lead singer says, do I recognize him. And I choke on my own spit.

"There you are," Shari shouts, suddenly appearing in front of me. Thankfully she's not dressed as a green alien. "I thought I recognized the back of your head."

Trying to clear my throat, I cough. "Hey." I barely eek out a whisper.

Her brows lift with worry. "Should I slap you on the back?"

I wave off her lifted hand. "No, I'm okay. Swallowed wrong."

"I'm so happy you made it. Isn't this a fun show?" Grinning at me, she reminds me of Boone's extreme handsomeness. Not even twins, the two have an other-worldly beauty to them. Exotic, yet familiar. Her long, dark hair is in messy French braids crowned by a headband sporting two alien faces on springs. When she moves, the little green ovals bounce around like insects circling her head. She's also wearing a T-shirt with David Duchovny's face covering the front.

"The whole UFO festival is . . ." I search for the word. Weird doesn't seem appropriate for Shari's obvious enthusiasm. "Crazy."

That works.

"I love it."

"Nice shirt. I didn't know I should dress to the theme." I pull one of the straps of my dress higher on my shoulder.

"Every alien story needs the pretty human heroine. Pretend that's your costume." She flashes a reassuring smile. "I think you look gorgeous."

Shaking off his admirers, Boone slowly prowls through the crowd in our direction.

I thought I could maybe handle Boone as a hot oil worker, a man who drives a dirty truck, a creature of habit, and a lover of pancakes.

Then he became the best kiss of my life.

I knew I was in trouble.

There's not a chance I can survive Boone the musician and local rock god. Not with knowing how his mouth feels against mine. Or the way he looks ninety-eight percent naked.

I'm doomed.

"I didn't know he was in a band." I sound a little breathless like one of the young fangirls.

"He's not the kind to brag. I'm telling you, he's shy," Shari says, almost convincingly.

"Right. And average looking, too."

She rolls her eyes. "I don't get it about his looks. It's not like he's perfect. There's that bald spot in his right eyebrow and his ears are a little big. Although they're better now that he grew into his head."

"Flaws give us character. You're both examples of superior genes." I mean it as a compliment but she gives me a funny look.

Making his way to us quicker than I thought possible given his swarms of fans, Boone steps beside me. Warmth spreads through my body from his proximity. It's been a week since the storm at the lake. Seven long days since I've been properly kissed. Insecurity and worry are dimming the glow. Maybe it was a onetime thing and he's changed his mind.

He leans close to be heard above the crowd. His lips brush my shoulder. "You look beautiful. I'm glad you're here."

Instantly I'm thankful for wearing this dress.

"What did you think of the band?" he asks.

"You were great." It's the truth.

"You think so?"

I nod enthusiastically. "I may never wash my shoulder again."

This earns me an eye roll from an embarrassed Boone.

A woman in silver robes takes the stage carrying a box with an antenna.

When she begins to sing, she waves her hands around the box and the strangest sounds come out.

My mouth drops open. "What is that? She's not even touching it and it's making music."

Okay, music might be a stretch of the imagination.

Boone answers, again speaking close to my ear to be heard, "It's a theremin. She plays themes from old sci-fi movies. I think this is from *The Day the Earth Stood Still*."

"Poor peace seeking aliens. So foolish to think humans would be friendly." Sighing, Shari shakes her head. "Too trusting and innocent."

The same tune as my text alert blasts from the speakers.

"Did the aliens invent it?" I ask because it's unlike any instrument I've ever seen.

Boone chuckles and kisses my shoulder again. "No, Mr. Theremin. As far as we know he was Russian."

"Russian alien?" I ask, undeterred.

"Probably a Vulcan." Boone jokes as the theme from *Star Trek* plays.

"How?" I ask.

"How what? I was joking about Theremin being a Vulcan. I've seen pictures of him and he definitely didn't have pointy ears. Of course, he could've had them surgically altered," he explains in a rational tone.

I twist my neck so I can look into his eyes to see if he's seriously believing what he's saying. We're standing close enough he has to duck his head to meet my stare. His dark lashes frame his too pretty eyes. Gazing at him, I get lost in the swirls of amber and green.

"You had a question?" Warm, minty breath skims my cheek when he speaks. He's leaned closer, and now his mouth is a few inches from mine.

I don't know my own middle name right now, I'm so lost in his eyes and the angles of his cheekbones.

Eerie music plays through the speakers somewhere behind us reminding me we're not alone.

"Wesley," I whisper, more breath than spoken.

Boone jerks away. "Who's Wesley?"

My lashes beat together as I blink away the Boone fog. "Me?"

"You're Lucy." Wrinkles line his forehead.

"Wesley's my middle name. Well, technically it's my father's last name, but Lucy Wesley doesn't sound as good as Lucy Halliday, so my mom gave me her name," I ramble, throwing the words together quickly to get to the end of the explanation as fast as possible. "Nice to meet you."

His attention flicks down to my extended hand. "Nice to meet you, Lucy Wesley Halliday. Boone Santos. No middle name. My sister, Sharyl, who prefers to be called Shari, Santos."

"What are we doing? Why are you two introducing yourselves again?" Shari lifts her eyebrows, confused. "I think the creepy alien music is affecting your heads."

Boone takes my hand, threading his fingers with mine. "We're getting to know each other. Out of order, but I'm going to change that."

"You are?" I ask, happiness lifting my lips into a smile.

"I'm going to take you out on a date tomorrow. For the whole day."

I swear Shari sighs. Or it could be me.

Eleven

"I CAN'T BELIEVE you've never been down to Carlsbad Caverns." Boone's voice holds a boyish excitement.

I want to say I can't believe he thinks bringing me to a giant hole in the ground is a good first date idea. Instead, I settle for telling him, "Caves and hanging out with bats aren't high on my list of things to do on my days off."

"You're missing out on one of nature's most splendid wonders." He bobs his chin to emphasize his brilliant idea.

"You sound like a brochure. Do you get a kickback for bringing in new visitors?" Bending my knee, I rest my foot on the edge of my seat in his truck.

"I've been coming here my whole life. My grandmother used to be a ranger here. Did you know the earliest explorers used lanterns and buckets on rope to get to the lower sections. Can you imagine being alone down there?"

"With the bats and the never-ending darkness? No way. Stuff of my worst nightmares. Like the black void of space, but with bats flying around."

He dips his chin and stares at me over his sunglasses. "You're weird, you know that, right?"

"Chiropterophobia is a real thing." There's probably a phobia of caves, too, but I don't know the word. I've never needed it before. I pull out my phone and look it up. "Speluncaphobia or claustro-phobia, which seems too broad because closets and elevators don't typically have bats hanging in them."

His lips curl into a smile. "I think bats are misunderstood. They're adorable. And eat mosquitoes. Which would you rather have? Bloodsucking insects or furry mini teddy bears with wings?"

My mouth pops open. "I'm weird? Pretty sure you're the only person who thinks bats and teddy bears belong in the same sentence."

"We should stay until dusk. You might change your mind."

"What happens at dusk?" I ask against my better judgment.

"I don't want to ruin the surprise." His grin is full of the kind of mischief that's a direct route to trouble.

"Tell me." I grab his wrist on his arm not currently steering the truck. The one resting on the top of his thigh right where his jeans crease. So essentially if he moved his hand a few inches, I'd be grabbing his crotch. At this realization, I jerk my hand away.

Thankfully, Boone doesn't seem to notice my almost threat-ening dick grab. "Since you asked so nicely, at dusk, thousands of bats leave the natural entrance to the caves and fly over the amphitheater to the delight of all in attendance."

"I'm going to stop you right there and say nope," I say this as I hold up my arms in defense against a swarm of invisible bats.

He laughs at my reaction. "I won't force you, but it's really cool."

"Can I wear a space suit? Better yet, a human-size hamster ball. Have one of those laying around?" My crazy ideas give me a small slice of comfort.

"Sadly, I don't think they rent those in the gift shop."

Widening my eyes, I shrug. "Too bad. Guess we'll have to be on the road before dusk."

We ride in silence for a few miles. Not sure about him, but my thoughts are still on caves and bats and how many phobias I have.

Wanting to break the lull in conversation, I try to focus on something positive. "That's kind of cool your grandmother was a ranger here."

"She's amazing. Back when she started, there weren't a lot of women who worked as rangers. By the time I was a kid, she was retired but would bring us here and encourage us to explore."

Twisting to get a better look at him, I try to process his words. "Your grandmother used to let you roam around caverns when you were a kid? In the dark? Unattended?"

"Shari was with me. Sometimes our parents joined us. And we had walkie talkies."

"My grandmother didn't let me ride my bike into town by myself, even in the middle of the day." Back then there wasn't a term for overprotective parents, but I'm definitely the product of helicopter parenting. Ironic that now I'm an orphan, completely on my own.

Boone follows the winding road from the turnoff to the visitor's center. Scrappy looking creosote shrubs and rock cover the craggy landscape, which gives no hint to the secrets hidden below the surface.

The landscape is beautiful but vaguely hostile. Kind of how I used to see the man sitting beside me. Maybe hostile is too strong. Unfriendly. Guarded. Disinterested. Dry.

Two of those things are no longer true.

"We're here," he announces when he pulls to a stop behind a single story beige building.

"Are we sneaking in the back?" I ask, peering around the dumpster for an entrance.

"I still have connections. We can go through the employee entrance and skip the lines. If you want, we can even take the elevator down to the bottom and avoid the bats entirely. Although some people," he points at his chest, "think you're missing the best part if you go that way."

"Save your judgment, Santos. I'm fine skipping the stench of the guano of a million bats."

"Suit yourself." He hops out the driver's side door.

I follow and find him waiting for me by the tailgate.

"If anyone asks, you're my cousin."

"Why?" I give him the side-eye. There's no way we're related unless one branch of his family tree is Wednesday Adams. I'm short, curvy, and pale next to his tall, angular, tanned self.

He glances around before tipping his head down and lowering his voice. "Lifetime family membership only applies to actual family."

"Got it. I'm Lucy Santos if anyone asks."

He grins down at me. "Lucy Santos works."

Works for me, too, but I don't tell him that.

As he leads me through the employee-only area, I mentally write Lucy Santos all over my imaginary notebook, sometimes drawing hearts or adding Mrs. before my new name.

I might be almost twenty-eight, but my inner teenager girl is alive and well.

The lobby is decorated like any other semi-generic welcome center. Pale stones lining some walls give a vague hint we're in the southwest, but the bland wood counters and fluorescent lighting make it feel like a government office. Out of the large picture windows, cacti fill planters and flower beds in case anyone forgets they're actually in New Mexico. Perhaps a necessary reminder once they ascend from the the depths.

Crowding near the elevators, tourists wait their turns to descend to the caverns.

"This reminds me of going to Niagara Falls when I was little.

You can take an elevator to tunnels behind the Canadian Falls." I'm not sure why I'm sharing this other than an elevator into the bowels of the earth is involved in both.

"Are you nervous?" Boone touches my shoulder, resting his hand there.

I shake my head no. "Yes."

He nods and then mirrors my head shaking. "Nothing to be afraid of. I know this place by memory. If you stick to the paths, it's impossible to get lost."

We join a group in an elevator, squeezing ourselves into the corner. More people crowd on and I find myself with my back pressed against Boone's front.

His natural spicy scent envelops me along with the warmth of his body where we make contact.

"We're like sardines in a can," an older man announces to the group.

We all laugh and the collective energy changes from discomfort to camaraderie as we descend.

I'm not sure how long I expected a journey to the center of the planet to take, but the elevator thumps to a soft landing and the doors open sooner than I imagined.

Boone slips his fingers between mine and I find myself returning his pressure.

"Ready to be amazed?" he whispers close to my ear as we wait for the others ahead of us to leave.

"As ever," I put on my fake friendly voice. I kind of sound like an overly excited cartoon character. I may have overdone it.

Like the elevator trip, what I see when I exit is not at all what I expect.

Directly ahead of us is a snack bar with tables and chairs straight out of a 1960s sci-fi movie. Round kiosks with illuminated circular roofs look like spaceships. Vintage down to the plastic chairs and shiny stainless steel of the counter where you place your order.

"What sort of trickery is this?" I ask, spinning around to take it all in. "Are we really underground?"

The "walls" are smooth rock and I feel like I've been transported to an amusement ride at Disney World where nothing is real and all part of a giant fabrication for our entertainment.

"Where are the Seven Dwarves? Is there a big theater with all the dead presidents around the corner? I'm so confused." I stop spinning because it's making me dizzy.

A woman exits the restroom directly across from the elevators. "There are bathrooms? In a cave?"

"You sound really excited about the bathroom." His eyes crease in the corners as he laughs.

"Be right back." I race over to the entrance and wave at him before I check out the restroom.

"I'm peeing underground," I say out loud, thinking I'm alone in the stalls.

"Me too," a small voice shouts from my left, followed by giggles.

Happy to share the moment with someone, I give the little girl a high five . . . after we thoroughly wash our hands.

I spy Boone sitting at a table with his legs stretched out in front of him. When he sees me he stands. "Everything you dreamed?"

"I'm not sure I'd survive living down here, but I'm feeling less panicked by the idea of being a few hundred feet underground than I thought I'd be."

"Who's asking you to move into a cavern?" From the grin on his face, I clearly amuse him.

"The whole place screams cold war bomb shelter of the future, only from seventy years ago." I stare up at the dark rock of the natural ceiling overhead. "Or a super villain's lair. This place has despicable Bond villain written all over it. Better yet, snack bar on the moon."

I finally end my rambling. I guess I'm still nervous.

"Except for the gravity keeping us from floating away." He smirks.

"Buzzkill." I pull the sleeves of my thin cotton shirt down over my fingers.

"Cold?" he asks.

"It's not exactly cozy down here."

"That's why I told you to dress warmly." He brushes his hands up and down my arms to create heat.

"I didn't believe you."

He begins unbuttoning his chambray shirt. "It's not a sweater, but another layer might help."

His nimble fingers slip the buttons out of their holes. The blue cotton falls open with his progress, revealing a white T-shirt underneath. Something about the faded denim and classic white tee make him fit in with the vintage decor. For a moment I can see him with his hair slicked back like one of the greasers in *The Outsiders*.

"Here." He hands me his shirt, which is still warm from his body heat.

"I can't. Won't you be cold?" I'm already slipping the cloth over my shoulders, but it feels more polite to protest.

"I'm always hot."

Understatement of the century. "Humble much?"

He tugs his shirt closed across my chest, his fingers brushing a few inches above my breast. "Thanks for the compliment, but I meant temperature wise. I never get cold."

"Still braggy." I roll the extra-long sleeves up to my wrists and button up. I'm not a thin, delicate boned woman, and still his shirt swallows me, hanging down to my mid-thigh.

"And you're adorable. Ready?" He gives me the softest peck, then rights himself and tucks his fingers into the back pockets of his jeans.

I'm still leaning forward, waiting for more until I realize that's all he's going to give me. There must be a dark corner around here where we can make out. It's a cave after all.

"Bring on the stalactites. Or stalagmites."

He flashes me a sexy, slow smile. "I can promise you both."

With his hand resting on my shoulder, he steers me down a paved path toward a sign that reads, "Big Room." A short walk down a dark tunnel brings us to the opening of a vast cavern, illuminated by white lights.

I take back my comment about Boone's "always hot" declaration being the understatement of the century.

"This place is a cathedral." Awe replaces my usual snark when we enter the enormous space lined with white limestone. "Only filled with penises of every length and girth imaginable."

Beside me, Boone chuckles.

"Let's pretend I kept the last part to myself and didn't actually speak it out loud. Because that would be embarrassing, even for me."

I stand by the statement, though. Great white phalluses hang from the high, domed ceiling while others rise up from the cavern floor like stone erections. Pools of water reflect the illuminated sculptures.

"This is the most bizarre place I've ever been," I tell Boone, who I assume is behind me. He must not be paying attention, so I grab his hand.

"Sure you don't want to stay for the bats?" Boone appears on my other side.

If he's on my right, how am I holding his hand with my left? Slowly, I slide my eyes to the side and see a middle-aged man sporting a yellow golf shirt over his dad bod. Glancing down, I confirm our fingers are laced together.

"Why are you holding hands with my husband?" a frazzled looking woman asks from beside the man.

"Mistaken identity," I apologize, releasing his hand and wiping mine on my jean-covered hip.

Boone watches me, fighting laughter with a twist of his mouth.

"Go on, let it out." I give his arm a gentle shove.

"I didn't figure you for the cheating type, Lucy. And now that I know you'd rather hold a stranger's hand than mine, my feelings are hurt." He pushes out his bottom lip in a pout and gives me sad dog eyes.

"I was talking to you and you weren't answering me, so I grabbed your hand to get your attention. It wasn't a romantic gesture."

"I hope not. That man's wife seemed pretty pissed." He snickers.

"Har har." I step around him to continue my exploration.

He follows me for a few steps before slipping his hand around my wrist and then interlocking his fingers with mine.

Afraid to ruin the moment, I don't say anything. Neither does he. We stroll silently among the giant sculptures almost a thousand feet below the desert.

This might not be my idea for a romantic date, and if this is romance to Boone, he's truly weird, but either way, I'm happy.

In this strange place, holding hands with him, I'm not thinking about the past or worried about the future. I'm content.

BOONE LURES ME outside to show me the natural cave opening. Families and couples are already claiming their bat viewing spots in the amphitheater carved into the hillside above the hole that leads to the bat cave.

"This is more than adequate. Right here. Got the idea." I dig in my heels and stop. "I can imagine the gaping maw spewing forth thousands of furry bloodsuckers."

A woman near me must overhear my description because her eyes bug out of her head and her mouth drops open. From her horrified expression, no one has explained the details of the event she's attending. I feel sorry for her.

"All good. Let's go." I use both the hand Boone is holding and my free one tugging on his arm to pull him away. "Sun's getting low in the sky. Best be on the road soon."

I'm growing to like the way his eyes narrow and his lips press together when I say or do something he finds funny in an odd, not ha-ha way. Like I'm a strange bird who suddenly appeared in his yard one day and he doesn't know what to do with me.

If he only knew how strange I am.

He'd run for the hills. Or down into a cavern to live with his bat friends.

For now, I amuse him. I'll take this moment even if it's all we get. There's no promise of a future, not when he finds out my past.

"I'll make a deal with you." He stands his ground. "If we leave now, we stop on the way home for the best chiles rellenos you'll ever have."

"Feeling pretty confident about these chiles." I scrunch up my face like I'm doubting him. I'm not. "What's the other option?"

"We stay for the bats." He smirks at me. "Your choice."

He's played me. So he thinks. Like going to dinner with him is a burden.

"Twist my arm. Let's go to dinner. Such a hardship." I grin at him.

We're far down the road when the sun sets, but I swear I see a flock of bats in the dusky sky as we drive back toward Roswell. Or maybe they're tiny black UFOs.

Today's one of those days when anything feels possible.

Twelve

ARTESIA SITS ABOUT halfway between the caverns and home. After turning off the highway and driving us away from the main drag, Boone parks the truck in front of a long, metal industrial building.

"Is this the part where the news channel reports the last place I was seen?" I joke as we walk to the front door. At least I assume it's the front door because there's a faded banner hanging next to it. The name Las Chicas is barely visible on the sun-bleached vinyl.

"You've got to learn to trust me." He rests his hand on my lower back.

If only he knew how impossible that request is for me.

I should have "trust no one" tattooed on my forehead. A warning to others as well as a reminder to myself.

Inside, Boone greets the woman at the hostess stand in rapid Spanish. I only pick up a few words, but smile and nod when he points to me. Colorful paper flowers and pompoms decorate the tables and walls in contrast to the nondescript exterior. Star-shaped lanterns hanging from the metal ceiling create a soft, dappled light in the large room. Most of the tables are filled with families and couples, who also greet Boone in Spanish.

I doubt many tourists would make it past the door to this

place, so I'm guessing they're all locals.

In fact, I spot Tony sitting at a large round table in the back. I wave when he sees me, not thinking of the company I'm with. He nods and grins, then not subtly at all, gives me a big thumbs-up.

Work should be interesting next week.

Lupe, as she introduced herself to me in English, brings over a plate of warm sopapillas and a squeezy bear of honey. The triangles of quick fry bread are my new favorite thing since moving to New Mexico.

After saying thank you, I drizzle a piece with honey and take an enormous bite. Mumbling with my mouth full, I declare, "So much better than bats."

A sticky dollop of honey slides off the end of the triangle, landing on my wrist.

Before I can reach for a napkin, Boone lifts my arm to his mouth. My eyelids peel back and my mouth hangs open when he gently sucks the honey from my skin with a soft, open mouth.

When he looks up at me, lips still pressed to my wrist, his eyes are dilated with intensity.

If lust has a look, Boone is mastering it right now.

"Do they have food to go?" I ask, my voice husky and my pulse racing beneath Boone's mouth. He must feel the rapid beat of my blood. All his talk of loving bats and caves and . . ."Wait, you're not a vampire are you?"

He lifts his head and stares. "Excuse me?"

"You love bats and took me to a cave on our first official date," I blurt out. Evidently all filters and rational thought have left my brain.

"You've seen me eat food and be in full sunlight." He doesn't fight his laughter, letting his head fall back. "You're not serious. Are you?"

"You're impossibly handsome and you were just kissing my

wrist and giving me a look like you wanted to eat me." My defense sounds crazy even to my own ears.

"Lucy, what am I going to do with you?" He picks up a sopapilla and bites it with his average-sized canines.

"Take me back to your bat lair and ravish me?" I suggest the classic end of a vampire's seduction.

"Once again, I'm failing at doing this dating thing in proper order. I took you to the bat lair after ravishing you in public, and in broad daylight, in case you forgot." He stares at me like he could undress me solely with the power of his vision.

I'm sure I'm blushing from the memory and can't meet his eyes. "I haven't forgotten."

Like I'll ever not remember.

"Me neither," he whispers so low I barely hear him. "This is a proper date, in case you missed the clues. We're going to have dinner first."

First.

My heart stalls for a beat before a thrill flutters through my body, settling between my thighs.

I am so doomed.

I'M THINKING ABOUT my underwear as we drive back to Roswell.

Boone's holding my hand and I'm trying to remember if I'm wearing cute panties.

Off in the distance a storm illuminates a thundercloud with lightning. Above us stars sparkle.

"I love how wide the sky is in New Mexico," I say, distracting myself from trying to covertly check what's going on in my pants.

"Isn't the sky the same everywhere? Same atmosphere, same planet?" he asks, glancing over at me. The dashboard lights cast him in a soft glow, which highlights the sharp angles of his face and the strong line of his jaw. He looks otherworldly.

And I might be wearing regular, old Saturday underwear.

"You haven't been to upstate New York. If there's a thunderstorm, the whole sky is gray. Not like here where there's room for stars and storms simultaneously. I love driving and seeing the line of rain off in the distance."

"Do you miss home?" he asks

Such a loaded question. "I miss my family."

The full truth, but not the whole story.

"But not where you grew up?"

"No. Too much snow and not enough excitement. My life felt like living in an old dream that belonged to someone else."

Taking his eyes off the road, he studies me for a minute. "That's an interesting way to describe your childhood."

"How would you describe yours?" Defensive Arts 101: Ask the questions, don't answer them.

"Normal enough." He laughs. "I wasn't super popular. Wasn't an outcast. Was in band. Played baseball had no illusions of going pro. Smart enough to go to college."

"Wow. You're really boring," I tease him because his description is almost as vague as mine. "You're so Archie."

"Is that good or bad?" he asks, completely missing my reference.

"Good guy. Almost too good."

"Hmm." He rubs his knuckles along his jaw. "Don't most women want the bad boy?"

"We want the bad boy who's good to us, which I think makes him the good guy in the end. I'm not really an expert."

We're passing the South Park cemetery and I get distracted by the lights glowing among the grave sites.

"Is it weird to love a graveyard?" I inquire, leaning forward to see around him.

He doesn't hesitate answering me. "Yes. Very."

"I love all the cheerful lights and the colorful, plastic flowers. Makes death feel less depressing. Too bad it's closed for visitors at night."

"You know this how?" he asks, eyes wide.

"I tried to go one evening at dusk. Got shooed away by some old guy locking the gates."

"You're a little obsessed with the dead, you know?" He twists to press a quick kiss on my cheek because I'm basically leaning over his lap at this point. Seatbelt be damned.

If anything, I'm obsessed with the undead or possibly dead, but I keep this to myself. I've shared enough weird for the day.

"How so?" I sit back in my proper seat.

"The whole vampire conversation earlier?"

"More like the undead, if that's your argument." I tip my head because it's the truth.

"Touché."

We arrive at my little apartment complex and I show him where to park in the back in my never used guest spot. Wanda might recognize his truck if she's peering through her kitchen curtains, but I'm hoping she's out or asleep.

"You want to come in?" I ask, realizing I assumed he would. Hence the underwear thoughts earlier.

"Are you inviting me to your lair?" He leans close enough I feel his breath against my lips.

Instead of answering him with words, I kiss him.

He unbuckles his seatbelt and shifts closer to me, sliding his arm between me and the seat to pull me against him. All the while, sweeping his tongue against mine and dominating my mouth with his. His large hand cups my cheek, angling my head to his liking.

The ghosts of my teenage hormones flair back to life and I

try to curl around him, needing friction, more kissing, and less air between us. I attempt this while still strapped into my seat.

Breathless, frustrated, and trapped, I pause mid kiss. "Not to be too forward, but I have an apartment right over there that's slightly larger than this truck."

He clicks the button to release me from my bondage. "I can't promise to behave outside of the confines of this cab."

I have my door open and I'm outside before he decides to be a gentleman. "I want the thunderstorm Boone, not a version who gives me a peck on the cheek at my door."

He follows me to my door and I'm so nervous I forget how to unlock it. I press my key fob at the handle and click.

"Here, let me." He inserts the key *in* the lock and twists to open the door.

"Right. Tab A goes inside Slot B. Got it." It's been so long since I've had sex, I needed a basic reminder.

Boone looks like a giant inside of the small space. My cool antique love seat looks like a couch for little kids next to him. "Have a seat. I'll be right back. Read a book. Or grab a drink. Glasses in the cupboard. Beverages in the fridge. There's water in the faucet."

I'm a terrible hostess.

I jog down the hall to the bathroom. With a sigh, I realize I'm wearing nice black underwear that even matches my bra, and won't have to make a quick switcheroo in my room. In the mirror, I notice my face is flushed and my eyes are extra bright. I look like I'm high, but in a good, happy way. A quick refresh and fluff, and I'm as good as I'm going to get without a full shower or spa day.

As I feared, Boone is perched on the settee. He's holding a book in his hand, which he returns to the shelf when I approach.

"Is it me, or is this thing small?" He stretches his arms along the back and can touch both ends.

"I think people were smaller when it was made." I stand in

front of him, not sure if I should squeeze next to him or sit on one of the kitchen chairs.

He makes the decision for me when he slides his hands around my thighs and pulls me forward. Guiding me to straddle him, he stares up at me. The lust I saw spark in his eyes at dinner is a brush fire now. He moves one hand to the back of my neck, bringing my mouth down to his.

"You're so beautiful," he murmurs right before pressing his lips to mine.

My heart is a hummingbird, beating so quickly everything blurs. The combination of his words, hands, and mouth should require an adult warning. The man knows how to kiss. He's not diving for lost treasure behind my tonsils or thrusting at me like an excited rabbit. His kisses are deep, long, and full of promise. I'm not sure I won't combust before we get naked.

Boone takes his time exploring my mouth while his hands roam over my body. He's a man with all the time in the world.

It's sexy as hell.

He may be taking his time, but my body is impatient for what comes next. It remembers how his bare skin feels and wants more.

Last time we made out, he was ninety-eight percent naked. Tonight, I want to go for a perfect score.

"Lucy," he whispers against my mouth, "I think a spring in your tiny couch is trying to violate me."

His words don't make sense to my sex clouded mind. I lean away and ask, "Violate you how?"

"I'm being poked in the ass by something. Did you grow an extra hand?"

I wiggle my fingers where they're twisted in his messy hair. "Nope."

He shifts and then grimaces. "We need to get up."

In a smooth motion, he grips my ass and stands. I wrap my

legs around his hips, then peer over his shoulder.

A small silver coil of a spring has penetrated the velvet. "You weren't kidding."

He spins around and glowers at the violator.

I so want to make a joke about little green aliens and their probe obsession, but I've made myself a promise to avoid all things aliens.

"Where's your bedroom?" He walks toward the hall that leads to my room and the bathroom.

A few steps later he lowers me down to the bed. I pull him over me, craving his weight on top of me. My thighs open to make room for his hips, and when he settles against me, I moan. Loudly.

He chuckles as he drags his scruffy face along my jaw.

The scrape of his one-day beard inflames my skin, but it's not the kind of friction I want.

I tip my hips up to meet him, slowly rocking against him. Now it's his time to moan.

He catches my grin with his mouth, kissing me until I'm breathless.

My hands slip beneath his T-shirt, and skim over his warm skin. After the caverns, I returned his shirt and now I curse the extra layer of fabric. I give up exploring his muscles to undo the buttons. He sits back on his haunches, allowing me better access. As soon as the last button is loose, he shrugs off the chambray and then pulls the white tee over his head.

"Your turn," he says, sneaking his own fingers beneath the hem of my shirt.

My bra is simple black satin, nothing fancy or sexy, yet Boone's eyes widen as he stares down at me. Guess he likes what he sees. Bending lower, he skims his lips over the peak of my nipple through the thin fabric. The warmth and pressures makes me arch my back in a silent plea for more.

Shifting back, he frowns.

"What?" I whisper, nerves sinking like rocks in my stomach.

"It's a beautiful bra, but I want you naked." He arches an eyebrow while he traces a line down to the button of my jeans.

A moment of shyness makes me hesitate. I have a squishy belly and my hips are too wide. He's perfectly proportioned and all muscles. What if he sees me fully naked and doesn't find me sexy?

"Lucy?" Softly saying my name, he cups my cheek to get my attention. "Are you having second thoughts?"

"No. Are you?" Waiting for his answer, I hold my breath.

"No, I've been fantasizing about seeing you naked since the afternoon at the lakes. I love that bikini but it's been torturing me for weeks. You're so sexy." His hand drops to my chest and he drags a finger over the arch of my bra, between my breasts, going lower until he traces a circle around my belly button.

Standing, he unbuttons his jeans and lets them drop to the floor. He's wearing dark gray boxer briefs and there's no way to ignore his erection tenting the soft fabric.

"In case you were having doubts about me finding you sexy, I think this is proof."

I love his shy but confident smile.

Lifting my hips, I shimmy out of my jeans and underwear. He pulls them off my body before dropping his boxers. My bra is the last to disappear.

Like the rest of him, his cock is beautiful. I reach out to stroke the hard velvet of him. He groans and twitches beneath my touch.

"Condom?" I ask.

"Not yet." He slowly crawls up my body and then drops kisses as he moves back down. A kiss to my belly button. A kiss to my left hipbone. When his mouth skims over the apex of my legs, I part them slightly in invitation. I feel him smile against my inner thigh before he places soft kisses over my center. His tongue presses against my clit and I arch my back.

Like his kisses earlier, he's not in any rush. Kissing and licking me in a slow, intentional rhythm until I'm a twisting, begging mess.

With a soft nip to the soft crease near my thigh, he slides in a single finger, then pulls out, before adding a second. His other hand finds my breast and teases my nipple. The combination of his mouth and fingers pushes me closer to the edge. I want to yell out how much I love his manual dexterity but bite my knuckle instead.

My hips rise to match the rhythm of his fingers. So close to breaking apart, I buck and squeeze my legs around his head. He flattens his hand on my sternum, stilling me. When he licks my clit, I explode. This is what a new star forming must feel like. Stars sparkle their light behind my eyelids as pleasure ripples through my body in waves.

His fingers still inside me as he guides me back down to earth.

"You're a dangerous man," I whisper, pulling him up to my mouth.

He's chuckling when I try to kiss him, but doesn't ask for explanation. "I'll be right back."

I'm not even sure what I mean. Sure, I could become addicted to the things this man can do to my body. But he's a bigger threat to my heart.

He returns with a condom and opens it.

"Let me," I ask, taking it from him. Stroking his length, I slip the condom on.

I fall back to the pillows and he follows, settling his body between my hips. I love feeling the weight of him. He brushes the head against my slick opening, once, twice before thrusting an inch inside. It's not enough. When he stills, I open my eyes.

"I'm already on the edge. Give me a second." His lids are closed and he moans, slipping in another few inches.

He couldn't have said anything sexier. Knowing I turn him on to the point of almost losing it within seconds gives me a heady rush. I don't want this be over, so I still, waiting for him to regain control. I'm rewarded with a deep thrust and a sexy groan from him once he's all the way inside.

"Fuck." The word rushes out on an exhale.

Finding a rhythm, he begins to thrust deep and hard. I wrap my arms around him, holding on as our bodies rock together. Still sparking small flashes of pleasure from my first orgasm, my body quickly builds up to a second one.

"You're close again?" he asks, slowing down, sliding almost all the way out.

"Don't stop. Please," I beg.

He thrusts in deep, and at the same time presses his thumb against my clit, sending a jolt of pleasure through me. "That. Do that again."

With a muffled grunt, he does.

It's all too much and I feel my body coil in anticipation of another release.

When I tighten around him and pulse, his rhythm falters. With two quick, deep thrusts he buries himself deeper. I open my eyes when he tips his head back with a deep moan. Watching him lost in pleasure is one of the most beautiful things I've ever witnessed.

Falling forward, he rests his head on my shoulder—his heavy weight a welcome crush that grounds me back in reality. "You okay?" he asks, placing a kiss against my collarbone.

"Mmm," I mumble. "When can we do it again?"

He laughs and gently rolls his hips. "I'm still inside of you, but I'm going to need a few minutes."

I kiss him before he slips out of bed to deal with the condom. When he returns, I stand and kiss him again, slipping by him to use the bathroom.

When I return, he's propped up on the pillows in my bed,

looking comfortable.

"Come back here," he commands, patting the spot next to him.

"How many condoms did you bring?" I crawl beside him.

His chest rumbles with his amusement. "Two."

"I like your optimism." I kiss his pec.

"I like your optimism better." He strokes his hand down my back.

"Huh?" I ask, drowsy and confused.

"I saw the new box in the bathroom," he whispers and pinches my butt. "We should pace ourselves."

I don't tell him I've had that box for months, never having a need to open it. Instead, I straddle him and begin kissing a path down his chest.

He's more dangerous than I first thought.

I'm going to need a tinfoil hat for my heart to protect myself from Boone Santos.

FOUR.

That's how many condoms we use.

I'm impressed with myself. Four is definitely a new record for me.

Twice last night, once at dawn, and one in the shower. Boone nearly cracked his head when he slipped on the wet floor getting the box.

If he wasn't already standing by his truck kissing me good-bye, I'd have to come up with some excuse to kick him out. My body is a tender buttercup after four rounds of sex with Boone.

The man has stamina. He must be part cyborg.

And I'm out of sex shape.

He's hard again as we make out in the parking area. My horny brain is suggesting I invite him back in for round five while my poor vagina is waving a white flag and calling for a time out.

I don't listen to my head.

"I need to go before I throw you in the truck bed and have my way with you again." His hand cups my breast underneath his shirt I'm wearing. Yes, I stole it again and I have no plans to give it back.

Twisting away from him, I peer into the back of his truck "I'm going to pass. Looks dirty and thorny."

He stares into the bed. "Yeah, that's a terrible idea. I forgot what a mess it is back there from driving on the dirt roads."

"Is that why your truck's always filthy?" I swear he has half a tumbleweed back there.

"Probably. I spend a lot of time on unpaved roads out in the desert. And honestly, I couldn't care less if my rig's clean on the outside as long as I can see out the windows."

I wonder what his place looks like. If he's a neat freak inside with a yard full of weeds. There's so much I don't know about him.

"When can we go on our second date?" he asks, kissing my cheek. "When's your next day off?"

"Saturday, and you're in luck because I have no plans."

"You do now." He lets his mouth linger over mine, not really kissing me until I press my mouth against his.

I hum into the kiss, but press my hands against his chest. "Be gone with you."

"See you in the morning for breakfast." He slowly releases me.

In my post sex haze, it takes me a minute to realize he means at the diner.

Thirteen

MONDAY MORNING TAKES a decade to arrive.

When I walk into the kitchen, Tony greets me with a extra big smile.

"You're late," he tells me, pointing at the clock.

"It's five-thirty. On the nose." I hold up my phone to prove the time.

"You're not early." He pretends to admonish me.

"If you want me here at five, pay me to show up at five." I rub my fingers together in the universal gesture for money.

"I'm paying you now." He taps his giant spatula on the grill before flipping some home fries.

"I'll bring you coffee when it's ready."

I drop my bag and pull on my apron. Silly me believes I've avoided him teasing me about my date on Saturday.

When I return with a mug of coffee, he grins at me. "You like Las Chicas?"

I nod enthusiastically. "Best chiles rellenos I've ever eaten."

"Handsome date enjoy them, too?" he asks, too innocently.

"He did." I give him nothing. "What happened to not wanting to know about our love lives? Should I stay after closing so we can braid each other's hair and gossip about boys?"

His spatula freezes mid air as he stares up at the exhaust hood. "Hell no."

"Didn't think so." I set his coffee on the shelf near the stove.

Wanda strolls through the back door, all frosted mauve smiles and extra high hair.

"Someone had an overnight guest," she announces to the room.

Tony mumbles something in Spanish and makes the sign of the cross over his chest. "Why am I the only one working this morning? Wanda, don't tell me why you're late. Get to work."

"Oh, I wasn't talking about myself. Lucy's the one with the truck parked in her guest spot."

Parking in her guest spot sounds like a terrible euphemism for sex. Leave it to Wanda.

Tony's eyes flick to me and then he shakes his head. "What you do on your own time is none of my business. Now will someone please set up the dining room before the customers have to do it themselves?"

Wanda opens her mouth to speak. Grabbing her by the arm, I pull her out of the kitchen.

"Tell me, tell me, tell me," she whispers excitedly.

I really don't want to and contemplate lying to her.

"I'm so happy for you." She hugs me before I can say anything.

Briefly, I hug her back.

Squeezing me tight, she starts to jump up and down. "I recognized Boone's truck."

I have no option but to bounce with her or have my shoulders pulled out of the socket.

Once I manage to escape her hold, I tell her, "Please don't make a big deal about this."

Her smile falls. "Oh, no. Was it bad?"

Wrinkling her nose, she holds her fingers about an inch apart.

"No, not that." Laughing, I avoid looking at her. "I just, I don't want to talk about it."

"Are you two gossiping out there?" Tony's voice carries through window.

As soon as we open the doors, the diner is packed with visitors for the alien festival in addition to the regulars. I barely have time to say hi to Boone and take his order.

When I pick up the plate of pecan pancakes, Tony jerks his head, indicating I should look behind me. I turn around. At his new spot at the counter, Boone's quietly smirking while tapping away at his phone.

"Tell him if he makes you cry at work, I have a baseball bat back here." He points to the corner behind him.

Lifting the plate, I roll my eyes. "I'm not going to tell him you're threatening paying customers with violence."

Unaware of Tony's ridiculous threat, Boone smiles and licks his lips when he sees his pancakes.

He pours syrup around the edge, then sticks his finger in the puddle and licks off the sticky liquid.

I want to suggest we meet up in the walk-in fridge for a quick make-out session, but Tony would probably fire me on the spot and chase Boone around with his baseball bat.

PLAYING TOURIST WITH Boone has been a fun distraction. He's already made plans to take me away this weekend for some sort of super secret adventure.

All week I've spent barely any time reading blogs or watching videos online. I've skipped going to the Center, making excuses to Zed about taking extra shifts at the Burger Joint in the afternoons. The lies are piling up all around me.

To make amends for being sucked into the Boone vortex, I

buy the ingredients to make cookies for Jim. In my little kitchen, which is just a wall in the living room, I mix up a batch of oatmeal dough while listening to one of my favorite podcasts. This episode is about the uptick in UFO sightings around the country.

I save a small amount of dough for myself that won't be sullied by raisins.

Once Jim's cookies are in the oven, I sit down and eat my dough with a spoon. Salmonella be damned.

The podcast's host, a guy named Bert, has a lovely soothing voice as he retells various stories about unidentified lights in the night sky. He reminds me a little of Cecil Baldwin, the narrator of *Welcome to Night Vale*, my all time favorite fiction podcast. At times, living in Roswell feels like a real life version of Night Vale. While Bert talks about orbs and triangular light formations, I open my laptop and find my bookmark for the Hudson Valley UFO site.

Years before I was born, small towns in upstate New York were inundated with UFO sightings over the course of one summer.

According to the debunkers and skeptics, the massive ship was a group of small airplanes flying in close formation over the rural areas at night. The same explanation has been used for other reported UFOS over Death Valley and in the Pacific Northwest.

I open another tab and scroll through a database of sightings in New York going back decades.

I've looked through the dates and locations dozens of times over the years, but I always hope if I keep going back, I'll discover something new. Or someone will add a new date and description to the collection around the time of my dad's disappearance.

Nothing catches my attention.

Blowing out a frustrated breath, I click on Wikipedia and reread about the Hill abduction in New Hampshire in the sixties.

Betty and Barney.

Just like the characters in the old cartoon, *The Flintstones*.

The two most interesting parts of the Hill story for me are the missing time and Betty's dreams about the abduction.

Somehow, somewhere, that fateful night in New Hampshire they lost three hours of time.

Why only three hours?

Why not a lifetime?

Like the Hills, hypnosis was used on my mom and me by a ufologist after my dad disappeared. We didn't experience missing time or strange dreams. Mom told me later the hypnotist tried to get her to admit to seeing gray-skinned, little men in military uniforms.

Just like the Hill's account.

Pretty shady stuff.

My timer dings and the cookies are done.

After sliding them to a cooling rack, I finish listening to Bert's soothing voice wrap up the episode.

He kind of reminds me of David Duchovny, which makes me think of Shari.

I text her to say hi.

I have more guilt about only hanging out with Boone and ditching her.

Bouncing dots appear on the screen and I wait for her response.

Let's all have dinner soon at place. Tell my brother he needs to share!!

I quickly type a response.

Sounds good. Check schedules and let me know. I'm free most evenings.

Smiling, I pile as many cookies as I can on a plate and loosely cover them with foil.

"There. Now you're protected from attack by electromagnetic rays."

Jim's door is open, so I knock on the frame. "Cookie delivery."

Through the screen, I can see him propped up in his recliner. The television's on, showing a baseball game from the announcer's voice describing plays.

"Knock, knock." I tap louder on the door.

"Who is it?" his thick voice asks as he jerks upright.

"It's Lucy. Halliday. Your neighbor," I add. "Were you sleeping?"

I know he spends a lot of his day taking cat naps, so I don't feel too bad for waking him.

"You say something about cookies?" he asks, flipping down the leg-rest of his chair.

"I brought the oatmeal raisin ones you requested." I hold the plate in front of my face.

"What are you doing out there with them? Come in already." Waving me forward, he tries to stand. Takes two attempts before he's upright.

"Don't get up, I'm coming to you." I swing open the door and step into the dim living room. It's a twin to my own apartment, but his space is cluttered with possessions while mine is a study in minimalism, aka what fits in a Honda Accord and being cheap.

"Did you put the raisins in them?" He accepts the plate and smiles. "Oh, they're still warm."

Peeling back the foil, he inhales. Before selecting one, he eyes them carefully.

"I added twice the recommended amount of raisins. They're in there."

Making his decision, he bites into one. "Mmm. Good job."

"Thanks."

"You haven't been sitting at home as much. You find yourself a fella?" He squints at me. "No need to answer. I can tell you do."

"How?" I press my hand to my heated cheek.

"For one, you're smiling. Two, Wanda came by yesterday all twitterpated about you having a truck in your guest parking."

Still sounds like a bad euphemism for sex. Worse when he says it and then winks.

"That's a lot of assuming based on someone parking in my spot. Could've been a random vehicle taking advantage of an opening."

"You've got a glow to you. Seen that before a few times when I fancied a lady and she fancied me back." He bites into his second cookie. "My advice? Enjoy the ride. Love's a rollercoaster without seat belts. Whatever goes up, is going to come down eventually. Hold on tight and you might get lucky enough to make it to the end with only a few bruises. Or you could get thrown for a loop and end up with your heart busted."

He coughs, sounding more congested than usual. With his thin, white hair slicked back from his forehead, I notice the hollow in his cheeks. Combined with the loose fit of his shirt, I worry he's not eating enough.

"That's a terrible analogy." I step into his kitchen to get a glass of water for him.

"So be it. Just came up with it on the spot." He sips the water. "Point is, life's more fun on the ride than sitting on the side watching."

My brow furrows as I try to get to that conclusion from his previous description.

"I'm old. You're too young to understand how this all works." He clears his throat and spits into a folded handkerchief he pulls from his shirt pocket. "I've got no one else to listen to me. Pretend I'm sharing nuggets of wisdom."

That's not true. I know Wanda checks on him and he has his goon squad down at the Legion.

"How are you feeling these days?" I inquire out of genuine concern. He reminds me a lot of my grandpa and I hate the thought of him being lonely.

"Doc says the COPD's getting worse." He spits again, and I look away. "I'm ready for what's coming next. Getting tired of dragging this tank around with me like a scuba diver on land."

"We could get you an astronaut's spacesuit. Might be more comfortable."

"And what? Piss in a bag? Or a diaper? Not as glamorous as it sounds. And I know from firsthand experience," he scoffs at my disgust. "Back when I was a pilot, not recently."

"Tell me a story about when you were flying planes." I perch on the arm of his plaid couch.

"Want to hear about the UFO I saw over the Atlantic?" Munching another cookie, he sprays a few crumbs when he speaks.

"You told me that one already."

"Fine. That's my best one. Give me a minute to make something else up." He sips his water and then finishes his cookie.

I sit on the couch for an hour while he tells me stories about his time in the Navy. When his voice fades out with another yawn, I excuse myself and tell him to set the plate outside his door when he's done with it.

Taking the short trip across the courtyard to my own casita, I stare at the evening sky lit with orange streaked with purple. I'll miss New Mexico sunsets.

Opening the door, I realize it's been weeks since I've thought about leaving town or where I'll go when my time here is up.

Fourteen

SATURDAY MORNING, BOONE shows up at my apartment to take me sledding.

In July.

While I think he's crazy, I happily go with him after he promises me there won't be caves or bats involved.

After an hour of driving us into the mountains, cactus gives way to trees. The air chills as we gain altitude. On either side of the narrow, two-lane road, tall pines jab the deep blue sky.

"Did you magically transport us out of New Mexico?" I lean my head against my window and stare up at the green tree tops.

He chuckles quietly. "No."

"No teleportation or apparition?" I shift my focus from the passing scenery to him.

Fighting a smile, he shakes his head. "Sadly, no."

I respond with an exaggerated sigh. "That was one of my favorite parts of *Harry Potter.*"

"Never read it."

"Okay, but you saw the movies, right?" I'm trying not to judge him on his entertainment choices.

"Negative," he says like it's no big deal.

My mouth hangs open as I attempt to formulate a response

that isn't full of shock and judgment.

"How is that even possible?" I screech, failing at my objective.

His lips twist to the side. "Wizards and magic and dragons aren't really my thing."

I can't see his eyes behind his sunglasses, but I swear his mouth twitches with a smile.

"It's all a metaphor for good versus evil and the triumph of love over evil, hope over despair." I cross my arms, gearing up to convince him he's made a grave error in his entertainment choices. "I mean, I guess if you hate those things and don't believe in a hero's journey, then, well, you wouldn't like them."

Grateful my own eyes are hidden behind sunnies, I blink away unexpected tears. My dad and I read them together. Well, he read them aloud to me before bed.

Boone's warm hand rests on my bare knee. "Sounds like I have some movies to watch."

"The books are better," I mumble as I turn to the window to wipe a tear from my cheek, hoping he doesn't notice.

"Tell me why you love them." He gives my knee a gentle squeeze. "Maybe you can convince me."

With an audible "harrumph" of disgust, I tell him, "If you can't see the amazing for yourself, it would be a waste of my energy and your time trying to convince you."

"I want to believe." He lowers his voice to a soft plead.

"You sound like one of the alien conspiracy guys in town."

"The little green men brigade? Those guys? Someone didn't love them enough as children."

I laugh despite my disappointment in his muggleness. "They are an imaginative bunch."

"That's a nice way of describing the whackadoodles and their grainy videos of big-eyed mannequins."

"Not a believer?" I ask.

"I think someone came up with a snappy bright green icon and people ran with it."

"Look at E.T.—he's neither green nor snappy. People think he's adorable."

"He was meant to be scary and creepy."

"Lies. He's even cuter than little baby Drew Barrymore in pigtails. And that's saying something. I loved that movie when I was a kid." The memory settles heavy on my chest. I forgot how much I loved *E.T.* At one point, I was obsessed with it. My brow furrows as I try to remember if it was before or after. All those memories are hazy, like I'm trying to see them through thick smoke that burns my eyes until I have to close them to block out the pain.

"Earth to Lucy." He taps my knee with his knuckles, pretending he's knocking on a door.

"What?" I shift my focus to him.

"Where'd you go?"

Blinking away childhood memories, I think of something generic. "Nowhere. Got lost thinking about other child actors who grew up to be good-looking adults."

Now I'm thinking about Ryan Gosling.

"O-kay." He stretches out the word, clearly thinking I'm a weirdo. "What about Britney Spears? Or Justin Timberlake?"

"Good point." I wedge my back into the gap between the side of the seat and the door. "You came up with those two really quickly. Is this something you give a lot of thought? Or do you have a secret crush on Ms. Spears?"

He checks the rearview mirror and his side mirror even though I'm sure we're the only vehicle on this stretch of road for at least a mile in either direction.

"Your hesitation says it all." I laugh and poke his side.

"I discovered her at a delicate age for boys." He keeps his hands at ten and two on the steering wheel, but his tell of bouncing his left knee gives him away.

"Was it the pigtails? Or the inappropriately short plaid skirt? Isn't she a little old for you?" I don't know how old she is precisely, but having a nightly act in Vegas à la Celine Dion and Cher would lead one to believe she's older than Boone.

"Can I plead the fifth?" he asks, a smile tugging at his lips.

"This isn't a court of law. Own your weirdness. Fly that freak flag high," I encourage him and demonstrate waving a flag. Because I'm a nerd.

"Now you are sounding like you live in Roswell." He grins at me and it's like the sun parting the clouds

"I'm going to ignore the implied insult and pretend you're complimenting me." I jab my index finger into his shoulder.

"You shouldn't attack a driver, especially while the motor vehicle is in operation," he deadpans. "We might crash."

"I trust your competency." I grin at him while humming "Hit Me Baby One More Time."

"No, uh uh. You can't hold that against me. I was young and impressionable, not fully formed. Blame my undeveloped frontal lobe. Pre-pubescent boys are the closest things we have to humans operating using only their lizard brains. It's why we don't bathe and can't remember simple tasks."

"Nice try." I frown, giving him my "sorry, you lose" face.

"Clearly you never spent a lot of time around boys," he grumbles.

"I tried to avoid them."

"Still do?"

His words hit close to my relationship avoidance. "Smelly, gross boys? Yes. Especially at work. Why are spit balls still a thing? Or an acceptable activity for a restaurant? I find them in my hair at the end of a shift way more than you'd think. And boys make the biggest messes. Splatters of ketchup everywhere. Lions are neater eaters."

"You're a poet." He loses the battle against smiling. "And what about men?"

Studying him, I try to guess his motivations. "Are you asking if I'm single?"

A frown flips his smile upside down. "I, uh . . . I guess I am. Doing this out of order once again."

I wiggle the fingers on my left hand. "No one's put a ring on it."

"That doesn't fully answer the question," he says.

"Why does it matter?"

"I guess it doesn't. Not in the grand scheme of the universe. Black holes don't care if you're single or dating a dozen guys you met online."

I ignore the online dating joke. "Black holes need a better range of options. But if the universe is asking, I'm single as in no, I don't have a boyfriend. Or twenty-four lovers on monthly rotation."

"A month is thirty days. What happens the other six days?"

I stare at him for a beat, hoping he won't make me bring up a woman's moon cycle, the monthly visit from our communal Aunt Flow. When he doesn't show any signs of comprehension, I cough. "A girl needs to rest and have time to binge watch entire seasons of shows while eating ice cream and salty snacks. Crying is optional depending on the subject matter."

And I hope we're going to leave it at that.

Changing the subject before he makes the uncomfortable connection between my random string of words and female biology, I ask, "What kind of name is Cloudcroft? Sounds like it should be Cloud-*craft* like a flying saucer."

He gives me side-eye. "You'll see."

We climb higher and clouds soften the light from the sun.

"Is it because it's always cloudy up here?" I peer out the window at the thick, swirling mist.

"Always is a long time. And no, that's not why. Have patience."

Passing through the thick layer of clouds, we once again drive into sunlight.

After about two hours, we round another curve in the road and the edges of a town appear. A few colorful wood buildings occupy land on either side of the ribbon of asphalt. Other than a gas station, none of the structures are from this century and I'm not sure if they were built in the last century either. A wooden sidewalk flanks their fronts, mostly cover by balconies on the second stories.

"Okay, at first I thought you'd teleported us to the Pacific Northwest, but now I think we've gone back in time. What is this place?"

"In the winter, it's a ski town."

"But we're in the desert. Mexico is like right over there." I point out his side window.

He bats my hand away from his face. "If you hadn't noticed, we gained about five thousand feet of altitude. We're in the mountains now."

"Har har," I say with full sarcasm accent. "You distracted me."

He makes a turn onto a side street that's even more ridiculously charming than the main highway.

"Is this my surprise?" I'm happy if it is.

"It's more of a pit stop."

"I don't see any snow. How are we going to go sledding?" I peer at the dusty ground peeking out between the pines.

"You'll see." He sounds so smug with his secrets and his sledding ideas when there isn't snow on the ground.

"Wanda knows I'm with you. So if you have nefarious motives, the police will be questioning you first." I cross my arms.

"You have trust issues, don't you?" he asks.

I hate that he sounds amused by this fact.

"It's good to be guarded. Don't take candy from strangers or accept rides from solo men. Who's going to say avoiding either of those things are bad advice?" I deflect from answering his question directly. Hell yes, I have trust issues.

"I don't have any candy, and while I might not be your average guy, I'm not a stranger. However, if I'm being forthcoming, I do plan to lure you with pie after we head out of town. Apple pie à la mode is as pure and American as it comes. What kind of monster would use it for, what was the word you used, right, nefarious purposes?" He ends his speech by dipping the bill of my hat low over my eyes.

"Hey," I cry, shoving it up so I can stare at him. "What was the part about pie?"

"What happened to not trusting me?"

"I'm here. I agreed to go sledding in the summer. And that was before anyone mentioned pie." I peer out the front window of his truck, looking for a bakery or pie sign.

I chuckle at my own pun.

"What's funny?" He unbuckles his seatbelt.

"I was thinking about signs and then looked around for a pie sign. Get it? Pi sign?"

He scrunches up his nose and closes one eye. "Ouch, that one was painful."

"Don't hate the pun." I'm out of the cab before he opens his door.

We wander down the block. One side is lined with modern, nondescript town buildings while the other is stacked with two story wood structures straight out of a western movie.

"What a weird town. Over here I expect a gunfight to break out any second." I point to the two storied hotel bearing the town's name. "And over here, I could be in any rural town in America."

"Then let's stick to the boardwalk and the fantasy." He presses his hand between my shoulder blades to turn me.

Back in the truck, I buckle in. "Ready for pie now."

"Is today going to be all about pie? I'm regretting mentioning it."

"No way, don't hold back. If you know other places, you need to tell me. I keep asking Tony why the diner doesn't have a decent pie on the menu. He waves me off and points out we have ice cream," I scoff. "It's not even frozen custard. I wouldn't be bragging if I were him."

I finish my mini-tirade and realize we're still parked. "Why are we sitting here?"

Boone laughs, filling the cab with the rich sound of his voice. "I wasn't sure how long you were going to talk. Figured if things escalated, and it felt like you might become agitated there for a while, best if we weren't moving at a high speed."

Narrowing my eyes, I stare at him. "If that was a roundabout way of accusing me of lady hysteria, Mr. Santos, you best check yourself."

A few miles down the road, he pulls into a gravel lot next to an apple-shaped sign shouting "PIE" in all capital letters.

While I find the bathroom, Boone orders the pie. When I return and see him holding a single plate with a single piece of pie, I realize I've misjudged him.

"Where's your pie?" I eye the plate and then him.

"I thought we could share." He holds out the solo slice.

Blinking and twisting my head like a confused dog, I try to comprehend his suggestion. He can't mean the words coming out of his mouth. I never figured him for being a cheap miser, but he does eat in a gas station five days a week.

"Or not," he finally admits. "Here, have this one and I'll get my own piece."

"That's probably for the best." I take the slice and sit at a picnic table a few yards from the walk-up window.

By the time Boone joins me, I'm half done with my slice.

"You weren't kidding." He points at my plate. "I guess it's acceptable?"

"So good." I finish the last bite and eye his slice.

Wrapping his arm around his plate, he says, "No way. I grew up with a sister who stole my food."

I take this as a challenge to at least steal a bite of his crust.

"Look at the size of that squirrel." I point over his shoulder. "Wow, I've never seen one that size."

Lame even to my ears, but he turns his head.

I think it's enough time to make my move, but without even moving his neck, his hand reaches out and grabs my arm.

"Hey," I protest. "Do you have eyes in the back of your head? You have super fast reflexes."

"No," he laughs. "Just years of practice."

After finishing his pie, he saves one tiny piece of the crust for me.

"Boone, you're a good man." I stretch over the table to give him a soft kiss, brushing my lips over his, tasting the cinnamon and apple on his breath.

He presses his mouth to mine, sweeping his tongue inside and tangling it with mine. "You're my favorite pie thief, Lucy Halliday."

Fifteen

WE SPEED THROUGH a tunnel and the radio goes to static. When we pop out the other side, I gasp at the view extending across a wide basin to another range of mountains. Below us on the valley floor is a huge expanse of white.

Boone chuckles. "White Sands. It can be seen from space."

By aliens, I think. "I've always wanted to visit."

"And today you will." He grins at me.

It takes another half hour for us to reach the valley and the town of Alamogordo. Despite being visible from the mountains, once we're on the desert floor, there's no sign of the white dunes. We pass the air force base and I'm reminded this is an active military area.

I read the sign as we drive by. "Holloman sounds like hollow man."

"Named for an early developer in rockets and aircraft that could be operated without pilots," he explains.

"Seems a strange place for a base." I crane my neck to check out the sky overhead for planes. "When was it opened?"

"Early 1940s. The Missile Range occupies thousands of acres of the gypsum dunes. If you wanted to test a nuclear weapon, middle of nowhere is the best location. Although El Paso and the

Mexican border are only a hundred miles south of here."

"I'm sensing a theme with our outings," I tease.

"What's that? Other than me being the best tour guide of southeastern New Mexico ever?" He grins over at me.

"Nuclear fallout," I say, totally serious because there's nothing funny about radiation poisoning.

"Not very romantic, eh?"

I tip my head in doubt. "Were you going for romance? Because end of the world puts a lot of pressure on us."

"Since it's not the end of the world, let's go sledding," he says, grinning at me.

Once inside of the official National Park, white dunes replace the flat scrubland like someone was filming a winter scene and left the fake snow behind. One second there's the flat, beige desert I've grown to expect in New Mexico. The next second, three story mountains of pure white appear. Space age looking shade structures add to the feeling we're on a strange, new planet.

"This is the second place you've taken me to that feels like being on another planet. I'm sensing a theme."

"New Mexico *is* the land of enchantment," he singsongs the state's slogan.

"And aliens," I add. This is the closest we've come to the real reason I moved to Roswell.

"There's more to it than the Roswell crash. I hope your custom tours are proving that." He sounds both defensive and bored.

I'm happy to drop any talk of aliens and Roswell.

We park in a turnout near several other cars. Dunes rise above us by at least twenty feet. I'm still confused about the sledding until I see two kids fly down another slope on plastic saucers.

I drop my mouth open and stare at Boone. "We're sledding on dunes?

He lifts his eyebrows and nods, laughing. "You just figured

it out?"

Opening my door, I climb out and yell, "I grew up in snow. Prepare to get your butt kicked."

He meets me behind the truck. "I didn't realize sledding was a competitive sport." He pulls two round saucers from the truck bed. "Do you want to race to the top of the dune?"

Before I can respond, he takes off with one of the sleds.

He makes running uphill look easy, but for every few steps I take, I slide down a foot or two.

"Climb diagonally. Like a ski slope," he instructs from his perch at the top of gypsum mountain.

His method works, and once I reach the top, I walk the edge to where he sits. As far as I can see are white dunes until they reach the mountains to the west. The breeze teases a faint briny scent. Surprisingly, the white powder is cool to the touch and slightly damp beneath the surface from the recent monsoon rains.

"This place is surreal," I say, shading my eyes from the silvery reflection of the sun off the dunes. My oversized sunglasses are more for face decoration than blocking all the UVA and UVB rays.

Slowly, he pours out a handful of powder. "I find it beautiful. There's something calm about the dunes."

With our shoulders occasionally brushing against each other, we sit side by side for a while. The rush to sled is forgotten.

"Have you ever lived anywhere else?" I ask after a few moments of comfortable silence.

"Other than college, no. And even then I only went as far as Austin."

As we talk, I scoop handfuls of the gypsum, the grains finer than sand. My feet dig into the dune in front of me. He's right, there is a calm to this place. Maybe it's the lack of modern life.

"Shall we have that sledding race?" He bumps his shoulder against mine.

We position ourselves on the edge of the dune. "Should I count down?" I ask.

"Go for it." He grins at me.

We both push off when I say, "One." Flying down the dune, I squeal when I pull ahead. My lead is short lived, and he flashes a grin at me when he zooms past.

"Two out of three," I shout as soon as I hit the bottom. I'm already racing back up the dune when I hear his laughter behind me.

I lose again and end up on my side after leaning too far to the left in an attempt to gain speed. "Three out of five." Undeterred, I stand, brushing powder off of my legs and arms.

"Want me to give you a head start?" He climbs up the dune beside me.

"No, I'm going to win fair and square." I'm breathless by the time we take our positions at the edge.

"Prepare to lose." I brace my fingers on the surface to push off and shimmy my saucer back and forth. "Ready to go?"

"Five, four." He begins the countdown. "Three."

Something tickles my left hand. I twitch in reflex and look down.

"Two," Boone says at the same time I scream.

A white lizard skitters over my hand and disappears behind us.

I flail my arm, sending myself off balance. The sled slides forward but I'm only holding on with one hand. Time speeds up. The sled drags me down the dune sideways until I release my grip. I have too much momentum and instead of stopping, I execute a gold medal somersault and roll to the bottom of the slope on my back. I have no idea where the saucer went.

With the last shred of my dignity, I raise my arm in victory. "I won!"

"Shit! Are you okay?" Boone jogs toward me, sometimes sliding and causing mini avalanches in the sand.

By the time he reaches me, I'm sitting upright and dusting off. "Everything survived intact. I might have a few scrapes and bruises, mostly to my ego."

His eyes hold genuine concern when he crouches in front of me. As he sweeps sand off my arms, his touch is gentle. The burn from the rough grains fades under his hand.

"Why aren't you laughing? I'm sure that was hysterical." I scan my arms and legs for scrapes.

His jaw ticks. "I was worried you'd break something. What happened up there?"

"A ghost lizard stood on my hand. I freaked out a little."

He squeezes his thumb and index finger close together. "A little."

Standing, he holds out his hand for me to use to leverage myself off the ground. A spark of static electricity shocks my palm where we touch.

"I still won. Lucy, one. Boone, two. Let's go again."

This makes him laugh. "I didn't figure you for the competitive type."

"I'm more stubborn. Once I set my mind to something, I'm laser focused." I make pew-pew sounds while pointing my fingers at him.

He must find this adorable, because he sweeps me into his arms and kisses me. It's not a casual peck. Oh no, Boone goes all in. He bends me back and sweeps his tongue against mine. Just when I think he might suggest we get naked and make love on the gypsum, he stands me upright. Clearly, he has more self-restraint than I do.

Head swimming from his kiss, I trudge up the hill in a stupor. I lose again, but I take comfort in my one, spectacular victory.

Ditching the saucers, we take a hike farther into the dunes. A few yucca plants jut out between gypsum mounds and other ghost lizards skitter across the surface. It's eerie and beautiful.

Holding my hand, Boone helps me up the final steep step of a dune. Spinning around, I try to spot the truck but see nothing other than white dunes in every direction. Without the mountains to the west, I'd be completely lost. In the quiet, with only the wind gently blowing through the valley, my stomach grumbles.

"Hungry?" He laughs, clearly hearing my stomach monster.

"Starved. I don't suppose there's a snack bar around the next dune, is there?"

"No, but I know a place."

A HALF HOUR later, Boone pulls his truck into a gravel parking area full of car-size potholes outside what looks like an old furniture store or small used car lot.

"Trust me?" he asks.

"No," I reply quickly. "Not at all."

"Still doubt me?"

"Yes."

"I promised sledding in the middle of summer in a desert and delivered."

"Yes, but you forced me to follow you into a hole in the ground where millions of bats live."

His shoulders lift when he makes his innocent face, all big eyes and closed mouth smile. "You loved it. In fact, if I remember correctly, you talked about living down there."

"In case of nuclear fallout. And if we could put up a giant net between the snack bar and the bats." I stand by my demands. Getting serious for a second, I tell him, "I loved the caverns and seeing them with you, knowing what a deep connection your family has to them."

I didn't even mean to make a pun, but he smiles. "Very deep."

"I was trying to say thank you."

He gives me a soft kiss and whispers against my lips, "I know. And you're welcome."

Because us kissing in his truck always leads to more, I take advantage of his proximity and kiss him back.

A breathless few minutes later, he ends the kissing with a quick peck to my lips.

"Come on." He opens his door. "I'm starving."

I eye the glass front of the single story building. Nothing about this place screams "best burger of my life" like Boone promised.

On the other hand, it's not underground and not a single green skin alien face decorates the exterior. And Las Chicas was delicious. I've had dreams about the sopapillas, honey, and naked Boone.

We slip into a booth along the back wall and wait for a server.

Boone rests his arm along the top of his banquette, looking like a supermodel in a jeans ad. Brushing a hand over my head, I feel the grit of fine grains of gypsum.

"I'll be right back. In a sign of trust, please order for me." I scoot along the bench and find the sign for restrooms.

Inside of the single bathroom, I lean close to the dingy mirror. My hair is worse than I imagined. A sunburn blooms on my nose and cheeks. White gypsum dots my hairline and a smear of it crosses my forehead.

How is it possible Boone looks like he stepped out of a magazine and I'm the after photo of someone who got lost in the desert for days? Bending at the waist, I run my hands through my hair and shake out my T-shirt. A circle of white appears on the floor around me. We dumped sand out of our sneakers before we got in the truck, and I'm still leaving half of the dunes in here.

If the bathroom wasn't the only one for the restaurant and also in need of a deep cleaning, I'd be tempted to strip naked and shake out all my clothing. I have a feeling there's white powder *everywhere*.

Wetting a stack of paper towels, I execute a quick wipe down of my exposed skin. The cold water feels good on my sun-heated skin.

Someone raps on the door while turning the handle.

"Occupied," I shout. "One minute."

"Lucy? You okay?" Boone's voice carries through the closed door. "Food's ready."

"Sorry. Be right out!" *How long have I been in here?* I'm either a bigger disaster than I thought or this place has the quickest service ever.

My dark hair is a fluffy halo around my head before I locate a ponytail holder in my pocket and do a quick braid. It's not perfect, but that's the look all the cool girls wear at festivals. Should be good enough for Alamogordo. Happy I no longer resemble the single inhabitant of a deserted island, I tell myself some words of encouragement in the mirror.

"Lucy, you're a mess, but at least you have a charming personality."

It's the best pep talk I can manage right now.

Standing next to our booth, a waitress leans her hip against the table, her full attention a laser beam focused on Boone. She's working all the angles of flirtation. I observe her master performance.

Hair twist. Check.

Forward lean to expose a little more cleavage. Check.

Biting on the tip of her pen. Check.

Giggling at everything coming out of his mouth. Vomit.

I can't blame her for trying her best, but she must wonder why he ordered two plates and has a purse sitting on the bench opposite him. Perhaps she's so completely mesmerized by his good looks, she hasn't noticed. It's possible. I've been standing behind her for at least a minute and she hasn't stopped talking.

Boone peers around her and gives me a wide-eyed plea for help. If I weren't so hungry, I'd leave him on his own. Instead, I take pity on him—and my growling stomach, but mostly him—and slide onto the bench seat in front of a messy burger stuffed in a plastic oval tray over-spilling with fries.

"This looks like heaven," I say, essentially blocking any further flirtation by my simple existence.

Or so I think.

Girlfriend slides her attention over to me, scans my nest of hair and disheveled clothes, and then goes right back to telling Boone about herself. While I munch on fries, we learn she grew up in Alamogordo, but left when she graduated high school and married a pilot. That apparently didn't work out since she's back where she started.

As fascinating as the story is so far, I cut her off. "Can you bring me some mayo when you get a chance? That'd be great. Thanks."

"Uh, sure. You need anything more, sweetheart?" she asks Boone, who hasn't touched his food.

"No, we're all set," he grumbles, his jaw set tight.

After she wanders off, he bursts into a fit of loud laughter. "Why didn't you save me?"

"I did. I asked for mayo. Classic waitress trick. Ketchup and mustard are typically kept on the tables or a nearby station, but she'll have to go back to the kitchen to get mayonnaise, which should be refrigerated. I bought us some time. Hopefully some other handsome man will want a burger and she'll move on to her next target."

"Smart. Then I guess I should thank you for your devious use of mayo. Thanks for coming to my rescue with condiments."

"As a waitress, it's what I do." I give him a nonchalant shrug.

"I'm surprised you of all people needed to be saved. Did you forget to be grumpy and ignore the help?"

He jerks his head back like I've slapped him. "Is that what you think I did to you? I was never rude."

I jab a fry into some ketchup. "I felt invisible to you for months."

"I was keeping things professional, being respectful. I always tipped twenty-percent," he says, defensively.

"And I appreciate that." I cut my giant burger in half with my knife. "If I had to choose, I'd rather get the silent treatment and a good tip than have to suffer through sexist jokes and overly friendly touching to get a crappy tip."

With his forearms on the table, he leans forward. "Are you kidding me? Who does that to you? The oil guys?"

I laugh. "You're sweet. Oblivious, but sweet."

"Seriously? Give me names." His eyes flash with anger, drawing out more amber from the green.

"Stop. Wanda and I handle them. If anyone were to ever get out of hand, Tony's there. He keeps a baseball bat in the kitchen. Wanda says he's only had to bring it out twice."

"I can't believe I've never noticed," he grumbles around his burger.

"Hard to see what's going on around you if you're staring at a screen." I pick up my burger and take a huge bite. Today's a good day and I don't want to think about how horrible men can be. Not when Boone is being amazing and I haven't laughed or smiled this much in a long time.

I'm starving and the burger is the best thing I've ever had in my mouth.

Until the heat from the hatch chile hits my tongue on the second bite. I barely manage to swallow around the sudden lava flow of heat.

"Wow." I drink half my bottle of Mexican Coke. It doesn't help. My eyes begin to water and I try a fry to soothe the blistering happening on my tongue.

"Too hot?" Boone bites into his own burger and swallows. I watch for beads of sweat on his forehead or a reddening of his skin color. He appears fine.

"A little." Would it be weird if I wiped off my tongue on my napkin? Or licked the outside of my Coke bottle?

Our waitress drops off my random mayo and I dip a fry into it with my last hope.

"You all right?" Boone's expression switches from amusement to concern.

"Fine, fine." I wave my hand in front of my mouth. "Why isn't your mouth on fire?"

"I like it hot." He shrugs and takes another bite. "You don't have to eat the chile."

He's calling me a wuss. And I'm fine admitting defeat.

"You need milk." He waves over the waitress and orders a glass for me.

Her eyes flash with judgment when she drops off the order. "Some people can't handle the heat."

Translation: she can.

And by heat, she means a hot guy like Boone.

Too bad for her we're not on one of those awful bachelor dating shows.

I happily drink the cold milk, letting it erase the oils from the pepper. With a satisfied sigh, I exhale. "Thank you."

"You're welcome. If you grew up eating chiles, you'd know that trick. Milk for your mouth. Butter for your hands. And never touch your eyes." He widens his eyes and shakes his head. "Horrible."

"Speaking from experience?" I ask, opening my burger and using a fry to remove the pepper.

"More than once. In some cases, I'm a slow learner."

I doubt that. He seems like the kind of guy who is naturally good at everything. Except maybe flirting with women. The thought intrigues me.

"How'd you end up working at the Rig?" he asks.

Sometimes I tell the truth about my dad and the aliens, passing it off as a joke when people laugh. Something tells me I shouldn't bring it up to Boone.

"I wanted a change of scenery. My parents met in college in New Mexico. What could be more different than New York than the desert?"

"What about your family? Still in New York?"

It's a common question to ask when you first meet or start dating someone, but I don't know how to answer it without spilling all my secrets. I bite into my chile-less burger and stall for time.

"Mom and I talked about selling the house and moving someplace warmer like Florida or South Carolina as soon as she retired from the school district."

"Why didn't you go? Those sound nicer than landlocked New Mexico."

I swallow down my rising emotions. "The doctors found a lump in her breast. Reassured of good survival rates and early detection, she kept working while going through chemo and radiation. And I stayed to care for her."

"I'm sorry." His eyes deepen to green and I swear they turn glassy with tears. He can't cry. If he cries, I'll cry.

"It's okay." There's nothing to be sorry for now. Pretending I'm not suffocating with the memories, I shrug. "We did make it to Florida. Once. Two years ago, after she stopped all treatments, we took ourselves to Disney World for an entire week to thaw out from the snowiest winters anyone could remember."

"That sounds nice. I've never been." He watches me intently

as if sensing there's more to my story.

I focus on talking about Florida. "It's flat, like here, but with swamps instead of lakes. Alligators instead of scorpions."

"You're really hitting the highlights. Maybe you should write travel brochures. So your mom's still in New York?" His dark brows draw up with hope.

I manage to shake my head no. My voice is hoarse as I fight back tears. "She died six months later."

Instead of speaking empty words about how sorry he is, he joins me on my side of the booth. Wrapping me in his arms, holding me tight, he gently rubs his hand down my back in a soothing oval. Down, across, up. Repeat. The contact soothes me in a way a token expression of empathy never could. I can't remember the last time someone held me like this. Not for sexual reasons, but to reassure me I exist and matter to someone in this world.

"What about the rest of your family?" he asks.

"Don't have any." I wipe a few stray tears with my fingers and feel the sting from the chile pepper. I swear its heat is going to haunt me.

"What happened?" He dips his head to be in my sight line.

"Dad left when I was a kid. Grandparents died a few years ago. No aunts, uncles, or cousins. We didn't really know my dad's family, and both his parents are dead, too. Now it's just me. The last of the Hallidays." I lift my bottle in a toast. "I know how to bring down the mood. I'm also available for kiddie parties."

"I'm sorry, Lucy." He touches my arm; warm fingers wrap around my wrist. "You're not a downer. It's your life. Facts aren't emotional."

"Said like a man," I snark at him. "Sorry."

"My gender has nothing to do with it. I'm a man. Fact. Why should my gender make you upset? It has nothing to do with you and isn't personal. It's a fact. True?"

I shrug. "True. You being a man doesn't make me sad."

It is the truth. He makes me happy, which is worse. Sorrow is my friend. I know sadness. Happiness is a stranger offering me candy and hollow promises.

"Your family dying is the same. They didn't do it to hurt you. They would've stayed with you if they could have. True?" He softly touches my chin to get me to look at him.

I nod, knowing he's trying to comfort me in his own, strange way.

"We all die. Everyone we know and love will die eventually."

"Okay, I may not be a downer, but you might." I'm basically pulling the kid trick of twisting his name-calling back around to him. *I know you are, but what am I?*

He smirks. "No, I'm not. Death is a fact. You decide how you react to the facts. You're in control of your emotions."

"What about falling in love? You think you can control that, too?" I tip my head, waiting for his answer.

"Why not? Who says it's impossible?" he responds with more questions.

"Generations of love songs and poems? The entire history of humanity?" I ask, drily.

"Romantic idealism isn't based on facts."

I've found Boone's major flaw, and the reason he's single.

The man doesn't believe in romantic love. He's too rational and reasonable to fall in love. This should be a welcome revelation, but my stomach sinks, and I lose the remainder of my appetite.

"Have you ever been in love?" I ask, already suspecting the answer.

"No. Have you?" he asks the same of me, curious, but matter of fact.

"Thought so. Why not?" I use his trick of answering a question with a question.

"It's never interested me." He shrugs. "You didn't answer my question."

"Once. Maybe. I thought I was head over heels in love in high school and freshman year of college."

"Thought?" He lifts an eyebrow in question.

"Looking back, I now realize it was mostly hormones and peer pressure. He was nice enough, but we were better off as friends."

"Nothing since?" he asks, and I find comfort in his curiosity.

"Nothing that came close to love. Or what I imagined love to be. So many people, who say they're in love, are miserable. No thank you. I've had enough misery on my own."

"Guess we're the same. Most women I know are consumed with falling in love and being in love. It's refreshing to meet some-one who's more like me." His happy smile tells me he means it as a compliment.

Disappointment burns my throat more than the green chile.

I should feel relief Boone Santos is emotionally off limits. I should feel better he's not going to fall in love with me. Beneath its layers of protective tinfoil, my heart tightens.

Crumpling my napkin, I place it over my leftover food.

Pointing at his empty plate, I use my chipper waitress voice. "Ready to go?"

"Did I say something?" he says, not moving to stand.

I shake off the unwelcome wave of disappointment. "You're right, facts shouldn't be emotional. Life's less messy when we stick to the facts."

DRIVING BACK TO Roswell, Boone takes us a different route through the mountains. I'm mostly quiet, mulling over our lunch conversation.

How different my life would be if my mother was able to let

my father go instead of clinging to the love she felt for him like a life raft. If she was Rose on the *Titanic*, she wouldn't have let Jack stay in the water. She would've pulled him on the door, willing to drown beside him rather than live a life without him.

Is that what love demands? To give up our life for another's?

Some days I feel like I'm slowly drowning while trying to hold onto my mother's raft.

I wonder what would happen if I let go.

Sixteen

NEEDING TO SHAKE off the melancholy from our conversation over the world's hottest burgers, I invite Boone back to my apartment.

When we arrive, I skip the pretense we're going to spend the evening having polite conversation on my tiny settee and I lead him directly to my bedroom. Sitting on the side of my bed, I expect him to join me.

Instead, he leans against the wall, gently dragging his index finger across the top of his lips, studying me.

He hasn't touched me. Yet my skin flames with heated anticipation.

He approaches, slowly.

On the outside I'm still. Inside, my heart gallops and blood races through my veins as my pulse quickens.

He triggers my flight instinct with his slow, steady pace. Somehow I remain seated on the edge of the bed.

"Lucy." My name on his lips sends a shiver down my spine. "What am I going to do with you?"

The tension between us is off the charts.

Honestly, he could tickle me or kiss me. Either one and I'll probably scream. I half expect him to pounce, closing the distance between us in a single move.

Of course he doesn't, because Boone never does what I think he will.

A few feet away, he stops and yanks his shirt over his head. The soft cotton drops to the ground.

Out of reach, I'd have to stand to touch him unless I use my foot.

"Are you going to stare or get naked?" His low chuckle and wicked smile break some of the tension between us.

After kicking off my shoes, I stand to rid myself of my shorts. I feel granules slide down my legs as I strip off my clothes. In the moment, I forgot about the gypsum.

"I need a shower." I shake and more white powder dusts my wood floor.

He drops his shorts and the same thing happens by his feet. "Can I join you?"

Leaving a trail of gypsum behind us, we strip off the rest of our own clothes and each other's. He kisses my shoulder while undoing the clasp of my bra. It falls to the floor, spilling more white powder.

I lean into the shower to turn on the faucets and Boone slowly peels off my underwear. Willing to do the same for him, I turn around and slip my fingers in the band of his boxers, bending at the waist to drag them down his thighs. Once free from its cotton confines, his thick cock bobs to attention. I give it a quick lick.

Boone's eyes burn a deep emerald before he closes them. Empowered by the effect I have on him, I sit on the edge of the tub and suck him into my mouth.

His moan of pleasure encourages me. With my hand wrapped around the base, I lick and suck as much as I can, using my hand to stroke the rest.

"Lucy," he murmurs. "I want to be inside of you."

I release him to say, "I'm still sandy."

"Then let's continue this in the shower."

He grabs a condom and sets the foil packet on the shelf next to my bath products.

We rinse and then he spends a long time lathering me with body wash. I do the same for him, paying special attention to stroking his shaft with my soapy hands, letting them wander to his balls. He grows even harder in my hand until the tip is an angry deep red. We rinse again before he pins me to the wall, lifting my arms above my head and grinding against me.

I want to live in this shower with him forever, as long as the water stays hot.

After teasing him with my mouth and hands, I expect him to be fast and rough, but once again, he doesn't do what I assume. He makes love to me with slow, steady thrusts, drawing out my pleasure quietly and deliberately until I'm a writhing, slippery mess before finally taking me over the edge with him into simultaneous orgasms. The unicorn of orgasms, and before this moment, completely mythical to me.

Still warm and damp from our long, hot shower sex, we collapse on my bed.

"What happened to your tattoo?" He sweeps his tongue around my nipple, then places a open kiss to the swell of my breast over my heart.

"Huh? I don't have any tattoos." My stomach drops. *Is he confusing me with another lover?*

"I thought I saw one here." He kisses my skin to mark the spot. "The first night we ran into each other at Pete's."

"Are you sure it was me?" I ask, squirming under the tickle of his breath over my nipple.

"Yes. It looked like a sun." With his tongue, he traces a circle and then lines on my skin.

I swear my heart stops beating. *He saw the symbol.* That's why he was doodling it on the napkin.

"No idea." My voice cracks with the lie.

"Hmm," he hums around my right nipple. "My mistake."

In spite of having his mouth against my chest, he doesn't notice the erratic thumping.

My breath shudders when I inhale and I hope he misinterprets it as passion.

Fear mixes with relief.

If he drew what he thought was my tattoo, he probably has no clue about the symbol's deeper meaning to me. Or its possible connection to aliens.

"How old are you?" I ask to change the subject.

He peers up at me from where he's kissing a path to my stomach. "Thirty. Why?"

"No reason. I'll be twenty-eight in December," I tell him even though he didn't ask.

"My birthday is in May." He places kisses around my belly button. "Am I doing this backwards again?"

"Driving me crazy with your mouth? No, I liked the direction you were going before." I run my fingers through his dark waves, confused by my sudden need to chat.

"I meant the dating business. We're naked and about to have sex, I hope, but we're also having a conversation. Should we talk first? I'm not sure how good I am at multi-tasking." He drops a kiss to my hip, then crawls up my body and places a soft, sweet kiss on my mouth.

"You asked a question, I answered." Blinking, I try to focus on his eyes when he's so close.

"Then you asked me how old I am, and I told you. That's what I meant by conversation. The back and forth. You talk, I talk." He drops a kiss on one cheek and then the other.

"I like your way better." I kiss his chin. "We say something, and then follow it with a kiss." I kiss the soft skin behind his jaw, below his ear.

His body jerks and he moans. "That tickles."

I nip his earlobe. "What about that?"

He rolls his hips, rubbing the tip of his erection against my thigh. "Doesn't tickle."

I kiss or bite various places on his body and he tells me how it feels. His inner elbows are surprisingly ticklish, as is the skin between his thumb and forefinger. Not ticklish over his ribs or his ankle.

Losing ourselves in the exploration of each other's bodies, we forget to ask more questions about each other.

And that suits me just fine.

Seventeen

"MY BROTHER WILL be late to his own funeral." Shari sighs and presses her phone's screen to check the time.

We're hanging out in her kitchen waiting for the guys to show up. Took us two weeks for our schedules to all align with a free evening. I don't mind Boone being late because it gives us time to catch up.

The house she shares with her boyfriend, Ray, is a small Spanish bungalow facing a park on the west side of town. I love everything about the house, especially the kitchen. The terra cotta floors, blue and white tile counters, and a bundle of dried red peppers hanging by the large window over the sink, give the space a warm, homey feel. I'd love to live here.

Taking a sip of the cider she poured for me, I lean against the island. "I've never noticed before."

He always shows up at the diner around the same time every morning like he has an alarm set.

"That's interesting." Her fingers tap against the glass as she sends a message. "We're talking about Boone, right? Tall, grumpy guy? Vaguely looks like me, but less attractive?"

"Sounds like the guy. Sometimes has weird facial hair?" I make a mustache with my finger above my mouth.

"That's the one." Laughing, she slightly shakes her head. "You apparently get another side of him."

"Unless he has a twin," I say as casually as I can. Do I really think he's an identical twin? No, but the man I know now doesn't act like the same cranky guy who barely spoke to me months ago.

"Lord no." Shari's dark hair flips in front of her face as she vehemently shakes her head. "One of him is enough. The world couldn't handle two. Might destroy the space-time continuum."

"I don't even know what that is, but it sounds bad."

"Never took physics?" she asks without judgment. "What did you study?"

"History. I like research, and I avoided science after finishing the basic requirements." Now I'm thinking I should've studied physics and quantum mechanics. Who knew conspiracy theories would require so much advance math?

"Boone's the math and engineering mind in the family. I'm better at the soft skills. Being a waitress, we get good at reading people, anticipating their needs, managing their expectations."

"I guess." I'm not sure I've mastered any of those skills. "What's up with the mustaches?"

She smiles and tents her fingers together. "I shouldn't enjoy torturing him as much as I do, but he keeps betting me and losing. At least he only wagers ridiculous facial hair. I tried to get him to get a tattoo, but he refused."

"What are you betting about?" I'm fascinated.

"Anything I know I can win. Mostly silly stuff. Were you around for the mutton chops?" She grins.

"Sadly, no."

"Handlebar mustache? He got really into that one, even bought the wax so he could have the sharp points. Hold on, I have a great pic." She picks up her phone and scrolls. "Here."

I stare at Boone's face on the screen. Not even the overgrown caterpillar can diminish his handsomeness. How is that possible? While I'm gawking at his face, a text notification appears on his forehead.

Don't scare Lucy away. Be there in 5

Laughing, I flip the phone for her to read it. "Why does he think you'll scare me away?"

"He's worried I'm going to spill all his secrets and shatter whatever illusion he's created of being a decent, kind, fun person. Or show you horrible pics of him." She snickers, mischief flashing in her green eyes. "Oops. Too late on the last one."

"Tell me more," I suggest, grinning back at her.

A few minutes later, Boone strolls into the kitchen, finds us laughing over Shari's phone, and grumbles, "I knew I should've picked you up myself. My sister can't be trusted. Has she spilled all of our family secrets?"

Holding her phone, I show him the ridiculous pic we're currently laughing over.

"Hey, I was really proud of that goatee." He takes the phone from my hand and sets it on the counter. Not caring his sister is a few feet away, he wraps his arms around my waist, and kisses me.

I feel him smile against my mouth before he gives me one more soft kiss. Pulling away slightly, he grins down at me. "Hi."

"Hello to you, too," Shari says somewhere behind me.

"I said hi," he repeats, gazing into my eyes like we're the only two people in the room and maybe the world.

"You're going to be insufferable, aren't you?" Shari asks

"Probably." He kisses me again. "When's dinner ready?"

"Enchiladas are in the oven and I need to steam the tamales. Ray's on his way, and as soon as he gets here, we'll eat." She opens the fridge and pulls out a salad bowl.

My mouth waters at the idea of homemade enchiladas and tamales.

Boone takes advantage of her back being turned and lowers his hands to my butt, giving me a squeeze. "I've missed you."

"Me too." Which is ridiculous because I've seen him every day for the past two weeks.

SHARI'S FOOD DOESN'T disappoint.

"This was amazing," I tell her, stuffed from eating two servings of enchiladas and a tamale. Even though my plate is empty, I'm tempted to lick the remaining sauce.

"Thanks. It's my mom's recipe." Boone sweeps his finger through the red sauce on his own plate.

"She must be an amazing cook," I say.

"We'll have to have her make us dinner sometime." Boone drops a casual "meet my parents" invite like it's not a big deal.

From Shari's wide eyes, she thinks it's a big deal. Her gaze meets mine and she mouths "wow" and then takes a sip of water to recover.

"What?" Boone shifts his attention to me.

"Nothing," I say.

Shari speaks up, "We like to play a game after dinner. It's a tradition."

"Like board games?" I ask, thinking how much I despise Monopoly and wondering if I can come up with an excuse to leave.

"I wish," Boone replies, sounding bored. "My sister has a small obsession with conspiracy theories."

"More of a fascination." She flips him off in a true little sister gesture. "I think what people believe says a lot about them."

Ray slings his arm around her shoulder and kisses her temple. For a guy with a shaved head and tons of tattoos, he's surprisingly sweet. "It's charming."

Now I know I need to get out of here before I blurt out my

family's story and come off like a crazy person. The Santos might live in Roswell, but that doesn't mean they believe in aliens. Most locals don't.

"I have a better idea. Lucy and I leave now." Boone squeezes my hand under the table and earns my vote.

"No," Shari deadpans.

"Can we at least sit outside and enjoy the evening while we torture our guest with the world's worst party game?" Boone couldn't sound less thrilled about his sister's plans.

"Excellent idea. You two can light the chiminea and pull the chairs together." Shari enlists Boone to do the grunt work. I admire her technique of flattering him and not giving him an out at the same time.

Grumbling, he obeys and steps outside through the french doors, which I assume lead to the backyard or patio. Ray takes his beer with him and follows Boone.

"Sorry about him. Do you have brothers?" Shari rolls her eyes at the open doors.

"Only child," I reply.

"Lucky." She sighs and gathers up our dinner plates.

I don't feel lucky. "I always wished for siblings. But it wasn't in the cards."

Swallowing down the rest of the story, I pick up my place setting and a couple of glasses. A benefit of waitressing is I can clear a table in one trip.

"Are you close to your parents?" I ask as I set the plates and glassware on the counter next to the sink.

"I guess." She shrugs. "They're . . ."

I wait for her to finish.

Staring out the window, she finally says, " . . . eccentric. I guess that's the best way of describing my family."

"Do they live in Roswell?" Curious, I want to know more

about their background.

"Outside of town, but they moved to their place near Santa Fe a few years ago."

"Can't blame them. Must get overwhelming around here with all the UFO believers and tourists."

Shari studies me as she turns on the water to rinse the dishes. Waiting for it to warm, she opens the dishwasher door. "Mind loading? It'll go faster."

"Not at all." I slide out the rack and load the washer as she hands me things.

"Why Roswell?" she asks me. "I can't imagine choosing to move here if you could live anywhere."

"Roswell kind of chose me. My parents met in Albuquerque in college. Or at least my mom was in school at UNM. After she died, I decided to see why she loved the southwest." None of that is a lie. Proud, I give myself a mental high five.

"Why not move to Santa Fe or Taos? I would." She hands me the final plate and dumps the silverware in the sink.

"Why don't you? What keeps you here? It's only a couple of hours away." Boone staying local makes sense, but Shari waits tables like I do. She could do that anywhere. Probably make better money in a more upscale town.

"I visit up there. I don't think I'll ever leave this area." Her shy smile surprises me. "I talk a big game, but I'm a hometown kind of girl."

"You don't feel trapped?" I blurt out. "Sorry. I don't know you well enough to judge your choices."

"No. You know Ray and I co-own the Burger Joint, right? He's an amazing chef and I run the front of the house."

"That's great." I had no idea. Impressive that they're my age and business owners. "I thought you were 'just a waitress' like me."

"Don't put yourself down. We're all on different paths and

journeys. You seem a little lost, but working on finding yourself. I have faith you'll find what you're seeking." She squeezes my hand.

"Glad one of us does." I contemplate telling her the real reason I'm in Roswell, but hold back. It's hard enough to make friends.

"Roswell is home for me. When you feel your roots sink into the ground, you'll know you found your true home."

"I'm not sure I know what that feeling is. I lived my entire life in the same house, at least up until a few months ago, and I couldn't wait to go anywhere else."

Her warm, soapy hands touch mine as she hands me the mess of forks and knives. "I won't pry, but if you need a friendly ear, you can always talk to me."

Traitor emotional tears prick my eyes. I believe her. "Thanks."

To hide the fact her offer is about to make me cry, I focus on slotting each piece of silverware into its own spot in the dishwasher. Blinking away the wave of sadness, I place the last of the knives in the basket and stand. A quick swipe of my sleeve over my eyes hopefully hides all evidence I'm a sappy, lonely crybaby.

"Fire's ready." Boone's voice carries from the doors. "You might want blankets. And you should—"

When I lift my eyes to his face, he stops talking. He glances behind me at his sister. "What did you do?"

"Pfft," she exhales the sound. "Why do you always assume it's something I've done? We were just chatting."

He glances at me. "Everything okay?"

I nod. "Sure. I think I got soap in my eye or something while we were loading the dishwasher. No biggie."

"You made her do chores?" he asks, incredulous. "She'll never come back."

"Why wouldn't I want to?" I glance between the two siblings. "The enchiladas were amazing, and I haven't laughed that much in a long time. I don't mind clearing a table or helping with dishes. I do it all the time at work. And as far as the game, I'm sure it can't be as boring as some of the dates I've been on in the last few months." At Boone's surprised expression, I add, "Not including you."

I think that makes it worse.

Boone's eyebrows drop as he furrows his brow. "You've been dating?"

Shari coughs to cover the laugh that snorts out of her. "Ignore me."

"Yes?" I have no idea why my answer comes out a question. "I mean, I've gone on dates since moving here."

"Hmm." He narrows his eyes at me for a beat before disappearing back through the door.

"What was that about?" I tip my head in the direction Boone disappeared.

"I think he's jealous." Shari stares out the window but I can see her fighting a smile in the reflection. "Maybe he doesn't like the idea of you seeing other men."

I follow her outside, my mouth partly hanging open at the idea of Boone feeling jealous. He wouldn't if he saw his perceived competition. A small frisson of excitement sends a shiver over my skin. Could he be falling for me?

Boone isn't like the conspiracy believers I use for information.

He's not even in the same galaxy.

Danger, danger, Lucy Halliday.

Boone Santos is nothing but trouble.

Eighteen

THE PATIO IS bigger than I imagined, surrounded by huge agave plants and other cacti. A group of low, wooden Adirondack chairs encircle a clay chiminea with a fire blazing behind the black metal grillwork. Smoke funnels out the narrow top and disappears into the night sky filled with stars. Slightly dulled by city lights, the starlight isn't as clear as it is farther out in the desert where the Milky Way is often visible.

I take a seat across from Boone, with Shari between us on my right and Ray to my left. The chair's cushions are thick and more comfortable than they looked. Settling in, I pull my knees up, rest my feet on the edge of the seat, and lean against the back.

Inhaling the smoke-tinged night air, I relax a bit more. While the rest of the group chats, I zone out, tipping my head back to stare at the sky, looking for constellations I can recognize. Our conversation in the kitchen was odd, and I feel a sense of guilt for going out with other men before dating him. I didn't mean to blurt out about my boring dates. I hate the hurt that I saw in his eyes; the beautiful sparkling green seemed to dull as he processed my confession. I don't want to hurt him.

When I'm around him, I turn into a fumbler of word salad, often blurting out what I'm thinking without a filter. I blame his jawline. It distracts me. Without the silly mustache, he's too handsome for his own good. And apparently his good looks short circuit my brain.

I've let him become a distraction. Imagining living in a house like this and hanging out with friends like them pulls me away from finding answers. After the summer, I think I should move to Albuquerque. Maybe Santa Fe. Put some distance between me and Roswell.

And most importantly, some distance between me and Boone Santos. It's for the best. Once he finds out my past, he'll run. I'm not sure I could handle another person leaving me. Better to beat him to it.

"Okay, who wants to go first?" Shari claps her hands together.

"How about you? It's your game." Boone takes a sip of his tumbler of water.

"Good idea since Lucy's never played before. It's easy. Pick a conspiracy theory and defend it like you believe it." She grins at me.

"Anything?" I ask.

"We try to avoid the really horrible ones like Holocaust denial or anything involving kids dying. Too depressing, not to mention too distasteful. Think more Big Foot or Loch Ness—"

Laughing, Ray interrupts her. "Aliens living among us is always a good choice."

Boone huffs. "Not very original."

"I want to go easy on the new girl." Ray gives me a friendly smile. I like him. If I met him in an alley, I'd probably turn and walk away based on his big size and the neck tattoos. He's a good lesson about not judging a book by its cover or a man by his shaved head.

"Fine, I'll start," Boone says, leaning forward and setting his glass on the wide arm of his chair. "I believe the Earth is flat."

"You did that one last time," Shari whines.

"But Lucy wasn't here, so it's new to her." He gives me a wink.

"Why that one?" I ask.

"I like thinking of Earth being a floating pancake in space. A defined edge instead of a globe appeals to me. Plus, I really enjoy the idea of being able to fall off if you got too close to the end."

"That's absurd," I say, my eyes bugging out at the thought he really buys into this.

"Why? What about the saying 'I'd follow you to the ends of the Earth?' Four corners and ends of the Earth are common expressions. Circles have no ends or corners. Or beginning. A circle is infinite. Round and round we go, never ending. Flat Earth means if we can reach the edge, we can hurl ourselves off into space."

My mouth hangs open. I totally believe he would jump off the planet if given the option.

"Seriously? There's nothing out there. Space is an empty, silent void," I say, supporting his nihilism.

"Is that your conspiracy of choice, Lucy? That we're alone in the universe?" Boone picks up his glass and raises it like he's toasting me. "Good one. Now defend it."

Shitshitshitshit.

I've stepped right into the one area I wanted to avoid. No way am I defending extraterrestrial life.

"No, I was going to pick the kraken." I'm totally lying through my teeth.

"Really?" Ray asks. "Go on."

"Uh . . ." I pause to give myself time to think of any facts I can think of related to the kraken. To buy more time, I sip my cider.

"I like the dramatic pause, but you've got to defend the kraken. Game rules," Shari encourages me.

"Well, we've only explored five percent of the ocean. It's totally possible that what we think of as the giant squid is a smaller relative to the kraken." I start to buy into what I'm saying, and sit more upright. "How tall is a giant squid? A couple of stories, fully extended? Why couldn't there be even larger creatures of a similar design hiding in the depths of the ocean? We have drawings and legends from ancient sailors showing huge tentacles. Why shouldn't we believe them?"

Ray begins clapping. "Totally convinced me. Unlike Boone. Bro, if Earth was flat, the lunar eclipse wouldn't happen. Way too easily disproven and dismissed."

Shari and I laugh at Ray's crossed wrists and buzzer noise disqualifying Boone.

A sore loser, Boone glowers at him.

"Okay, okay, no gloating," Shari admonishes Ray. "Excellent job, Lucy. Now my turn!"

She taps her fingers against her bottle of beer.

"You're going to pick the moon landing, so get on with it." Boone sips his water. I don't know if he's not drinking because he drove or if he never drinks. And if he doesn't drink, is it because he's in recovery or for some other reason? Not that it's any of my business.

"I was, but now I'm picking dinosaurs." Replying to his teasing, she sticks her tongue out. "T-Rex, specifically."

"Oh, I've heard this one. How it's an invention in some sort of paleontological aspect of world domination and the bones are fake." I slap my hand over my mouth. "Sorry. Go on."

Boone's warm laughter breaks the silence first, then Ray follows.

"I'm so sorry," I mumble to Shari, too embarrassed to even glance at Ray.

"You're really good at this," Boone says, drawing my attention.

Even in the low light from the fire, his green eyes spark with amusement. "If we're ever playing on a team, I'm calling dibs on you."

"No fair," Shari groans. "I knew her first. If anyone can call dibs, it should be me."

My eyes flash to Boone. Doesn't she know he's been eating breakfast with me for months? Although why would he tell his sister about the new waitress at the diner south of town? They must have better things to chat about than who's serving his pancakes.

He tips his head to the side as if he's debating revealing our connection. "Uh, if that's the basis for dibs, I win."

Shari's head turns back and forth like she's watching tennis. "How?"

Catching the hint of betrayal in her voice, I jump in to explain. "I'm a waitress at the Rig out on the road to Lovington. Boone eats breakfast there most weekday mornings."

Shari's forehead wrinkles and she asks her brother, "What are you doing way out there?"

He gives her a quick glance. "Working."

Her face scrunches up and she opens her mouth to say something but must change her mind because she presses her lips together with a shake of her head.

"I heard y'all have really good chicken fried steak," Ray says, either ignoring or breaking the growing tension. "Kind of out of the way, but a man's gotta eat."

"You should come down. I'm there during the week for breakfast and lunch. The coffee's not the best, but food's good." I pretend Shari and Boone aren't having a silent conversation mostly with their eyes and eyebrows.

"Sure, if we ever find ourselves on our way to Lovington, we'll swing by." Shari smiles at me, but it doesn't reach her eyes.

Confused, I open my mouth to ask about Boone working in the oil fields, but Ray speaks first.

"Now I'm craving some huevos."

Shari laughs. "We just ate."

"I'm a growing boy." Patting his flat stomach, he gives Shari a flirty smile. "Gotta keep up my strength to keep up with you."

"Sister," Boone mutters into his glass.

"Okay, on that note. Should we declare Lucy tonight's winner and call it a night?" Shari brings the conversation back to safer waters. She's really good at changing direction and managing people. I wonder why she's wasting her talents slinging burgers.

I guess the same could be said for me, but I bet she hasn't spent her life chasing a ghost.

After saying our good-byes, Boone and I step out the front door together. His dirty truck is parked behind my car on the street. The majority of the evening we were fine, but something changed once we finished dinner. His reaction to me dating and his sister's strange response to Boone being in the oil fields every morning have put a weird spin on the end of the night.

We walk to the sidewalk in silence. I count the steps to keep from blurting out a question. At number twenty-three, he cracks the awkward silence by clearing his throat.

At the sound, I stop and face him, slapping a smile on my face while my insides churn. "That was fun."

It's a partial lie, but for someone who doesn't get out much—or never—I had fun tonight.

"Really?" He laughs, clearly disbelieving me.

"For the most part. It's always a little awkward being the new kid in a group that knows each other well. I was honest about the good food and enjoying the evening."

Studying me, he purses his lips and lowers his eyebrows.

I chuckle at his ridiculous face. Either he has no ego or his ego is so huge, he doesn't care about looking weird. Proof: the mustache.

"I was about to apologize for my sister, but evidently no apology is needed if you had a nice time."

"What did she do? I thought she was a great host."

He hums in response but doesn't speak. "Nothing, apparently."

"Well, I have an early morning. As you know." I add the last part hoping he'll bring up the weirdness about him eating breakfast at the Rig. Or the change in his mood. Or ask to come over. Something, anything to keep me from what I'm about to do.

He doesn't bite. Not buying what I'm trying to sell.

If that's the right metaphor. I'm not sure what I'm selling. We're standing at the curb and the location feels ripe for a goodnight kiss. Yet it's like we're strangers.

When he still doesn't say anything, I fill the silence. "Guess I'll see you in the morning."

His steady gaze makes my skin feel hot, so I dig around in my bag to give myself something to do other than stand here and be awkward.

"Lucy, what's going on?" His hand brushes my arm.

"Nothing." I try to swallow down the words rising in my throat.

"Is it my reaction to you dating other guys?" He steps in front of me on the sidewalk, blocking my escape unless I jump the hedge.

Yes. "No."

"I shouldn't assume we're exclusive, but I guess I have. We've only gone out a few times. When you were telling Shari about all the boring dates you've gone on, first I thought you meant me. Which I was going to call bullshit on, but then it hit me you meant other men. I'm not a big enough jerk to think I'm your first anything, but something came over me. Jealousy, I guess. Although I've never felt it before. There's something different about you. And I like it. Because I like you. A lot."

At his heartfelt apology and declaration, alarms start going off in my head where I should feel joy or happiness. Because I'm a weirdo.

"I'm not really the relationship kind of girl. So no worries."

My words sound like a lame line from bad advice column on playing hard to get. "Remember our conversation about not being the kind of people who fall in love?"

Throwing his words back at him hit my target. I hate myself.

He narrows his eyes at me, looking for the lie. "What have we been doing?"

"Hanging out? Playing tourist?" I ask where I should be giving an answer, using his technique against him.

"Right. Just hanging out, seeing the sights with me as your tour guide." He grinds out the word between clenched teeth.

No. No. No. I want to cling to him and make him swear he'll never leave me because if I fall in love and he leaves me alone, I'll break into dust and fade into nothing.

Walking away now is the only option to protect myself and to save him from the truth of my reality.

"Thanks for taking me to the caverns and sledding in White Sands. I loved it." I try to swallow down the word bile burning up my throat, but there's no stopping what's going to come out. "But I'm not sure it's smart if we go out anymore. Things are getting . . . complicated."

My words hit him like I shouted them. He jerks back. "What?"

I have to get out of here before I tell him everything. He'll laugh at me. How can I tell him the conspiracy theories they make fun of are the structure I've built my life around? Even if I doubt aliens exist or crashed north of here, I've spent years of my life looking for answers instead of living. Rather than expose my truth, I'm going to walk away.

Lightning flashes in a giant thundercloud to the west. "Storm's coming."

"I don't give a fuck about the weather. You're insane if you think I'm going to let you walk away without giving me a chance." He's pissed and I don't blame him.

When I don't say anything, he whispers, "Lucy."

Turning away, I stare at the wind moving through the leaves.

He sighs loudly, the sound full of exasperation. "I forgot I have meetings out of town next week. I won't make it to the Rig."

That's a first. I can't think of a single day over the past five months he didn't show up for breakfast.

It's better to make a clean cut than to open up the big box of cray-cray inside of me. Attempting to put on a casual, everything's fine façade, I swing my car keys off my finger. "Okay. Have a nice night, Boone."

"Lucy."

I pause at the sound of his low whisper, so quiet I'm not sure he meant for me to hear it. Only when I hear his footsteps walking back to the house do I run to my car, barely making it before the tears fall and a sob chokes me.

Nineteen

BOONE'S LONG LASHES brush together when he glowers down at me from the stage at Pete's. He's pissed yet the anger intensifies his good looks. That fact adds another layer to my annoyance.

His sneer curls his lips, and he flashes his canines like a feral dog about to lunge.

Everything about him screams pissed off, and at first my body responds to some primal caveman possession reaction. I shut that down as swiftly as it hits me.

No, he doesn't get to call me out in public. Nope. No way.

Ignoring Boone's glaring, I turn to a petrified looking Brayden, who's the color of a cherry and frozen in place like a human popsicle.

"Are you dating him?" Boone shouts above the music, which goes quiet at the same time.

The rest of the band stands silent, instruments still in their hands.

"Are you fucking her?" Boone snarls out the question, this time low enough only me, Brayden, and about ten people closest to us can hear.

This is the first time I'm seeing Boone since the night of the kraken incident, also known as the night I destroyed everything.

He's feral, his eyes more amber than I've ever seen them.

My first instinct is to ignore him, turn, and leave Pete's. Maybe get in my car, drive and never come back.

I have no ties to this town.

Or to Boone.

Instead, my mouth opens and my brain bypasses the flight urge and speaks for me. "None of your damn business."

Way to defend my honor, Brayden. Not only does he believe aliens are demons and dark angels, he's pretty terrible at being a gentleman. I gently touch his arm, trying to break whatever trance he's in. Apparently having a band member yell at your "date" in the middle of a show can freak some guys out. "I'm leaving. You're welcome to stay."

"Huh?" Brayden's glassy stare meets mine. It's like he's been hit with a tractor beam that's rendered him stupid.

"I'm leaving," I tell him.

In the awkward silence of the room, the drummer begins to play a steady beat on his drums. The crowd is growing restless and some random guy behind us yells, "Play 'Free Bird'."

A bunch of the audience laughs and begins shouting random song requests.

Then a half-eaten chicken wing sails through the air and lands at Boone's feet.

He breaks his one-sided glaring contest with me to glance down at the chicken bone.

"What the hell?" he mumbles right before a carrot stick hits his shoulder.

"I'm out of here." I tug Brayden's sleeve, giving him one more chance before things escalate.

More carrots and some celery sails by my head, reminding me of eighth grade. Back home, the Great Food War of Washington Middle School is the stuff of legend. Having witnessed it firsthand,

I know things are about to get messy.

Brayden doesn't budge and I make the decision to leave him behind to save myself. When a hamburger bun smacks Boone's leg and sticks, I know it's now or never.

Shoving my way through the crowd toward the emergency exit to the left of the stage, I hear one of the band members tell people to calm down.

Too late.

That ship has sailed.

The guitarist, whose name I think is Melo or Mallow, begins playing random notes. Behind me, someone shouts my name. I'm a foot or two from the door and freedom, there's no way I'm turning back now.

Brayden is on his own and Boone can go fuck himself.

"Lucy Halliday!" the voice shouts again from the open door behind me. Even with the blast of music and shouting from the inevitable food battle, I recognize Boone's voice.

I could stop, face him, and tell him where he can stuff his masculine possessive bullshit. Or I can start to jog, holding on to hope I can outrun him, and get to my car before he catches up. A third option hits me as I speed-walk down the side of the building: I can keep on walking. Because I didn't drive. Brayden did.

Wanda set me up with Brayden. He's the son of a cousin or a cousin's cousin or her dental hygienist. She said he had information about people who go missing after abductions. Not thinking it was going to be a real date with a dinner and a show, I agreed. And broke my rule about always driving myself.

As much as I'm annoyed at Wanda, I blame Boone. I got used to him driving when we went on our real dates.

Brayden picked the place. When we arrived at Pete's, I should've suggested somewhere else. I didn't. Instead, I sat through dinner trying to steer the conversation to abductions while Brayden talked about aliens in the Bible. I saw live music as my escape from the alien Jesus believer, and dragged him up to the stage before realizing who was playing.

My evening has been a Jenga tower of bad decisions.

It hits me Brayden hasn't followed me. I wonder if he's still standing in the same spot by the stage. Or if Boone knocked him out.

If he did, he can get his pecan pancakes and huevos someplace else. I'll amend our "no shirt, no shoes" sign to read "no shirt, no shoes, no assholes."

"Lucy, stop."

Hell no. I'm not a dog he can command.

I speed up.

"Lucy." The tone of his voice switches from demanding to pleading.

I'm not moving that quickly. He could definitely catch up to me if he wanted.

From the sound of his footsteps, he's a few yards behind me, not closing the distance by running, or even jogging.

On the other hand, I'm feeling a little winded. We've passed the parking lot of Pete's and are now a two person parade down the sidewalk, heading back toward Main Street.

"Lu-cy, please stop and talk to me."

I keep stomping in the direction of downtown.

"Lucy, you can't walk home. It's too far."

Pfft. What does he know? It might take me over an hour, but I'd do it just to spite him.

"Loo-cy," he whines. "Stop running away from me."

If I thought him saying please was a game changer, arrogant, cocky Boone whining is a whole other level.

Honestly, I'm not sure I like it.

I stop and wait for him.

Not because he whined and said please. My feet are killing me in these boots and there's a sharp stab of a cramp in my side.

Waiting the few seconds it'll take for him to catch up, I glance around and am surprised to see we've gone farther than I thought. Main Street is the next intersection. The marquee of the UFO museum peeks around the corner.

I didn't realize I was so close. For a flash, I think about dashing across the intersection to the alley that'll take me to the secret entrance.

Glancing behind me, I realize Boone's stopped walking, too. Rather than approach me, he's standing still, eyeing me like I'd watch a prowling coyote—little bit afraid, but also fascinated from a safe distance.

We stare at each other, both of our chests rising and falling in sync.

"Lucy," he says again, a small smile tugging at his lips.

"No." I hold up my hand when he takes a step forward. "Stay there."

He freezes, obeying my order.

I'm half-tempted to tell him "good boy" for listening. Just to piss him off.

"You don't get to speak to me the way you did back there. Ever. In fact, you shouldn't speak to any woman like that. Who the hell do you think you are?"

"I—"

"Don't answer that. It was rhetorical!" I shout at him.

He dares to smirk at me.

"If you want to keep that smirk, you better lose it. I am not in the mood for your beautiful mouth tonight. Not when you act like a giant manhole, jerk face, caveman, sexist prick." I pause to think of more insults.

"Are you finished yelling at me?" He crosses his arms and waits.

"No." I mirror his posture.

"Then by all means, continue." Rolling one of his hands in a circle, he calmly encourages me.

"Ugh, you are so infuriating. I don't need your permission to speak my mind, Boone." My voice drips with sarcasm when I add his name at the end. Petulant and pissed, that's me. "Jealousy is ugly, even on you."

He presses his lips together and then drags his bottom teeth over his top lip as he listens. No mustache to hide his full lips or the way the pressure of his teeth turns the skin from pink to white to deep rose.

Ugh, ugh, ugh. I hate his beautiful mouth.

That's a lie I wish were true.

Sounds of traffic from the main drag behind me fills the growing gap between my words and his silence.

I'm about to turn around and keep walking when he finally speaks. "Can I say something?"

"You've never needed my permission before." I'm in full snarky, teenage girl mode and I can't seem to care enough to stop myself.

"Touché."

A white pickup speeds by us and a guy yells out the passenger window, "Get a room!"

And in this moment I hate all men.

That's not true. Only the men on this street in this moment.

"I'm sorry."

And with those two words, as much as I'm mad at him, I can't hate Boone Santos.

Inhaling slowly through my nose, I absorb this revelation and his apology. "Why are you apologizing?"

He slides his fingers into the front pockets of his dark jeans and rocks back on his heels. "I was a jealous bastard."

I notice the hamburger bun left a stain on his right thigh.

"You were."

Lips pressed together, he nods. "Right. And there's no excuse. If a guy spoke to my sister like that, I'd deck him. I don't know what happened to me back there. Did you show up tonight to rub it in my face? Make me jealous? Shari told me she met you when you were on another date."

"No, no way. I told you I don't play games."

"Then why bring a guy to Pete's?"

"He picked the place." I hate that I'm defending my actions. "I didn't know Alien Autopsies was even playing tonight."

"Do you like him?" The question has a bitter bite to it.

"Why does it matter?" I have no feelings about Brayden, but I'm not telling Boone because he's being an asshole.

"It does. All I know is it does." This realization makes him frown. "You didn't answer my question."

"No, I don't like him. I just met him. And since he didn't follow me outside, I won't be seeing him again." I debate telling him my true motivation for hanging out with Brayden. Misleading guys for research doesn't make me a good person even if I never lead them on, or go on second dates ever. Except with Boone.

"Good." He glances at my face and then around us as if noticing our surroundings for the first time. "How are you getting home?"

I bite back the urge to tell him it's none of his business again, but the fight has left me. My feet hurt and I'm stranded.

"I can text Shari and have her drive you." He pulls out his phone and taps the screen.

"There's no reason to bother her. I'm an adult and can find my way home."

One of his dark eyebrows lifts in question, but before he can ask it, his phone chirps with a text alert. Reading the screen, he frowns, then nods. "Shari can be here in five minutes."

"What did she say?"

"Want me to read it to you? She asked what asshole move I did now."

"Is this a habit of yours? Insulting women and having your sister clean up your messes?"

"No. After my behavior tonight you have no reason to believe me, but I swear, this is a first."

I want to believe him.

I also want to forget this evening all together. "You don't have to babysit me. I'm sure the rest of the band is wondering what happened to you. Don't you have a show to finish?"

His eyes widen and his mouth pops open. "Oh, shit. I left in the middle of a song, didn't I?"

His reaction surprises me. "Uh, more like at the end of a song, but yeah, if you're out here, you pretty much left the gig in the middle."

"Fuck." Running his hands through his hair, he blows out a big breath. "I suck today."

"Should I comment on that?" I ask, attempting humor.

"Please, no. I'm going to go back to the bar and resume playing. Axl is going to rip me a new one. He'd probably fire me if I were an actual member of his band."

"Axle? Like a car? Poor guy."

"Worse. Axl like the lead singer of Guns 'n Roses. I guess his mom was a groupie."

"That is worse. Hold on, what do you mean you're not in the band? I've seen you play with them twice now."

"I'm filling in for Garcia. He broke his wrist climbing near Taos. Can't play bass with a cast."

"So you randomly filled in for him?" Curiosity takes over and I forget to be mad.

"We played in a band together in high school. I'm a little rusty, but bass is pretty simple if you know what you're doing. I have good rhythm."

I know he does. The sun set already, but I'm feeling flushed like I've been sitting directly in its rays.

"You're a pervert, Lucy Halliday."

"Why do you always say my name?"

"Do I? I like Lucy. Lucy Halliday has a good ring to it. Solid, a little quirky, unique. Like you."

"Solid?" I throw major side eyes at him. Sounds like heavy. Boone needs to work on his compliments.

"If I called you beautiful and sexy, you'd probably do me bodily harm after the manhole stunt I pulled on stage. I'm trying to make amends."

Shari's car pulls to a stop next to the curb.

"Oh good, there's no bloodshed and Boone still has all his appendages," she shouts out the window. "I worried I'd be too late for the fun."

Boone groans in reaction to his sister's comment and interruption.

"Quit scowling at me, dear brother. You're the one who sent out the SOS text." She waves at me and pops open the lock on the passenger seat of her Jeep. "You still need a ride home?"

"I do, thanks." I reach for the door handle but Boone's hand on my arm stops me.

It's the first time we've touched since the dinner at Shari's. My skin lights up with a billion tiny sparks of electricity, flashing a welcome message like a roadside motel advertising vacancy.

Out of spite, I resist the urge to be the first to pull away.

"Or we can hang out here all night," Shari offers, sounding both amused and annoyed.

"No, I'm coming." I manage to open the door and then Boone swings it wide for me, holding it while I climb in the SUV.

"I'm sorry," he says. "I promise what happened back there won't happen again."

Once I'm settled, he closes the door and steps away, pausing for a beat or two when our eyes meet. I want to believe him, but I need to protect my heart. Pretending he isn't there, I stare out the windshield. Out of sight, out of mind, right?

"You're a weirdo," Shari tells him as she shifts from park to drive.

Boone responds with a shrug before turning around and heading back to Pete's.

At the intersection she takes a left, heading in the direction of my apartment.

"How do you know where I live?" I ask, shifting in my seat to stare at her.

She slows down for a red light, but doesn't answer me right away.

"Shari?"

"I'm sure you told me. Probably when you came over for dinner."

"I don't think I did."

"Hmm," she hums to herself. "I don't know exactly where you live. I guessed you were south of town because of where you work."

Could be plausible, but also sounds like she's backtracking.

"Fine. I know where you live. It's a small town, people are friendly."

"Did Boone tell you?" My heart squeezes at his name.

"No, I swung by the diner when you weren't there and chatted up Wanda. She's a sweetheart, but really needs to learn how to keep a secret."

I don't know who to be mad at. "Wanda gave you my address just like that?"

"I told her I wanted to send you some flowers." She flicks her attention to me, then sighs. "Fine, it was Boone. He gave it to me in the text he sent. You can be mad."

"Thanks, but I don't need your permission. I'm already mad."

"Sorry. It comes from a place of caring. We don't let a lot of people into our circle, but when we do, we get overly protective."

"You grew up here. You must have tons of old friends and family around."

"Not really. We mostly keep to ourselves. Close knit, small family. If you haven't noticed, people are weird in this town."

"I guess Boone didn't tell you about our conversation after dinner at your place." I twist my head to watch her expression for the truth.

She bites her lip. "He came back inside after you left."

"I—"

She interrupts me. "We don't have to talk about it, but since I'm his sister and I feel obligated to tell you, he seemed pretty hurt. He doesn't open up to new people, especially women."

"Probably for the best." I'm still stinging from his bizarre behavior.

"What happened tonight?"

I give her the condensed version while she drives me home.

"Are you sure he doesn't have an evil twin?"

"He's going to wish he did." Pulling up to the curb in front of my complex, she turns off the engine. "I'm going to kill him."

"Please don't. You'll go to jail. At this point you're my only friend besides Wanda." The thought makes my eyes sting.

"Boone's a good guy, Lucy. And he likes you. Even if he can be a stupid caveman idiot like tonight," she grumbles. "If I can't kill him, would you be open to serious bodily harm?"

The idea makes me smile. "Just don't ruin his face."

Reluctantly, she agrees, "Fine."

I wipe a few tears from the corners of my eyes. "I'm fine. I swear."

"Want me to come in? I can stay over and help you make effigies of my brother, then we can burn them in the early light of dawn." She grins at me. "I'm really enjoying thinking of new ways to torture him."

"You have a dark side." I smile back. "I like it."

"I'm here if you need me. Text me and I'll help you hide the body."

I dip my chin and level a serious look at her. "Shari."

"Fine, fine. Can I give you a hug?" She opens her arms.

Returning her hug, I fight back more tears.

"You're going to be okay. I know it." With a final squeeze, she releases me.

Twenty

BY THE TIME I toss my bag in my cubby by the back door of the diner, I'm officially five minutes late for work. I barely slept at all last night.

Prepared for Tony's comment, he surprises me by not calling me out on my tardiness.

"Morning," he says without turning from the grill. "Wanda's already made coffee. Get yourself a cup."

That's it.

Inhaling the combined scents of bacon and sausage sizzling on the griddle, I stand frozen behind him. "No lecture?"

He glances over his shoulder. "You want one? We're about to be slammed by the early birds, but sure, we can stand around while you give me an excuse about being late. Or how about this option? We move on with our days, and pretend we did."

I finish tying my apron and dash out of the kitchen. When I pour myself a cup of coffee, I make one for him, too.

"Thank you," I say, placing the full cup on the little shelf near him.

He grunts his thanks and I know I can stop fretting over being late.

In the dining area, Wanda's finishing the last of the place

settings. I grab the bin of ketchup and hot sauce bottles. After saying hello, we work in silence. She places a paper placement and a mug in front of each chair, me following behind with the condiments.

"Late night?" she asks once we finish.

"Yeah, but not for the reasons you think."

"Didn't see your lights on." She gives me a knowing smile. Today's lip color is a frosted pink the shade of raspberry sherbet. "How'd it go with Brayden?"

"We didn't have a connection." I don't want to tell her more details and I hope Brayden won't share his version with his mom's cousin or cousin's cousin.

Wanda's frosted coral lips press into a thin line of disappointment, but her voice is sympathetic when she asks, "Still stuck on Boone?"

I don't know how to answer her. Not after last night.

The door opens and a group of older oilmen walk through it.

"Showtime," Wanda mumbles behind her smile.

"I'll take their table. Make up for being late." I pat her shoulder, and then pick up both the regular and the decaf pots of coffee.

A young family with a squawking infant sits at table five. Part of me wants to reseat them at another table in the hope he'll walk through the door soon.

Wanda and I hit our stride as the tables fill and empty with the breakfast rush.

Still no sign of Boone.

Every time the front doors open now, I glance up, hoping for him to walk through them.

He doesn't.

I'm clearing dishes from a four-top table when the door opens and again I look up. A dirt covered oil field worker stumbles into the room and yells for someone to turn on the local news. "Sinkhole opened up south of Artesia. Brine well collapsed."

At his announcement, the room erupts into chatter. Oil workers make calls and start talking over each other, one hand covering their ears to hear whoever's on the other end of the line.

Wanda finds the remote and changes the omnipresent business channel to a local station.

An aerial shot of a hole fills the screen. It's hard to tell scale given the flat scrubland, but compared to the white pickup parked nearby, the hole must be almost a hundred feet across and who knows how deep. Reminds me of one of the smaller cenotes out at Bottomless Lakes.

"Turn up the volume," one of the regulars shouts.

"Don't get your undies in a bunch." Wanda presses the volume button while glaring at him.

"Anyone hurt?" the guy who ran in with the news asks.

"Doesn't seem like it." Another man glances up from his phone. "Not near any roads or buildings this time."

Once I know no one is missing or dead, I tune out the gossip and the broadcast.

Boone's not missing because he's trapped in a hole.

He's avoiding me. Like I asked him to.

That doesn't make me feel better.

For the rest of the morning, every local who comes in talks about the sinkhole.

I nod and half-listen to their comments, but I couldn't care less about a hole in the ground.

When my shift's over, I'm ready for a nap. A sleepless night and a long morning having the same conversation on repeat have left me with a headache.

Unfortunately, I can't go home and sleep the afternoon away. Today's one of my shifts at the Center.

I order a turkey melt for Zed and pour myself a giant iced tea, hoping the caffeine will wake me up.

I can't even text Boone to make sure he's okay. I doubt he wants to hear from me after last night.

I assume if something happened to him, Shari will tell me eventually.

Waiting for Tony to make the sandwich, I pull out my phone to check my texts.

Nothing.

"SINKHOLE," ZED SAYS when I walk into the cramped office of the Center.

"Hello to you, too." I drop the plastic bag on top of a pile of file folders on his desk.

"You hear about it?" He moves the bag to the floor. That's a first. Usually he begins inhaling his lunch as soon as I set it down.

"Everyone in the diner this morning was talking about it. We even switched one of the televisions over to the local news." Also a first. "Is there a full moon or something? People are acting freaked out about a random hole appearing in the desert. Don't sinkholes happen all over the world?"

Zed removes his glasses and folds them before blinking up at me. I'd never noticed he actually has pretty eyes.

"Do you know what a salt cavern is?"

"Huh?" I shake off my thoughts about Zed's pretty eyes. The moon must be full or some planet goes retrograde today.

"Salt cavern?" he repeats.

"I'm guessing it's a cave full of salt. Or made from salt." I feel a lecture coming on, so I lean against the row of file cabinets opposite his desk.

"You've heard of Carlsbad Caverns?" he asks, ignoring my simple explanation to his question.

"I've been there. They're part of an ancient coral reef from a

prehistoric ocean that used to cover this area in the Permian era."
My heart twinges as I repeat the lesson Boone taught me about
the caverns.

"Impressive." He bobs his head. "See? I knew you were a
smart girl."

"Woman," I say. "We've gone over this, Zed. Not a child,
therefore, not a girl."

Leaning back in his chair, he rests both hands on the top of his
head. "Fine. Between here and Carlsbad are layers of salt as well
as other limestone caves. Some of them collapsed and formed the
Bottomless Lakes. Years ago, oil companies figured they could fill
the salt layers with freshwater and then pump it out for their own
usage, creating brine wells."

"Why?"

"If you haven't noticed, we're landlocked around here. No
access to saltwater from any existing ocean."

My feet ache from working a full shift at the diner. Zed's
obviously just getting started so I reluctantly give up and sit in the
chair opposite his.

"Go on," I encourage him, hoping he'll wrap it up quicker
if I show interest. "Wait, skip the details on mining and drilling. I
won't remember them."

He frowns in disappointment. "This is the third collapse in
two years."

"Is that unusual?" I ask, because who knows what's the normal
rate of sinkholes around here.

"Very. Remember the article I pulled for you a while back?
With the perfectly round hole intersected by straight lines?"

Remembering how it recalled the symbol, I sit up straighter.

"You do. Did you pay attention to the one that appeared this
morning?"

I shake my head no.

"Same pattern."

The hairs on my arm stand up straight. It has to be a coincidence. "Doesn't that make sense? Same area so the roads and terrain are the same. Both were salt cavern collapses."

"All three of the most recent cave-ins have been on SFT, Inc. owned property."

Reason and cynicism tell me there's a simple explanation. "Sounds like SFT is overworking their land."

"That would be the obvious explanation," he sneers. "The one the media will latch onto and the public will accept."

"But?" I add for him.

"What if the answer isn't to blame an oil company? What if the truth can't be found below ground?"

I'm tired and still reeling over my actions last night. Today is not the day I want to play hypothetical conspiracy games with Zed. I'm already thinking about swinging by the liquor store on my way home, buying margarita fixings, and spending the evening watching *10 Things I Hate About You* while I wallow in my feelings.

"You're not even listening anymore." Zed taps a pen on the desk.

I yawn and try to cover it in my elbow. "Sorry. It's been a long day. Can you repeat it?"

"Never mind." He dismisses me by picking up the bag with his lunch. "Just don't accept the explanation SFT or the local government feeds everyone via the media."

"Got it. Trust no one and nothing." I push myself out of the chair. "Got a new box for me today?"

"Found some files about abductions in the late nineties. Mostly in the Tennessee and Ohio areas, but there might be something in there of interest to you."

My tiredness fades and is replaced with interest. "Thanks, Zed. Much better than another hole in the ground story."

His mouth full of turkey, he mumbles, "Eh, you never know how the two could be related."

Inside of the tiny closet of a room, I open the top of the banker's box and quickly flip through the articles.

An hour later, my back aches and my neck is stiff from being bent over the table, sorting and scanning clippings, journal pages, and photos.

Rolling my head in a circle, I press my palms against my lower back to stretch out sore muscles.

A masculine voice carries from Zed's office. Turning off the hum of the scanner, I still my breathing to hear better. We never have visitors, so whoever is out there must be another member of Zed's group. I've never met anyone else. My curiosity is off the charts.

Still listening, but unable to understand what's being said, I creep closer to the door.

Zed's visitor isn't another person but an old transistor radio sitting on his desk. Tuned to the local talk radio station, a man's voice fills the office with an update on the sinkhole.

Disappointed, but still curious, I step into the hall.

Zed spots me and turns a dial to lower the volume.

"Radios are okay?" I ask, a snarky edge to my voice.

"Passive listening. No one is tracking if I'm receiving radio waves."

All I can think of is the old images of men wearing tinfoil hats to protect themselves from transmissions. "What's the media saying about the hole?"

"Listen for yourself." He turns the volume back up.

A male voice is speaking about cooperating with local authorities and the EPA.

Zed interrupts, "Feds are involved already. Don't you think that's interesting? Why should the government care about a hole on private land in the middle of the desert?"

The announcer continues speaking, but it's difficult to hear under Zed's ramblings.

"Shh," I hush him.

"Thank you," the voice says.

"Did you shush me?" Zed interrupts.

" . . . Spokesperson for the Santos Family Trust, owners of the land where the sinkhole appeared earlier this morning."

"I can't believe I'm being told to be quiet in my own office," Zed continues speaking while I flap my hands at him to shut up.

"What did he say?" I ask, wishing radio had a rewind button like online clips.

"Blah, blah, blah, nothing to see here. I think that summarizes everything." Zed's cranky now.

"No, the Santos part." It's not that unusual a name, but what are the odds?

"SFT is the Santos Family Trust. They own a ton of acreage around Roswell. Couple hundred thousand acres. Most of it's leased out to the oil companies, cattle ranchers, or big agro."

Something clicks into place. "And the name of the company spokesperson?"

Zed studies me for a moment. "The great-grandson. Boone."

Twenty-One

"EVERYTHING OKAY, HUN? Something wrong with the pancakes?" The older waitress in a neat vintage, uniform dress and apron hovers over my table, one hand holding a coffee pot. Her short, gray hair is neatly curled and tidy.

"No, they're delicious." The words come out all watery as more tears fall.

"If it's man trouble, he's not worth it. They never are. Trust me. I've had five husbands and not one of them was worth the salt I lost crying." She moves the napkin dispenser closer within reach. "Let me bring you some pie."

With a pat to my shoulder, she moves away. I glance down at the half eaten plate of pecan pancakes. They're amazing, but the worst choice I could've made. I'm not sure pie can help at this point. I'm too miserable.

Sun splashes off the windshields of the cars parked in front of this little diner in the mountain town of Capitan. Only I would go to a diner to escape my life. Different diner, same problems.

A slice of blueberry pie with a huge scoop of vanilla ice cream on the side is slid in front of me.

"Thanks, but—" I start to decline her sweet gesture.

"On the house," the waitress waves me off. "Trust me. It'll help."

Pitifully sniffing, I dab my eyes with a fresh napkin. "Thank you."

"Don't you worry about it." She squeezes my shoulder before moving to the next table.

Purple juice from the warm pie mixes with the melting ice cream on the plate. *Maybe one bite,* I tell myself.

I'm going to need my strength when I drive back to Roswell this afternoon.

Boone's not some random oil field worker who plays in a band.

After Zed told me about Boone's role as family spokesperson, he spilled the whole story about the Santos family. The patriarch showed up in Roswell in the early 1940s and bought several small plots in the area from struggling ranchers. A year later oil was discovered on his property south toward Artesia. Family's fortunes grew as they amassed more and more acreage.

Excited to share local gossip, Zed started pulling out maps and land charts, but I'd heard enough.

I know I'm being a hypocrite about Boone's family. He never lied to me about who he was. Just like I've never lied to him about why I'm in Roswell.

We just omitted some of the important stuff.

Leaving the Center last week, I went straight home and packed a bag. I asked Tony for some days off and Wanda found a cousin or a niece to cover my shifts.

Then I took off, no destination in mind.

When I hit Santa Fe, I found a little motel with a vacancy on the edge of town. I thought about driving through the night to Colorado or Arizona. Instead, I cried in the bathtub. Fully clothed and sitting in a tub without water in it seemed the right place for a sob fest.

I turned off my phone and locked it in the glove box in my car.

Strolling through Santa Fe's historic downtown didn't help ease the ache in my heart.

Ropes of red chiles hanging everywhere made me cry.

Corned beef hash advertised on a sandwich board outside a café sent more tears spilling down my face.

Not even seeing the famous floating staircase that might've been built by a mysterious alien carpenter could cheer me up.

Now blueberries reminds me of the pancakes Boone ate after our first official date and the first time we had sex. Made love. Because as much as I don't want to fall in love with Boone, I'm on the rollercoaster.

This blueberry pie is delicious, but it doesn't change the painful fact I did the right thing in ending it with Boone.

He's an heir to millions.

I'm a penniless orphan with an alien obsession.

We're not meant to be together.

"WHERE'VE YOU BEEN?" Zed closes a file folder and tucks it under a stack of papers when I enter the office. "Thought you'd left town."

"I missed a couple of days." I tip my head to one side, attempting to read some of the papers on his desk upside down.

"It's been over a week." He leans an arm on the stack closest to me. "Not to mention all the time you took off earlier in the month."

"Do you have an absence policy I missed in the employee handbook? Oh wait, I'm a volunteer."

"Handbook? You're kidding, right? Imagine if that got into the wrong hands." He's completely serious. And seriously paranoid.

"Well, I'm here now. Brought you lunch even." I hold up the plastic bag. "Turkey club and an extra scoop of fries."

Honestly, I thought the extra fries would smooth over the fact I skipped my shifts here. Apparently, Zed's forgiveness cannot be bought with food.

"In your messages you said you were doing some sightseeing."

"I wasn't sure you got the texts."

"My cell phones all have texting capacity." He crosses his arms and glares at me.

"I'm not judging your revolving collection of flip phones from Walmart. You never responded, so I wasn't sure if I had your current phone numbers."

"Is that sarcasm I detect?" He unknots the top of his white, plastic lunch bag.

"No, why would I be using sarcasm right now?" I lay it on thick.

"Are you going to be taking more vacations or can I rely on you to show up for your commitments? I'm beginning to think you're not a true believer." The styrofoam squeaks when he opens the box.

Standing to the side of his desk, feeling like a scolded child who didn't do her homework, I stare at him while he squeezes a packet of ketchup all over the top of his fries. Who does that? A monster that's who. Everyone knows you make a puddle of sauce and dip fries into it. Sticky red ketchup clings to his fingers now.

"I think I'm done here." I manage to keep the disgust out of my voice.

"There's a half dozen boxes waiting to be scanned. Better get to it or you'll never catch up." He doesn't bother making eye contact while cramming fries into his mouth.

I wait for him to notice I haven't responded or moved before speaking again.

Finally, he lifts his attention from his food and stares at me. "Yes?"

"I meant, I think I'm quitting."

He swallows thickly a couple of times, then takes a long sip from his cup of pop. "You can't quit."

"Or whatever you want to call it when a volunteer stops volunteering. I'm doing that."

"Why?" He finally, mercifully wipes his messy hands on a couple of thin paper napkins. The image reminds me of a murderer cleaning blood.

And that's when it hits me how foolish I've been coming here in secret. No one knows I'm here and the general population doesn't even know the Center exists.

I could be kidnapped and forced to join a cult, and no one would know.

My eyes land on the large "I Believe" UFO poster on the far wall.

It might be too late about the cult part.

"You signed a non-disclosure agreement and a confidentiality contract, Lucy. I'm not going to beg you to stay, but you should know you can never tell anyone about knowing me or anything about what we do here at the Center." He sips from his straw again. "Ever."

I imagine Zed and his messy desk and his stacks of banker boxes set up in an office off of the snack bar at Carlsbad Caverns. Going to bet cellular waves can't penetrate almost eight hundred feet of limestone. I can't think of a better location for the Center. And if anyone needs a secret underground lair, it's Zed. Throw in a hairless cat and he'd be perfect.

"No one will believe me. And if I tell them how I spent hours and days scanning old articles from tabloids, reading random strangers' emails and journals, they'd think I was a nut job. And maybe I am."

"What about finding out the truth? What about finding out what happened to your father?"

Low blow. He knows that's the one reason I'm even here in New Mexico.

"I'm not sure I'll find answers in these boxes. Maybe there aren't answers to some mysteries. Who built the pyramids? Aliens or some brilliant, hardworking Egyptians? Perhaps the moon is just a rock and not a secret mining site for intergalactic companies. Maybe the simplest answer is the truth and Occam's Razor is true.

"All I know is for the first time in years, I want to live my life without constantly thinking about aliens and abductions and the man who donated half of my DNA. I'm almost thirty and what do I have to show for all the time I've spent on this planet? What's wrong with wanting to have some fun? Make friends. Be normal." My chest heaves with emotion when I finish my impromptu monologue.

Zed removes his glasses and then rubs his eyes. "Fine. Take a break. You're not fired. When, I mean if, you want to come back and help out, you'll be welcome."

"That's it? You're going to cave that easily?" My jaw drops open.

"You made a good argument. I'm not some evil overlord who will force you to work for me with threats and coercion." He gives me a weak smile and I'm reminded he could be handsome with a little sun and a haircut.

Zed's not evil. Just a little, okay, a lot, obsessive.

"I'm still going to leave now. But I'll keep in touch. Maybe come in once in a while and check in."

"You can still bring me lunch." He lowers his glasses.

"Deal." I take a step backward.

"And, Lucy?" He meets my eyes. "If I find anything directly related to your father, I'll let you know."

Even though we're leaving things on a positive note, I still get the feeling I've been used. My own obsession turned against me to help Zed find the truth he thinks is out there.

It's not him, it's me.

I'm changing and discovering new parts of myself, or redis-covering old parts.

As I walk down the stairs, momentarily feeling free, I sense a strange suction of relief leaving my body like water disappearing off a beach right before a tsunami hits. In my case, a wall of grief slams into me when I open the door to the alley.

I'm giving up on my dad. If I stop searching, I'm accepting he's never coming back, gone forever.

Like my mom and my grandparents.

I've held out a sliver of cynical hope I could find him and not be alone.

My knees almost buckle with the power of sorrow that slams into my chest, punching a hole through my ribs before squeezing my heart. Breathing becomes a challenge and dark shadows grow at the edge of my vision.

I've never had a panic attack, but I'm either having my first one or dying.

The latter seems most plausible.

I can't die in the back alley behind a UFO museum that also houses a secret research center.

The headlines would be too absurd.

Struggling to draw in enough air to keep from passing out, I focus on putting one foot in front of the other to get to my car. I can pass out in my car. I won't face-plant or hit my head if I do.

Step. Inhale.

Step. Exhale.

Step. Inhale.

Step. Exhale.

Almost to the sidewalk. I curse Zed for making me park a block away. I don't even have my phone to call someone. Who would I call? Shari? She'd come get me. Boone? He's probably down in the oil fields. By the time he'd get here, I'd be a headline in the local paper. Or maybe no one would notice my crumpled, barely sentient or lifeless form in the alley. At least not for hours. No one comes back here.

I make it to the sidewalk and inhale a deeper breath. My right hand rests over my heart and I press it harder against the wild thumping.

Tears skitter down my cheeks and drip off my jaw onto my arm. Focused on breathing and not dying, I didn't realize when I started crying.

With my head ducked, I weave between clumps of tourists. My sunglasses are on the seat next to my phone in the car. I swipe below my eyes, only half caring I must look like a crazy person.

Another few yards and my car comes into view. I can make it. *Hold it together, Lucy.* A few more steps and I'm standing by the driver's side, bobbling the keys out of thy pocket. It takes me two tries to click the right button on the fob. I accidentally hit the panic button, setting off the horn and lights. How ironic.

A few heads turn toward the disruption before I can turn it off. If only there was a button to stop real panic.

Finally inside, I slump down in my seat, letting the tears flow freely. A loud sob rips out of my mouth and I heave forward in pain. Resting my forehead against the steering wheel, I let the wave of grief suck me into its undertow.

I'm alone.

My mother is dead.

My father is gone.

Neither are ever coming back.

Parked cars are the perfect place to have an emotional breakdown. Like sturdy, nearly soundproof containers for emotions. Despite having large glass windows, people rarely bother looking inside of them as they walk down the street. I make this observation while resting my cheek on the steering wheel. The worst of my sob fest has left me exhausted and in dreamlike sleepy place. However, I'm numb and unmotivated to start the car to drive home. This is my life now and I'm okay with sitting here forever.

Staring out the passenger side window, I watch people stroll down the sidewalk. Families with small children, sullen teenagers in alien T-shirts, men in cowboy hats, women in clusters, old people shuffling alone—an oddball parade passes by my window. None of them would ever notice if I disappeared. Their lives will continue on as happy or sad as they are.

I need to go home.

Soon.

Turning the key, I scan through radio stations until I find something I don't hate. I'm still scrolling when a car pulls alongside me and honks. A man makes a gesture for leaving. I wave him away while mouthing, "no."

I guess my car bubble isn't as invisible as I'd thought.

My phone plays the sci-fi music I set for text alerts.

I flip it over and see a text from Shari. *This day sucks!!! Want to meet at Pete's in 30?*

Another text pops in the window as I read the first.

Just us. In case you were worried about seeing Boone

Promise

Please???

It would be so easy to ignore her messages. Pretend I didn't get them. But I read them, and she'll see that. Against my heart telling me what I need is my bed and a gallon of ice cream, I say yes.

A glance in the mirror reveals splotchy skin, mascara smudges, and pink-tinged eyes.

I'm not fit for other humans or being in public. If I show up looking like a train wreck, Shari will ask questions.

I send one more text.

Make it 45. Need to change

I PARK AT the curb in front of my complex instead of driving around to the back. Passing Jim's screen door, I shout, "Hello!"

and wave. His TV blares *The People's Court*, so I know he's home. I don't wait for a response. He often naps with the TV at top volume.

Inside my apartment, I strip off my work clothes, leaving a trail behind me in the hall to the bathroom. Hot water pours over my head and down my back in the shower. A smaller tsunami of grief washes over me and I rest my forehead against the pink tile.

I can cancel on Shari. Stay here. Maybe stand in the shower until the water runs cold.

I think about Jim. He's alone. In fact, he's the older man version of me. And he doesn't seem miserable. He has his routine and the guys down at the American Legion. Nothing wrong with his life.

The difference is he's lived a whole existence before now. He has stories and memories. A lifetime behind him.

I shiver as the water turns tepid.

Still a hot mess, but at least I'm clean now. Wrapping a towel around my chest, I quickly dry my hair with another towel. I find eye drops in the medicine cabinet and decide to skip makeup. More crying is highly likely.

Ignoring the trail of dirty clothes, I step into my bedroom to find something to wear. My bed is a siren in the corner, luring me with soft pillows and the promise of sleep.

I could lie down for a minute or two. Let my hair dry more.

Fighting the pull to nap, I pick out a soft T-shirt dress from the closet. Just because it's from the sleepwear section at Target doesn't mean I can't wear it as a dress.

Once I'm dressed, I glance at the clock on my nightstand. Plenty of time to lie down for a minute.

Twenty-Two

I JOLT AWAKE.

Blue light flashes through the dim, late afternoon light in my bedroom and eerie Theremin music fills the room. For a second, my mind goes to UFOs. Because of course it does.

Then I realize my phone alarm is going off, muffled by my pillow. Fully awake, I decide the lights are from a police car on the street.

The clock says I've only been asleep for an hour, but my body feels heavy like I've slept for days with the flu.

I'm super late to meet Shari.

Peeking out the bedroom curtain, I spy a police car as I suspected. Parked in front of the cruiser is an ambulance.

Dread settles on my chest like a heavy weight. Given there are only three units in this complex, and I'm fine, that means it's either Jim or Wanda. Unless it's for one of the neighbors on the other side of the street. I cling to that hope as I dash through my apartment and outside.

The screen door to Jim's apartment is propped open, and an EMT is walking inside, donning rubber gloves.

Oh no. *No no no.*

"Is he okay?" I practically leap across the courtyard to get to Jim's.

"Are you family?" the EMT asks. He's a young, blond guy with round, ruddy-colored cheeks that give him a baby face.

"No, I'm his neighbor. He doesn't have any family."

"Are you listed as a medical proxy? Or have a Power of Attorney?" Turning his back to the door, he blocks me from entering into the living room.

"I don't know if he has one." I'm ducking and weaving in front of him like we're in a boxing match.

He stands still, managing to prevent me from seeing past him.

"I can't let you in, miss. We need to do our jobs and you'll be in the way." His answer is a definitive no.

It sounds bad, really bad. Jim is alone like me. Who's going to go with him to the hospital and help him? If only family can visit, he won't have anyone.

Tears spill down my face again as I jog over to Wanda's. Pounding on the door, I call her name. There's no way she can't hear me if she's home. When I don't get an answer, I look for her car in her spot. It's not there.

Not wanting to leave Jim alone, I go back to my casita and sit on the small step where I can keep an eye on the whole complex.

I'm not a religious person but for some reason, I begin to recite the Lord's Prayer from memory. I might not have all the verses in the correct order, but it feels right to say it while I wait.

A few more men go in and out of the apartment. One is a police officer, and another guy is also an EMT. I'm not sure about the third because he's not wearing a uniform. Finally, the baby-faced guy I first spoke to brings a gurney from the ambulance to the door.

That's got to be a good sign.

After some maneuvering, he manages to get it through the door.

I stand, waiting to let Jim know I'm here for him and I'll be at the hospital, too. From the time I spent in hospitals when my mom was sick, I know I can occupy a chair in a waiting room for hours without anyone bothering me. The doctors might not give me medical information, but they won't kick me out for waiting.

The police officer is the first to exit. He gives me a nod that is neither sad nor happy. Walking to his car, he speaks into the mic on his uniform. The man in plain clothes meets him at the car and they shake hands.

A few seconds later, Baby Face backs out of the door, pulling the gurney over the threshold while his partner pushes from the other end.

I take a step forward, ready to speak to Jim.

But when I see the sheet pulled all the way over his head, I freeze.

A weak sob obstructs my throat. Unable to take a deep breath, I crumple to the ground.

"I'm so sorry for your loss," baby-faced EMT tells me in a professional monotone. "He never regained consciousness. The police will notify the landlord to come lock up the apartment."

The words make sense, but I can't comprehend the meaning behind them.

Still crying, but not sobbing, I quietly observe them wheel Jim away.

I'm still sitting on the step in front of my door when Wanda comes home.

Seeing me there, she runs over. Her eyes widen when she sees Jim's open door and empty chair.

"What happened?"

I try to speak the words, but my throat keeps closing.

"Oh, sweetheart." Sitting next to me, she envelops me in her arms and her sweet, floral scent. "It's going to be okay. He's too stubborn to die."

"He's not," I finally manage to choke out. "He died. I should've checked on him when I walked by earlier, but I was too caught up in my own head."

Her tears join mine. "You should've called me when you found him."

I stiffen. "I didn't find him. The EMTs were here and working on him when I woke up from a nap."

"He must've pushed his alert button." Wanda squeezes my hand.

The explanation only makes me feel worse. He was suffering enough to call for help and I was a dozen yards away, oblivious.

The parallels to my dad hit me like a kick to the stomach.

"Breathe, sweetie." Wanda's voice sounds far away. "Put your head between your knees."

She sounds like she's underwater, but I'm the one drowning and can't get oxygen into my lungs.

Following her instructions, I lean forward.

The darkness continues to encroach as I struggle to inhale. Wanda rubs circles on my back until my breathing normalizes.

"You're okay," she speaks in a soothing voice. "I've got you."

My tears return harder than before at those two sentences. Boone said the same words when he found me in the storm.

"Lucy?" someone calls my name.

I lift my head at the familiar voice and see Shari standing in the middle of the courtyard.

Seeing my face, she rushes over to us.

"What happened? I called and sent a hundred texts when you didn't show up. Are you okay? Was it something Boone did? Do I need to get a shovel?" Her words fly out of her. "Hi, I'm Shari."

Wanda manages a weak laugh. "I'm Wanda. And I like the way you think."

I forgot about meeting her tonight.

"My neighbor died." I point at Jim's casita.

Shari crouches in front of me and Wanda. "I'm so sorry. Did

you know him well?"

I think about her question. "Not really. We talked occasionally and I made him cookies sometimes."

"I'm so sorry," she repeats.

"Nothing to be done about it now," Wanda says. "I'm going to lock up his place, then have some tequila. If you want to join me, good. If you don't, I understand."

She pats my knee, then stands.

Shari takes her place next to me. "Want me to stay with you?"

Resting my head on her shoulder, I shake my head no. "It's been a really shitty day and I think I need to go to sleep for a week. Maybe then I'll wake up and feel okay."

"You can sleep and I'll hang out in case you change your mind. How does that sound?" She leans her cheek on the top of my head.

"It's really sweet of you, but my couch is old and uncomfortable." I think about the spring poking Boone and suddenly wish he was here instead of his sister. "Please don't tell Boone. I . . . I would prefer it if he doesn't know about Jim."

Something tells me Boone would be here in minutes if he knew I was hurt. Even the last time I saw him, when he was a complete and utter asshole, he still stayed with me until he knew I'd be safe.

Rubbing my eyes, sleep settles heavy in my body. I feel a million years old and completely empty.

"Promise you'll call or text if you need anything. Or you wake up at three and want someone to be here. You don't have to be sad alone, Lucy."

I nod and shift so I can stand up. "Thanks."

She also rises, brushing off her bottom. "I'm going to call you in the morning. If you don't want to talk, text me back so I know you're okay. Otherwise, I'll be on your doorstep again."

One more tight hug later she leaves.

If grief had an official holiday, today would be the day.

I notice the glow of the full moon rising over Jim's roof.

We send people to the moon, but we can't cure cancer, heal broken lungs, or restore memories.

I flip off the glowing disk. Sadly, it doesn't help me feel better. It's not the moon's fault.

Memories from when I was little float into focus as I stare up at the sky.

Images of Dad and I in his car, driving at night, especially during warm summer nights with the windows down and rock music playing on the car's stereo.

Neither of us cared where we went or if we drove around in circles, being in the car was special. Something about the glow of the dashboard, headlights illuminating the dark, made the time together feel magical. Like we were the last people on Earth. Some nights he'd pretend we were in a spaceship, flying through the stars.

And at some point during all of our drives, he'd ask if I could see the moon.

"I see the moon and the moon sees me," he'd say.

"No, Daddy, I see the moon, so the moon sees me," I'd argue back.

"If you see the moon, you'll see me," he'd sing to me. "The light of the stars shine on me, let them shine on you, my love."

Even now, when I see the moon, I think of those drives.

Returning to the step outside of my front door, I gaze up at the sky, indigo to the east, still bright with violet and red in the west as the sun sets.

"I see the moon," I whisper. "Do you see me?"

Twenty-Three

FOUR DAYS LATER, I pull myself together. I manage to take a shower and put on fresh clothes that aren't the leggings and Boone's shirt I've lived in for the past three days.

Per her request, I've checked in with Shari a couple times a day. Wanda's stopped by with food from the diner after her shifts. No word about how much work I've missed lately, so I assume I still have a job. At this point, I'm afraid to talk to Tony. He might fire me for being a flake. I'm also avoiding the diner in case Boone's decided to return to his regular schedule.

It's been two weeks since the scene at Pete's and I haven't seen or heard from him.

I know I asked Shari to not talk about me, but I wonder if the warning was even necessary.

Deciding that I need to get out of my apartment, I drive into downtown. Without a set agenda, I circle Main Street and look for parking. I can window shop the tourist stores for a while. Little green aliens plastered on boxers, mugs, hats, and bras will be a good distraction from my woes.

When I don't instantly find a parking spot, I keep driving north, passing the spaceship-shaped McDonald's and the cutout of a woman holding a pie while she welcomes a flying saucer full of green aliens.

I wonder what kind of pie she made for them.

Leaving the last buildings of Roswell behind me, I hit the interstate. Jim's death has me thinking about my dad. I'm mourning both men, and pissed I never got to say good-bye to either of them. It's time to come to terms with this abduction bullshit that brought me to New Mexico in the first place.

Utility poles break up the endless flatness of the grasslands flanking the road. After passing mile marker one-thirty-three, I pull off the road, sending a spray of dust and gravel into the air from my tires. A semi roars past me, buffeting my car with wind. As far off the highway as I can be without getting myself stuck in the ditch, I slow down to make the sharp turn onto the narrow dirt road. A hand-painted white sign tells me I'm in the right place. Passing through a gate, my wheels clunk over the cattle grate.

Bouncing down the dusty, red dirt road, I head west toward the Capitan Mountains in the distance. A few miles later, I come to a parking area with a small shed and tall, red stone rectangles marking a path.

After triple-checking my surroundings, I open the door and step out.

What do I think is going to transpire? Best case scenario, nothing. Worst case, my search for answers is somehow answered. Or the other way around, depending on the outcome.

I'd like to think of aliens as the benevolent, long-lived glow worms from *Cocoon*, but I'm doubtful.

Aliens aren't little green men and they're not E.T. or whatshis-face from *American Dad*. Not the angry bitch mother as portrayed in *Alien*. They aren't blue-skinned sex gods or short, gray men with probing fetishes. Nor the goofball horn dogs from the eighties classic, *Earth Girls are Easy*, aka intergalactic slut shaming. For what it's worth, I totally thought Jeff Goldblum was super buff and completely believable as an alien in love. Although Boone is ten times as handsome as Mr. Goldblum at his hottest. Maybe Boone should play the sexy alien if they ever do a remake.

Great, now I'm casting Boone in alien movies. I'm not sure he wants to give up his life as millionaire for a shot at fame in Hollywood.

I'm the mayor of Crazyopolis.

Evidenced by my current location, I am willingly tromping through the desert in an area populated by scorpions, snakes, and ranchers with guns and low tolerance for alien conspiracy theorists. I'm not even sure what I expect to find at the crash site that's been scoured by the army, FBI, local sheriffs, and multiple generations of obsessive truth seekers.

Ahead, I can see a rocky ridge where a spacecraft from a far-away galaxy may or may not have landed. Faded flags mark two spots on the cliff.

That's it.

Wind whips my hair around my face as I stand still, waiting for some sign or feeling to tell me this place is special. I'm ready for answers.

There's no moon in the sky for me to talk to, so I speak to the emptiness.

"If aliens are real and they kidnapped my dad, give me a sign," I shout.

Nothing happens.

A pair of turkey vultures circle off in the distance.

"Is that my sign? We all die and become carrion?"

I wait for a better sign.

Nothing comes, so I ask another question like I'm standing at a wishing well instead of a rocky outcrop.

"What am I meant to do with my life?" I yell into the silence.

Besides the whistle of the wind through the grasses, I'm alone.

"Thanks for the reminder," I shout, flipping off the sky.

The truth may be out there somewhere, but it's not here.

GIVING UP ON a sign from the universe, I drive back into town.

I press the buzzer at the Center, fully expecting to be ignored.

"Lucy?" Zed's disembodied voice squawks from the intercom.

I face the camera and wave. "The prodigal daughter returns."

He buzzes me through the door.

Halfway up the stairs, I know this is a bad decision. I have zero interest in scanning firsthand accounts of unexplainable phenomena. Nor do I want to be lectured about responsibility and gratitude. I pause and debate turning around before I have to face Zed.

"Why are you taking so long?" He appears at the top of the staircase. "Are you not taking Zumba classes anymore?"

"You remember me mentioning that?" I gape at him in surprise.

"I pay attention more than you give me credit for." He disappears from view. "If you decide to join me, I promise I'll be nice."

I'm here, I might as well do what I came to do.

He's sitting at his desk by the time I enter the room. His very neat desk.

"Where are all your files and top secret folders?" I scan the empty desktop and floor for the usual stacks.

"I did some spring cleaning." His chair squeaks when he leans back too far.

"It's August."

"End of winter in the southern hemisphere."

I'm not buying his explanation, but I take a seat opposite him. "I probably owe you an apology for my outburst."

"You're not the first to freak out on me. This life isn't easy." He rests his hands on the top of his head. "Feeling better?"

Inhaling a deep breath, I fight back the tears. "Having a small nervous breakdown, but otherwise my health is good. My neighbor, Jim, died."

"I'm sorry. You want to talk about it?" he asks, dropping his hands and leaning forward.

"Are you a therapist now?" I respond, sarcastically.

"Former psychologist, actually."

My mouth drops open again.

"What shocks you the most? The profession or that I had a career before doing this work?"

"Both? I always figured you lived with your mother." I cringe. "Sorry."

"Some stereotypes exist for a reason." He shrugs off the insult.

"Why do you do this?" I gesture around the perimeter of the room.

"After years of listening to people complain about their relationships and how awful their lives are, I started wondering what the point of it all is. There must be something bigger out there. Guess I fell down a rabbit hole."

"And you believe all of this?" I need to believe he does.

"I do. The more I started digging, the less the official stories made sense. I wanted to find as many anomalies as I could to counteract the truth we're spoon-fed all of our lives."

"And the paranoia?"

"Justified. Big Brother is real, and always watching. Hell, people don't even realize how much of their privacy and life they happily hand over to the government. Siri, Alexa, Google. They're all listening, watching, tracking us. Manipulating us with algorithms. We're living in a sci-fi novel."

There's the Zed I know.

Surprisingly, he cuts himself off mid rant. "You didn't come back to hear my thoughts on the world."

"No."

"Still looking for answers about your dad?"

"I'm trying to move forward, but I'm feeling more lost than ever. I've spent my whole life both doubting and wanting to believe there's a grand scheme behind his disappearance. Now I'm not sure I'll ever get answers."

"Pretty scary stuff. Living in a world of infinite possibilities. Are you okay with not knowing?"

Pressing my lips together, I think about his question for a moment. "I guess I'll have to be."

"If you think about it, you've been living most of your life with this uncertainty. Do you want the truth or do you want to be happy? And can you accept the two may not exist in the same reality?"

After digesting his words of wisdom, I answer, "I think I choose happiness."

"Now you're at a crossroads. You don't have to continue down the same path you've been on."

"When did you get so wise, Zed?"

"Woke up one morning and stopped buying into bullshit."

I laugh at his passion, knowing it's not mine. "Speaking of crossroads and paths, I went out to the UFO crash site earlier today."

"Find what you were looking for?"

"Nope."

"You go to the real one or the 'official' site off of 285 past mile marker one-thirty-three?" he asks, lifting his eyebrows.

"The sign said official." From his expression, I already know I've gone to the wrong place.

"Lucy." His voice is full of disappointment. "have you learned nothing from me? Official is code for cover up."

"Do you mean the debris field? I've been there before," I try to recover.

"More like field of planted evidence." He rolls his eyes. "Hold on."

He spins his chair around and pulls a long tube off the mostly empty shelf.

"I tried to show you this during our last chat, but you left." He unrolls several maps and charts. "See this? You were over here."

I follow where he points. A red circle has been drawn around the "official" site. Two more circles form a triangle on the map. "This is the debris field, but what's this area?"

"Some call it Boy Scout Mountain. Others know it by the ranch owner's name. My people refer to it as the one, true crash site." He jabs his finger on the third circle.

"What's the ranch name?" I ask, a strange certainty settling into my bones. "Never mind, just tell me how to get there."

Twenty-Four

HEADING WEST OUT of Roswell, I drive into the foothills of the Capitan range. Dark rain clouds block the sun, turning afternoon to evening dusk.

I flip on my headlights as the light fades.

Following Zed's instructions rather than using the map feature on my phone, I turn off the main road before reaching the town of Hondo. Oblivious how close I was to the truth, I drove right by this turn on my way down from Capitan last week.

The narrow county road twists farther into the mountains. Along the road, fencing marks private property and a few ranch homes break up the landscape.

Among a small grove of mesquite trees, a sign declares I've reached Arabella. Below it is another sign warning about a primitive road for the next six miles.

"Huh, wonder what that means?" I ask myself out loud, because apparently I talk to myself now.

The pavement abruptly ends and my car jolts when it hits the rocky dirt.

"Thanks for answering my question," I tell no one.

According to Zed's directions, I'm right on track.

To my left, thunder flashes in the sky, illuminating a triangular mountain peak. *Must be getting close.*

Fencing continues to run alongside the road, but houses and other structures peter out.

Static overtakes my radio station and I hit the other presets, finding the same problem with each of them. I hit the scan button and the radio flips through numbers in a loop.

"Must be the mountains." I turn off the radio.

Talking to myself helps with my nerves as raindrops splash on my windshield.

"No big deal. Just a thunderstorm. Been in plenty. Wipers activated."

With no radio playing, I can hear the thunder rumbling and try to count the time between flashes of lightning and the clap of sound. "One one-thousand, two one-thousand, three one-thousand, four one-thousand . . ."

Boom.

I peer at the sky out of my side window, watching for the next bolt of thunder. My tire hits a bump, drawing my attention back to the road.

I slam my brakes, pumping my foot to stop the car.

Directly ahead of me, the dirt is gone. No more road.

It disappears into a void. The only thing between me and certain death is a rustic "X" made of crossed pine logs. A single orange flag flutters in the wind. Definitely not the world's strongest barricade.

"Why would Zed send me out here if there's no road? Does he expect me to hike into the wilderness on my own? With the snakes and the scorpions and gun toting ranch owners?" I lean forward, trying to see through the rain. My wipers are at top speed and they're not able to keep up with the deluge as I focus on the gap in the surface of the earth.

"It's a sinkhole," I whisper.

My headlights show there's land up ahead, so I'm not at the edge of a cliff. The hole has swallowed the road and a few dozen yards on either side. Barbed wire fencing cuts across the road, marking the border of someone's property. It disappears at the edge of the hole.

I'm pretty sure I didn't get lost. I haven't made any turns since the pavement ended. No wrong forks in the road to take.

I pick up my phone to call Zed. "No service. Of course." Tears of frustration burn behind my lids.

Staring out through the rain at the sinkhole, I decide to wait for the storm to pass.

Then I'll get out and explore the area to see if I can continue.

I'm fine. Sitting alone at the edge of a sinkhole, in a storm.

Alone.

In the middle of nowhere.

Only Zed knows where I am.

Maybe it's a practical joke. Get the mark to drive herself out to the middle of nowhere based on a random map with red circles.

My eyes shift side to side as I contemplate Zed wanting to off me for quitting my semi-fake internship.

How far would he go to protect his secret work? Why were all his files and folders gone?

Who is Zed really? I don't even know his last name.

Zed, if that is even his name, seemed genuinely concerned about me today.

Maybe the Center was a front, and I am a naïve dupe.

A front for what though?

Sex trafficking would be the obvious answer.

Too horrible to even contemplate.

My mind spirals into dark places.

I check my breathing and pulse to see if I'm on the verge of another panic attack.

"Okay, this is crazy. I'm going to turn around, drive home, and pretend this didn't happen. Or drive up to Capitan and get a whole pie first." I shift the car from park to reverse and glance in the rearview mirror.

My foot slips off the brake and I quickly slam it back down when I see the gray truck pulling up behind me. Setting the car in park, I ease my foot off the pedal.

"No way." Mouth hanging open, I'm shocked. No, something more.

Gobsmacked.

"Zed, you snake!" I shout at the roof of my car while shaking my fists.

Boone knocks on my window.

I ignore him.

"I can see you, Lucy." Bending over until his face is parallel with mine, he makes the universal gesture for rolling down my window.

"It's raining," I tell him, refusing to meet his eyes.

"I know. I'm getting soaked."

I will not gawk at his thin cotton shirt clinging to his chest.

Definitely not.

"Stop staring and come out. Or unlock your doors and let me in." His soft tone emphasizes the double-meaning.

I click the button and point at the passenger side. He jogs around the back, dashing through the red glow of my tail-lights.

Immediately regretting the offer, I inhale his warm, spicy sandalwood scent mixed with the fresh rain and wet mesquite from the storm. He takes up too much space and air in my little car.

"What are you doing here?" he asks, sliding his seat back to accommodate his long legs. He doesn't sound upset, just surprised.

"Sightseeing."

"More like trespassing," he chuckles.

"You own the county roads, too?" I ask, dropping a not so

subtle hint I know about SFT owning the majority of land out here, while deflecting from my awkwardness about him discovering me on his property. And I miss him. Seeing him again makes my heart ache like a bruise I want to keep pressing.

His tiny baby caterpillar mustache twitches. Yes, it's back. I need to find out these bets he keeps losing.

"This section of the road's closed. If you didn't notice, there's a sinkhole across right over there." He tilts his head in the direction of the hood, but keeps his eyes on mine.

"I noticed." I cross my arms. "How'd you know I was here?"

"You're parked at the edge of my family's ranch. I saw headlights and came down to make sure some lost tourist didn't end up in the hole. For some reason, people keep stealing the 'Closed Road' sign where the pavement ends. Most people see the dirt road and turn back. Not you, though." He gives me a small smile that reaches his eyes.

I don't return the smile because I'm still rolling around in my sadness like a dog. "I'm more stubborn than the average tourist."

"That you are. But it doesn't explain how you found your way here." He lifts an eyebrow.

"Zed gave me these directions," I blurt out, feeling like I've been sent on a fool's mission.

"Zed?" His eyes widen.

I slap a hand over my mouth. "No one. Nothing. I'm clearly lost. I thought this might be a shortcut to Capitan."

"From the Center?" he asks, studying me.

"What center?" I play dumb.

"From the Ufology and Universal Intelligent Life Center. He's the only Zed I know."

"Hold on, you know about that place? And you know Zed?" The idea of the two of them hanging out is stranger than visiting seventy-year-old crash sites and expecting answers.

He nods, completely unfazed we're talking about a top secret organization. "Roswell's a pretty small town."

"He sent me out here with a wild story that the UFO crashed on your family's property," I confess, since he already knows about the Center.

"Did he?" Unaffected, he runs a finger over his upper lip. "Interesting. Never figured him for the sentimental kind."

"Zed? Sentimental?" Confused, I narrow my eyes at him. "Spill."

Adjusting the vents and turning on the AC to clear the steam from the windows, he avoids answering me.

"Boone?"

Finally shifting his attention to me, he confesses, "I knew who you were when I first started coming into the Rig."

"What?" I gape at him, my chin tucked into my throat like a pelican.

"My family's known Zed for years. When you first showed up, he didn't trust you and asked me to keep an eye on you. From a distance. Not engage with you," he says, managing to rush through the words and simultaneously sounding nonplussed.

"You were spying on me?" I screech, but softly like a baby bird.

All I can think about are birds. Maybe the turkey vultures at the other crash site were a sign.

"I guess, in a way. A man needs to eat, and I do like the pecan pancakes there."

"Is that why you never spoke to me other than to order?"

Nodding, he gives me an apologetic smile that only lifts one side of his mouth. "I failed at the first rule."

"The first rule of Stalker Club? This is really creepy, you know that, right?" Not like randomly showing up at his house unannounced like I'm doing right now. Which is both creepy and pathetic.

"I know. I'm sorry I didn't tell you sooner, but Zed asked me to keep his secret." He sounds sincere. "And if I kept to the rules, you wouldn't be here with me now."

I'm still stuck on Zed sending Boone to keep track of me.

"I have a question. More like a bunch of questions." He rests his hand on the console between us. Even though he's not touching me, I feel the static electricity build.

"Can I reserve the right not to answer?" My voice cracks.

"Lucy."

He knows what it does to me when he whispers my name.

"Boone," I mimic him.

"Ready? First, are you still mad at me from Pete's? Because I need to know how much groveling I have left to do before you forgive me. If it's a lot, I'm going to suggest we drive up to the house so we'll be more comfortable."

Rain thumps down on the roof as my gaze drops to his wet T-shirt and jeans. Ignoring the invitation to his house, I whisper, "I'm not mad, but what would you do to grovel?"

He touches my chin with his finger, tipping my face up to look at him.

"Anything. I'd do anything." His deep green eyes search mine, focus bouncing over my face. "I can't stand being apart from you."

It's a good thing I'm not standing because I feel my body turn to jelly at his words. One minute I have bones and tendons, the next, nothing but jelly.

Unfortunately, I'm still in defense mode, too tender from Jim's death and my recent realizations to melt into his arms. Instead of swooning, I say, "Jim died."

"I'm sorry." He cups my cheek, his eyes full of compassion. "How did you know him?"

"He was my neighbor." My chin wobbles and my breath quivers when I try to continue.

"I'm so sorry, Lucy." He doesn't ask how or if we were close or anything about Jim, but the words he speaks are enough.

"Thank you."

"I feel like a jerk."

"You didn't know."

"I should know these things. I want to know everything." He catches a tear as it slides down my face.

"My life's too messy and complicated. You don't want to get onboard this crazy train."

"Fuck that. No one's life is easy." Boone pins me with an intense look. "Do you see me as just another complication?"

I hate the bolt of hurt that flashes across his face.

"I never said that," I say, quickly, not wanting to hurt his feelings.

"Worse. You decided we shouldn't even date. That was pretty harsh." He stares out the rain-covered window.

"I never used the word *even*. And if you'd listened, you'd have realized that I was trying to protect you from my crazy. You don't know the depth of my weird."

He leans closer to me in the small space. "I do know you. And you're my favorite weirdo. I shouldn't have let you leave that night on the sidewalk. I should've kissed you and told you nothing you could say would drive me away. I never should've let you go. Because I was already falling in love with you."

This is the most outrageous outcome for my already strange afternoon of trying to visit UFO crash sites. Never did I imagine sitting in a car with Boone in another thunderstorm while he tells me he thinks he's falling in love with me. This is beyond impossible. I'm probably home asleep in my bed dreaming this moment.

"I was horrible to you," I mumble my apology.

"We both had our moments, but I'm not going to let fear and jealousy win." He picks up my hand and slides his fingers between mine. Neither gripping nor holding, more like he's testing our connection.

Warmth spreads up my arm as I feel the familiar spark.

"You can't fall in love with me."

"I'm not asking your permission. Anyway, it's too late to give it. The past weeks have been torture staying away from you. Every morning I drive by the diner, hoping to see you through the window."

"You do?"

He nods. "I'm pretty pathetic these days."

"Why me?" I whisper.

"Because in all the world, there's only one of you. Think of all the factors that clicked into place in the universe for us to meet. Each piece had to happen in the order they did for our paths to cross. The odds are millions to one, and yet here we are."

"I thought you didn't believe in love?" my inner cynic asks because I can't get out of my own way and accept what he's saying is true. I'm the ultimate skeptic who wants to believe, but can't.

"Where'd you get that idea?" He jerks his chin back.

"You said as much when we were in Alamogordo. You asked if I'd ever been in love. I told you I didn't think so, and think most people who believe they're in love are miserable."

"I agree with all of that, but that doesn't mean I'm incapable of falling in love. Although this is a first for me, I'm all in. I'm also confident I'm doing it wrong." His shy smile cracks open the layers protecting my heart.

What I believed was the truth isn't.

Not even close. My mind flips through memories of our time together in a new light. I even reexamine his reaction at Pete's when I showed up with Brayden through his eyes. *Ouch.*

"Earth to Lucy." He squeezes my hand.

"I'm sorry about Brayden." I feel tears prick my eyes. "I swear

I wasn't trying to hurt you."

"Do not apologize. You'd ended things between us. I had no claim on you and acted like a jealous caveman."

"I'm sorry I told you I didn't want you." Shit, now tears spill from my eyes in a steady stream.

Boone wipes them off my cheeks with the pads of his fingers. "Truth?" he asks.

I nod, afraid to open my mouth and start bawling.

"I didn't believe you. Not at all. But I wasn't going to force you to see me if you needed space and time to work out your issues."

I mumble, "I might be unloveable."

"Now that's the biggest crock of shit I've ever heard." His laugh fills my car. "And I live in Roswell."

"I have a lot of issues." I press my hand over my mouth.

He gently pulls it away and kisses my palm. "We all do. It's what makes us interesting."

"You're so normal. Except the mustaches." I do the thing I've been dying to do forever. "May I touch it?"

He stills.

Inhaling another shaky breath to stop my tears, I slowly reach out and stroke my finger over the prickly baby caterpillar riding around on his upper lip. The hair isn't soft like fur, more like a bottle brush. "That's going to leave a burn. How long do you have to keep it?"

"Tell me more about the location of this burn . . ." Smirking, he catches my finger. "Can we get out of here now that the storm's passed? There's something I want to show you."

Bright sunlight spotlights the mesquite trees and scrub against the black clouds of the storm north of us.

"One thing first." I lean close. "Kiss me?"

"What is it about you and kissing in cars?"

He doesn't give me the chance to answer before he melds his

mouth against mine, sliding his tongue between my parted lips and making me forget my middle name all over again.

BOONE DRIVES HIS truck and I follow. Less than a quarter of a mile back the way we came, he stops at a gate and opens it with a remote. When the two sides swing ajar, I gasp.

The doodle symbol, he drew on a napkin and I found in my Dad's book as well in an old article, is welded to medallions on both sides of the gate.

"What the—" I freeze.

Boone's truck pulls through the opening and waits for me. After a minute or two, he leans out his window and honks.

My mouth remains hanging open as he guides us up the slope of the mountain. I'm barely aware enough of the drive to pay attention to the scatter of barns and metal outbuildings we pass along the way.

He parks in front of a single story, adobe ranch home flanked by a couple of casitas around a large courtyard.

We both get out of our cars. He's smiling. I'm impersonating my dead goldfish, complete with bugged out eyes.

"What? How? What, what is going on?" Apparently, gobsmacked is my new normal.

He taps his finger on my chin. "Close your mouth, Lucy. I'll explain everything soon, but I need to show you something first."

I snap my mouth closed.

Taking my hand, he gives me a soft kiss before leading me along a gravel path between the main house and one of the casitas. Cactus and succulents fill the garden beds against the house, which extends back in two wings, creating another courtyard around a large patio.

"Wow," I say when he steps to the side. "The view is incredible."

Nothing obstructs the sightline from the patio east to the horizon. A few pine trees dot the hill around the house, but below it's all gently rolling grassland crossed with rocky ravines.

"We have the best sunrises. I can't wait to show you." He pauses to kiss my hand.

"It's not even sunset, we have a long time to wait for sunrise." I can't help myself.

"Always the cynic." He grins at me. "Ready for your surprise?"

"No. I hate surprises."

"Come on." He pulls me by the hand to the low, stone wall bordering the patio. "Look."

I don't get too close to the edge. Instead, I stand behind him, leaning forward to peek over the side.

"Holy shit."

Twenty-Five

HONESTLY, AFTER ALL the talk of knowing Zed and the Center, when he said he wanted to show me something, I thought he might mean spaceship wreckage on the hill.

Which makes no sense. Why would they leave it there for seventy years? Wouldn't someone else have noticed the shiny metal, intergalactic spacecraft?

What I do see is even more shocking, strange, and unexplainable.

The road I followed runs below the house in a straight line until it gets to the sinkhole. A row of fencing intersects the perfect circle at a right angle. My breath turns to stone in my lungs when I see a narrow riverbed cut through the middle diagonally.

"Breathe, Lucy." He strokes his hand down my spine, grounding me in my body again.

"How?"

"The sinkhole's been here for decades. Technically, it's on our property and we've never bothered to fix it. That's why the county road didn't get paved. There's a turn shortly before where you ended up that bypasses it. You must've missed it in the rain."

"But, the same design is on the gates, too," I whisper because it's all I can manage.

"Yeah, it's become the ranch's brand as kind of an inside joke for our family."

All logical, rational explanations. Except it doesn't explain the connection to me. "I doodled the same pattern in one of my dad's books when I was a kid, and then saw it drawn in the margins of an article from the fifties about crop circles. I drew it on my chest to smuggle it out of the Center."

Boone's eyebrow lifts. "Is that why you had it on your breast?"

"Wait, did you think I had a tattoo of your brand? That must've freaked you out." I widen my eyes at the realization.

"It was too odd to be a coincidence."

"Is that why you were a jerk at Pete's?" I ask, missing pieces falling into place.

"Which night? The first? Partly. I didn't know why you'd have a tattoo of the ranch's brand. The second time? No, that was all me. Through Zed, I'm familiar with Brayden and his demon theories. I couldn't believe you were with him after complaining about all of your boring dates before me." He twists his mouth. "Maybe we need to avoid going back to Pete's."

"Can we call that night the Brayden Incident and erase it from our collective memory?" I want to forget it ever happened. "I promise I'll never go on dates for research again."

His brows furrow. "Research?"

I sigh. "We should probably sit down for this part."

HE LEADS ME over to a sitting area in front of a large outdoor fireplace. When he takes a seat in a deep chair, I sit on one of the adjacent outdoor couches. I need space for the tale of crazy I'm about to unload on him.

He listens while I retell the stories of my life. Never once does he laugh at my beliefs or doubts. At one point, he reaches over and laces our fingers together, holding my hand to show his support.

"And that's me. I'm a waitress with daddy issues and a cynical obsession with aliens."

He chuckles. "Is that what you put on your dating profiles?"

I glare at him, but I laugh, too. "What happened to our pact about the Brayden Incident? I thought we promised to not discuss my online dating life ever again."

"Truce. Just so you know, Axl, from the band, won't shut up about that night. Says he's writing a new song about it and the working title is, 'Lucy, Are You Sleeping with Him?'"

Too soon.

"Delightful. It'll probably become a one-hit wonder. Next year's 'Gangnam Style'." Maybe I can get a job inside Carlsbad Caverns and hide in there. Apparently living in the middle of a desert isn't isolated enough for me to avoid notoriety.

"What are you thinking about?" He touches my knee.

I skip sharing my snack bar fantasy and ask something I'm curious about. "How does your family know about the Center?"

Shifting forward, he rests his elbows on his thighs. "Can you keep a secret?"

I lean closer and nod.

"As you know, Zed's focused on documenting every published account of UFOs and aliens, from a blog post to a YouTube video or a NASA press release. We're interested in the same information."

"Why? Do you really believe Zed and the rest of the ufologists are the ones with the answers?" Not once did I guess he would be a believer.

He shakes his head no. "I think the only one who truly believes Zed is himself. Staying on his good side is the easiest way to know the latest chatter and conspiracy theories, which helps us track the current feelings about aliens—the ones from space, not the humans who immigrated outside of the government systems."

"As what . . . hobbyists? Is this why Shari loves her conspiracy game?"

"I hate that game," he grumbles. "We own a lot of acreage in the area, including the land around one of the alleged crash sites, so it's important to know what the ufologists are doing."

Tears prick like tiny needles in the back of my eyes. "The deeper I delve, the more questions I have, and the less certain I am about anything. Zed and his circle have devoted their lives to finding the truth. If they don't know, who does? I truly believed I'd come to Roswell, restore my faith, and find my people in the true believers and zealots. I even imagined them welcoming me with their silver, robe-covered arms wide open, and I'd finally have answers."

"That hasn't happened." He states without hesitation or doubt. His long fingers brush against my wrist as he listens. "What if you're asking the wrong questions because you're working off of false information? You were led here based on a lie."

In my head, I curse Zed again but also thank him for meddling. "Usually I assume everything is a lie, and through elimination, I'll be left with the truth."

"You're a cynic." He grins, flashing his perfect teeth between his perfect lips.

"I'm a realist." I counter.

"Are you sure? Wouldn't it be easier to believe in the possibility of the unknown?"

"Aren't you a pocket full of sunshine?" I grumble.

He laughs at this. "You're the only person to ever refer to me as sunshine."

"I was being sarcastic. I thought you were fluent in sarcasm." I frown, making an exaggerated disappointed face.

"I am. And you're deflecting. I offered you an alternate solution and you mocked me, leaving me to conclude you don't want answers. Are you afraid of the truth?" He gives me a pointed look.

"That my father left of his own free will and was enough of a scumbag to hide himself from us?"

"What's the other option? The one that brought you to Roswell?" He attempts to refocuses me with his question. "He was kidnapped by aliens who decided to keep him?"

It still sounds crazy when I hear it spoken out loud.

"Why are you here if part of you doesn't hold out hope for aliens?" He pins me with his stare, green dominating amber in his eyes.

"Process of elimination?" I don't intend for it to be a question, but my voice lifts at the end. "Over the years, I've hired multiple private investigators, spent money I don't have, and none of them have definitive answers. When I first drove out here, I stayed in Albuquerque for a couple of months, retracing my parents' early life together. Nothing came of it. Roswell was my last option. A final stand. My Alamo."

Brushing his finger over his micro-stache, he thinks for a moment. "What about a third outcome?"

"Between aliens and scumbag?"

"Somewhere more to the left of scumbag."

I furrow my brow.

"Can you live your life without an answer? Accept that there are events for which we'll never have conclusive answers? This world is full of theories without proof. Hell, even proven facts can be debated and discredited by opposing factions."

"Accepting uncertainty feels like giving up." I have to wipe away the tears of frustration that have trailed down my cheeks as I speak. Finally composing myself, I focus on him again. He's not laughing, not even smiling.

"You don't need your beliefs to be validated for them to be real. Faith doesn't operate on tangibles. Ask any major religion.

Look at all the people who believe in green aliens in flying saucers. The government has given a reasonable explanation of the crashes, yet people still believe in the impossible.

"What do you want to happen, Lucy? To find a grainy video of your father caught in a glowing beam, being levitated into a hovering spacecraft? Or discovering he's been dead for almost twenty years but buried as John Doe? Would you feel better knowing he walked out one night, recreated himself, and has been happy for decades in a new life without you? Which is the better outcome?"

Inhaling to the point I feel my ribs forced to expand to accommodate my breath, I mull over his options. I hold my breath for a second before exhaling.

"Honestly?" My voice sounds small to my own ears, almost childlike.

He nods and touches my cheek.

I concentrate on the warmth where his skin makes contact with mine.

"Aliens." It's the twisted, ridiculous truth. "I'd rather believe he's somewhere in outer space than in the ground or still walking this planet. Because if he was abducted by aliens, that means my mother's loyalty and love meant something. She didn't cling to her love until her last breath for some loser who abandoned her and their child. It means I'm special, and not some throwaway kid whose dad left and never looked back."

He rubs his thumb along my jaw as my tears quiver along my bottom lid, threatening to spill over.

Discarded.

Unloveable.

"So aliens it must be," I say out loud, barely above a whisper.

Has to be.

The other reality sucks too much.

"Then that's what happened. You can decide what is true,

what is real, and if you believe it, who cares if anyone else does? There's no proof aliens *don't* exist. Millions of people believe we're not alone in the galaxies that make up the universe. We're all energy, made up of the same material that exists in the stars. You're contain the same stardust as I do. Why couldn't someone from a planet far, far away travel here? It's not impossible. "

Processing his words, I stare out at the valley still in the sun while shadows from the mountain have crept across the patio. A peace settles over me, like being cocooned in one of my grandpa's cardigans.

"I've been rambling for too long." I stand and stretch. "I crashed your house, and you probably have things to do or family hiding from the unexpected guest."

"Crashed? Nice pun." He stands as well. "I'm the only one of the family who lives here now. Shari's in Roswell and our parents stay in Santa Fe most of the year. Want the tour?"

Thinking of the here and now, instead of the past, I grin at him. "You have this huge house to yourself? With no neighbors? Do you run around naked all the time?"

"Of course," he deadpans, stepping closer, crowding my space. "And I expect my guest to do the same when she spends the night."

Images of his beautiful body naked send a buzz through my body. There's nowhere, no other place where I want to be in this moment. Even with his ridiculous mustache.

I squeak when he scoops me into his arms.

"I think we'll start the tour with my bedroom."

"BOONE?" I WHISPER in the fading light inside his bedroom. Dusk casts a purple glow on the white sheets on his large wooden bed. Curtain-free windows reveal an indigo sky outside. I never want to leave this room.

"Yes, Lucy?" he asks, quiet as possible.

"I'm falling in love with you, too."

He kisses my neck, right below my ear, making me squirm a little. "That's good to know. I want to tell you—"

I cut him off by pressing my finger against his lips. He kisses the tip. "Can I ask for a timeout on the love talk? I'm feeling raw and vulnerable, and all squishy today."

"I love your squishy side." He nips the tender spot where neck becomes shoulder.

Swallowing my nerves as well as a moan of pleasure from his mouth on my skin, I continue, "Please don't make a big deal about it. At least not yet. I'm still getting used to the idea."

"Deal." He smiles against my naked shoulder where he's currently kissing a trail from my arm to my chest. Placing a kiss over the spot where I drew his symbol, he whispers, "I promise to always protect your heart. Promise me you'll stay?"

"The night?" I ask.

"That's a start." His eyes meet mine.

I see nothing but love in his beautiful, strange, ever changing eyes. I've never seen anything like them. Except Shari's.

I still, my pulse thrumming in my veins, my breath frozen in my chest.

"Earth to Lucy?" he chuckles. "Where are you?"

"You always ask that. Like I'm floating in out space when I'm right in front of you. Why?"

With a shrug, he continues trailing his mouth along my skin. "It's something my family always says."

"Because one of you isn't on Earth at the time?" A funny feeling tickles my gut.

"Right, because we're aliens." His laughter bursts out of him as he climbs over me. "Lucy, what am I going to do with you?"

"Anything is possible," I tell him, laughing between the words as he tickles me.

"Believe in the impossible."

And I do.

Because I've fallen in love with Boone.

A Note about the Epilogues

TINFOIL HEART IS a story about choosing love and letting go of the past, especially the beliefs that hold us back from living our best lives. We create our realities based on what we believe is true about ourselves, others, and the world we live in.

In that light, I'm giving you two epilogues. Two different truths about Lucy and Boone.

One is for skeptics.

One is for believers.

Read both and then decide for yourself which one you believe is true.

xo
Daisy

Epilogue for Skeptics

Two months later . . .

WANDA AND I are preparing tables for the morning rush. Over the months, we've settled into a comfortable routine and friendship.

She's old enough to be my mother, but I think of her as more of a friend.

Before I met Shari, she was my only friend in Roswell.

Between her, Tony, Shari, Ray, and Boone, I now have a friend family. I'm including Tony because he's the cranky relative you invite to all of the family gatherings because he shows up, mans the grill, and feeds everyone, grumbling the entire time. He's also the one you want on your side if anyone does you wrong. Thankfully, he's never threatened Boone with the bat, or had reason to.

Zed's more like the weird cousin you pretend isn't related by blood.

I'm still working five days a week waitressing. Just because my boyfriend owns half of the county doesn't mean I'm quitting and watching telenovelas all day with Tony's mom and aunts. Every once in a while, I'll pick up a shift or two at the Burger Joint with Shari. She's offered me a job more than once, but for now, I'm good at the diner.

I'm going to look into getting my master's degree online so

I can apply for teaching jobs in the school district. Finally put my history degree to work. Use my research powers for good and not evil.

I have a little money saved already. Not paying a retainer on private investigators means I can sock some away as savings.

I've given up on finding out what happened. The last investigator suggested my dad was using an alias when he married my mother. He said for a few grand more, he could possibly get a lead through a guy he knew in the black market of selling stolen social security numbers.

I turned him down.

And I'm okay.

More than okay.

I'm happy.

Wanda pours us both mugs of coffee. "How long have you been working here?"

"I started in February." I count out the months in my head. "Eight months, give or take a couple of days. Why?"

"No reason. It's nice to see you finally settling in." She gives me a motherly look of pride. Today's lipstick is a bright coral.

"I guess I am." I grin at her. I do that a lot these days. I no longer have to fake being chipper and upbeat. I'm annoyingly happy.

"You were so lost when you arrived. Always asking about aliens and talking about crazy conspiracy theories. I was worried you'd be indoctrinated into one of the UFO cults and end up eating poisoned pudding." Wanda touches my arm.

"I was pretty obsessed, wasn't I?" Cringing, I wrinkle my nose. "And I do like pudding, so you were right to worry about me."

"When you kept asking if anyone had direct information about the crashes, I asked Zed if he'd take you under his wing. Keep an eye on you so you didn't fall in with the crazies."

"You did? Does everyone know Zed?" It's a small town, but he doesn't seem like the kind of guy who gets out much.

"Known him most of my life. We were in high school together. But he's a few years older."

"So you're familiar with his work at the Center?" I question her, trying not to stare at the smudge of coral lipstick on her teeth.

"What center?" she asks, her eyes wide with confusion.

"Zed's organization?" Not wanting to betray his confidence, I don't tell her the name or location.

"I thought he was a therapist. Last I knew at least. Figured he could help you through your grief over your momma."

"He told me he retired." I'm so confused.

She frowns and two parallel lines appear between her eyebrows. "I'm not sure. I'll have to ask his wife next time I'm at the hair salon."

Hold all the horses. In shock, I screech, "Zed's married?"

Wanda pats her fluffy hair. "His wife does my do. They have a couple of kids, too, but they're out on their own now. Moved to California. Or one of the Carolinas. I can't keep track."

"Wow. I totally misjudged him."

"You two going to gossip all morning or can we serve some breakfast to customers?" Tony shouts from the kitchen.

I laugh and flip on the lights. Wanda unlocks the front doors.

The rest of the morning my mind reels from the information bomb she dropped on me.

Boone's at meetings today, so I'll have to wait until I get off work to ask him about Wanda's version of events.

AT DINNER WITH Boone, I bring up my conversation with Wanda.

"Did you know Zed's married?" I swirl my fork through the red enchilada sauce on my plate.

"Sure." He shrugs like this is common knowledge. "Why?"

"I thought he lived in his parents' basement."

With a shake of his head, he chuckles at me. "Did you ever ask him?"

"No, because I thought it would be an invasion of his privacy. And he might be embarrassed he still lived with his mother."

"Why would you think that?" He smothers his smile with his hand.

"Because he's the king of the alien conspiracy theorists."

"Stereotype, much?" he asks, dipping his head.

I stand by my observation and he can give me judging-eyes all he wants. "Fitting. He talked about using the computers at the library and all sorts of paranoid ideas about the government watching him."

"He piled it on a little thick for your benefit." Laughing, he places his fork and knife across his plate.

"What does that mean?"

"Truth?" His smile fades as he becomes serious.

"Emotionless facts, please." His switch from laughter to somber worries me.

"After Wanda introduced you to Zed, he called me and asked for my help."

Knowing this information already, I nod and say, "Right, he wanted you to keep an eye on me at the diner. You told me that part already."

"There's more to it. Said he wanted to help you get over your missing father."

"What?" My voice lifts with surprise.

Boone carries on, calmly explaining, "He wanted to know if I could help him set up an office downtown where he could have you intern. He came up with the ridiculous The Ufology and Universal Intelligent Life Center name. I didn't think you'd buy it, but you did."

"He doesn't research aliens and UFOs?" I'm officially confused.

He flinches when he looks into my eyes. "He does, but not above the old theater. He has an outbuilding on his property he turned into an archive and office. He's as fascinated with the conspiracy theories as you are."

My whole version of events implodes. "Why would you all lie to me?"

"No one lied to you. Wanda and Zed liked you and wanted to help you find your way."

Anger slams into me so hard, I set my butter knife as far away on the table as I can so I won't be tempted to stab him. "So you knew my whole sad sack life story before we ever spoke? My dad's leaving and my family all dying?"

He holds up his hands in the universal gesture for innocence. "No, I swear I didn't know anything more than you were looking for answers in Roswell."

I throw some major shade at him. "How can I believe you?"

"Because you love me and love involves trust."

"Trust no one." I give him the stink eye. "Did Shari know?"

"Only what you've told her. She thought it was weird I was driving down to the Rig to have breakfast every morning. It's over an hour drive each way, as you know."

I've made the same trip almost every weekend since I got lost and then found Boone's ranch. During the week, we alternate between my casita and his new house in the same neighborhood as Shari's. I even bought an adult-sized couch made in this century for the living room. The red velvet loveseat is now in my bedroom.

"Since tonight's conversation theme is all about shattering Lucy's delusions, how do you think I knew about your ranch's brand?"

He drags a finger over his smooth upper lip. "I've been thinking about that."

"And?" I ask, bracing for some weird twist of fate story.

"You said your dad was from New Mexico, right?"

Nodding, I roll my hand to keep him talking.

"Stick with me, okay? Did you ever visit your grandparents down here? Maybe take a family road trip when you were little? The symbol shows up on our gates and fencing, even the cattle have it branded on their sides. Is it possible you saw it and drew it on the only paper you had available?"

I scrunch up my forehead. "I don't know. I have no memory of being down here before I moved. Mom destroyed most of the pictures with him. His father died when he was little, and I think his mother passed when I was seven or eight, before he left, I do remember that."

"But is it possible, even if you don't remember?" he says, patiently.

"I suppose it's not impossible," I mumble. "I have more questions."

"Ask away."

"Have you ever worked a day in an oil field in your life?" I'm pretty sure I already know the answer.

His hazel eyes crinkle with amusement. "I've done work in an oil field, but no, I've never been an oil worker. Most of the guys at the Rig work on land leased from my family."

"And the constant staring at your phone and the television every morning?"

"Watching commodity prices and making trades. Or coming up with clever things to say to you to get your attention. I'd type them out in the notes app and then save them."

"You did not." Wanting proof, I reach for his phone on the table but he's too fast for me. "You have freakishly fast reflexes, you know that, right?"

"I played baseball for a long time. Always keep your eye on the ball." He tucks his phone into the pocket of his shirt—the chambray one he stole back from me after I stole it from him.

"You won't show me the love notes?" I pretend to pout even though I know my powers don't work on him. "I don't believe you. The first time we spoke more than a few words was when you ordered corned beef hash. That's the brilliant opener you came up with?"

"It worked, didn't it? Simple *and* brilliant." He winks at me. "And I'm not going to show you the notes. A man should have some secrets."

"That reminds me." Pushing back from the table, I tell him to hold on for a minute. "Look what I received in the mail today."

I hand him the envelope with a law firm's name as the return address.

"What is it?" Not waiting for me to explain, he reads the single piece of paper and his eyes widen. "Jim left you something in his will?"

"Apparently, I get the contents of his safety deposit box. Want to go to the bank tomorrow afternoon with me and find out what's inside? Maybe it's the real alien autopsy video. Or material from the debris field. Or a million dollars."

"Which one do you want it to be?" he asks, smiling at me. "Until you open the box, the possibilities are endless."

"I'll go with option C. A million dollars. Imagine what I could do with that kind of money," I say, my mood shifting back to happy, its new normal.

"Tell me how you'd spend it."

"The possibilities are endless. New cars for me and Wanda because ours are old and falling apart. Get my master's degree so I can teach. Travel more. Volunteer as a Big Sister or maybe get licensed to be a foster parent to other orphans. Or train to be a grief counselor. I've had enough experience with death and grief, I should put it to good use."

"You can do that all now. I have the money." He means it.

"I imagine you do, but I don't want you to develop a complex I'm only using you for your handsome face and your millions. Total gold digger material right here." I sweep a hand from my messy bun down over my Target dress and mustard-colored old man cardigan. "Plus, I'm really in it for your hot body and stamina."

"No wonder Jim left you something. He fell for your charms." He gives me a quick peck.

My heart squeezes with the memory of Jim's passing.

INSIDE OF THE private room at the bank, I hesitate to open the box.

Boone squeezes my thigh above my knee. "You don't have to find out today. Rent the box under your name and wait until you're ready."

His suggestion is completely reasonable, but I'm too curious to put this off.

Stuff in the long narrow box is a stack of letters, a few silver dollar coins, and an engagement ring with a small, but sparkly, round solitaire diamond.

The top envelope is addressed to Miss Lucy Wesley Halliday.

"I don't think I ever told him my middle name," I say.

"Is he proposing?" Boone picks up the ring between two fingers like he's examining a scorpion that might sting him any second.

"Worried you have competition?" I pluck the ring from him and slip it on my right index finger. The small, gold circle won't pass my second knuckle.

The beautiful green of his eyes flares and he sets his jaw. "If anyone is going to put a ring on your finger, it's going to me."

I kiss him because I want to, and I can.

"Let's see what Jim has to say." I tear a corner of the envelope and slip out a piece of yellow, lined paper.

As I read, tears well in my eyes. I've cried a lot in the past three months. *Who knew happiness came with endless waterworks?*

"What does it say?" Boone rests his chin on my shoulder in an attempt to read the note.

"Dear Lucy, thanks for the cookies," I read aloud.

"That's it?" he asks, incredulous.

"No, there's more." I clear my throat. "You're probably surprised I left you anything, given we didn't talk all that much. When I heard your dad left you as a kid, I changed my will to make sure you received the contents of this box.

"We all have a stories we tell about our lives. In your story I was a side character, your neighbor, a lonely, old Veteran with no family. But I had a whole life before our paths crossed. Why am I telling you this? Well, you remind me of my own daughter. Bet you didn't know I once had a family, too. Wife left me and took our daughter. Never saw them again, and didn't go looking for them either. Figured she had a good reason to do what she did. I always hoped my daughter would want to know me when she got older, but unlike you, she didn't look for me."

I stop reading as tears thicken my throat.

Boone slips the paper from my hands and drapes his arm around my shoulders, then continues where I left off. "These envelopes are letters I wrote to my little girl but didn't send given I had no idea where to mail them. I was thinking you might want to read them to get a different perspective on your life. I can't make right what your dad did by leaving, but if he had a beating heart, he loved you. A lot of us men don't know how to express ourselves when it comes to emotions, but that doesn't mean we don't have them.

"If you're still reading these ramblings of an old guy, trust me when I tell you your dad loved you. You were loved, Lucy. The ring belonged to my mother and I held onto it in hopes of one day giving it to my daughter. I'd like you to have it now. Keep it if you want. Or pawn the ring and the coins if you need the money. They're yours now. I hope you have a good life and find the love you're looking for. Sincerely yours, Jim."

Boone wipes his eyes.

"No, you can't cry, too." I sniff and rub my hands over my wet cheeks. "You're supposed to be a rock of emotionless facts in moments like these."

"He's right, you know." Boone clears his throat.

Unlike me, a current factory of tears and snot and ugly cry face, he still looks composed and handsome.

"About which part?" I ask

"You are loved and wanted, Lucy."

"And I love you," I manage to say without sobbing.

He gives me the softest kiss, not seeming to mind the current state of my face.

"I love you. I'm the luckiest man in the world because I'm the one who gets to be the one you love."

I used to compare myself to a potted plant, but now I transplanted myself, and I'm putting down roots.

I may not have found the answers to the questions that brought me here.

What I did find in this quirky desert town is more than I ever dreamed. I've found a home, a new family, and a hope for the future. Most importantly, I've found love.

Epilogue for Believers

Two months later . . .

WANDA AND I are preparing tables for the morning rush. Over the months, we've settled into a comfortable routine and friendship.

She's old enough to be my mother, but I think of her as more of a friend.

Before I met Shari, she was my only friend in Roswell.

Between her, Tony, Shari, Ray, and Boone, I now have a friend family. I'm including Tony because he's the cranky relative you invite to all of the family gatherings because he shows up, mans the grill, and feeds everyone, grumbling the entire time. He's also the one you want on your side if anyone does you wrong. Thankfully, he's never threatened Boone with the bat, or had reason to.

I'm still working five days a week waitressing. Just because my boyfriend owns half of the county doesn't mean I'm quitting and watching telenovelas all day with Tony's mom and aunts. I'm going to look into getting my master's degree online so I can apply for teaching jobs. Put my history degree to work. Use my powers for good instead of evil.

I've given up on finding out what happened. The last investigator suggested my dad was using an alias when he married my mother. He said for a few grand more, he could possibly get a lead

through a guy he knew in the black market of selling stolen social security numbers.

I turned him down.

And I'm okay.

More than okay.

I'm happy.

"How long have you been working here?" Wanda asks while pouring us both mugs of coffee.

"I started in February." I count out the months in my head. "Eight months, give or take a couple of days. Why?"

"Seems longer. It's nice to see you finally settling in." She gives me a motherly look of pride. Today's lipstick is a bright coral.

"I guess I am." I grin at her. I do that a lot these days. I no longer have to fake being chipper and upbeat. I'm annoyingly happy.

"You were so lost when you arrived. Obsessed with aliens. I was worried you'd be indoctrinated into one of the UFO cults and end up eating poisoned pudding." Wanda touches my arm.

"I was pretty obsessed, wasn't I?" Cringing, I wrinkle my nose. "And I do like pudding, so you were right to worry about me."

"When you kept asking if anyone had direct information about the crashes, I asked Zed if he'd take you under his wing. Keep an eye on you so you didn't fall in with the crazies."

"You did? Does everyone know Zed?" It's a small town, but he doesn't seem like the kind of guy who gets out much.

"Known him most of my life. We were in high school together. But he's a few years older."

"So you're familiar with his work at the Center?" I question her, trying not to stare at the smudge of coral lipstick on her teeth.

"What center?" Her eyes widen with confusion.

"Zed's organization?" Not wanting to betray his confidence, I don't tell her the name or location.

"I thought he was a therapist. Last I knew at least. Figured he could help you through your grief over your momma."

"He told me he retired." I'm so confused.

She frowns, and two parallel lines appear between her eyebrows. "I'm not sure. I'll have to ask his wife next time I'm at the hair salon."

Hold all the horses. In shock, I screech, "Zed's married?"

Wanda pats her fluffy hair. "His wife does my do. They have a couple of kids, too, but they're out on their own now. Moved to California. Or one of the Carolinas. I can't keep track."

"Wow. I totally misjudged him."

"You two going to gossip all morning or can we serve some breakfast to customers?" Tony shouts from the kitchen.

I laugh and flip on the lights. Wanda unlocks the front doors.

The rest of the morning my mind reels from the information bomb she dropped on me.

Boone's at meetings today, so I'll have to wait until I get off work to ask him about Wanda's version of events.

AT DINNER WITH Boone, I bring up my conversation with Wanda.

During the week, we alternate between my casita and his new house in the same neighborhood as Shari's. When not traveling on the weekends, Boone and I spend as much time as possible at the ranch.

Tonight we're at my house. I even bought an adult-sized couch made in this century for my living room. The red velvet loveseat is now in my bedroom.

"Did you know Zed's married?" I swirl my fork through the red enchilada sauce on my plate.

"Sure." He shrugs like this is common knowledge. "Why?"

"I thought he lived in his parents' basement."

With a shake of his head, he chuckles at me. "Did you ever ask him?"

"No, because I thought it would be an invasion of his privacy. And he might be embarrassed he still lived with his mother."

"Why would you think that?" He smothers his smile with his hand.

"Because he's the king of the alien conspiracy theorists."

"Stereotype, much?" he asks.

"Fitting. He talked about using the computers at the library and all sorts of paranoid ideas about the government watching him."

"Who says they aren't?" Setting down his fork, he grins at me.

"Not you, too." I roll my eyes. "I thought we settled this when I visited the ranch."

"Fine, no truth for you tonight."

I stick my tongue out at him.

"Speaking of the truth, have you ever worked in an oil field in your life?" I'm pretty sure I already know the answer.

His hazel eyes crinkle with amusement. "I've done work in an oil field, but no, I've never been an oil worker. Most of the guys at the Rig work on land leased from my family."

"What were you doing there five days a week?"

"Watching commodity prices and making trades. Eavesdropping on conversations. Fantasizing about you. All while eating a tasty breakfast."

"Money, knowledge, sex, and food. At least you have your priorities streamlined." I laugh.

He adds his laughter to mine. "Man's a simple creature."

"Said no woman ever," I say, drily. "That reminds me."

Pushing back from the table, I tell him to hold on for a minute. When I come back, I hand him the envelope with a law firm's name as the return address. "Look what I received in the mail today."

"What is it?" Not waiting for me to explain, he reads the single piece of paper and his eyes widen. "Jim left you something in his will?"

"Apparently, I get the contents of his safety deposit box. Want to go to the bank tomorrow afternoon with me and find out what's inside? Maybe it's the real alien autopsy video. Or material from the debris field. Or a million dollars."

"Which one do you want it to be?" He smiles at me. "Until you open the box, the possibilities are endless."

"I'll go with option 'C.' A million dollars. Imagine what I could do with that kind of money," I say, my mood shifting back to happy, its new normal.

"Tell me how you'd spend it."

"New cars for me and Wanda because ours are old and falling apart. Get my master's degree so I can teach. Travel more. Volunteer as a Big Sister or maybe get licensed to be a foster parent to other orphans. Or train to be a grief counselor. I've had enough experience with death and grief, I should put it to good use. Endless possibilities."

"You can do that all now. I have the money." He means it.

"I imagine you do, but I don't want you to develop a complex I'm only using you for your handsome face and your millions. Total gold digger material right here." I sweep a hand from my messy bun down over my Target dress and mustard-colored old man cardigan.

"No wonder Jim left you something. He fell for your charms." He gives me a quick peck.

My heart squeezes with the memory of Jim's passing.

STARING DOWN AT the key, I hesitate to open the box.

Boone squeezes my thigh above my knee. "You don't have to find out today. Rent the box under your name and wait until you're ready."

His suggestion is completely reasonable, but I'm too curious to put this off.

Inside is a piece of silvery, metallic material, a stack of black and white photos, an old Army ID card, and the front page of the *Roswell Daily Record* with the headline: "RAAF Captures Flying Saucer on Ranch in Roswell Region."

And an envelope addressed to Miss Lucy Wesley Halliday.

"I don't think I ever told him my middle name," I say, opening the envelope and then reading the text on a plain white piece of paper, "Lucy, thanks for the cookies. Hope this helps you find answers. Believe. Sincerely, Jim."

More confused, I pick up the ID card with a younger version of Jim staring at me from the black and white picture. "I swear he said he was in the Navy."

Dead silent, Boone stares at the box.

I don't think he's breathing. To check, I press my hand to his chest. "Breathe."

His ribs expand with his inhale. "What did you say Jim's last name is?"

"I didn't. It's Walter."

Boone nods his head once.

"What is this?" I pick up the material and try to crumple it in my hand. It won't stay crumpled. Nor does it have any weight to it. Lighter than Mylar or Tyvek, but thicker. "Check this out."

He refuses to take it when I try to pass it to him.

"Boone? What's wrong?" Worry churns my stomach at his odd behavior.

With a quick glance around the room, he lowers his voice. "Close the box. We need to get out of here."

When I start to laugh, he silences me with an intense glare.

"I'm serious." He slams the box closed and locks it. "Let's go."

I follow him out the door. We don't get far before a smiling bank employee stops us.

"You're not allowed to take the boxes out of the bank. I can give you a bag if you need help carrying the contents out to your car," she says, blocking our exit.

"I promise to return it," Boone tells her, his voice almost a growl. Amber dominates his eyes and he reminds me of a lion about to pounce.

"Don't tell my boss you took it or I'll get fired." She steps to the side.

"We won't," I reassure her. "I'll bring it right back."

Once we're in the car, Boone moves everything from the box to a metal toolbox he had in his backseat. He locks that, too.

"You're being weird," I tell him, unsettled by his behavior. "Did you just rob the bank? Because I'm feeling like Bonnie to your Clyde. I love you, but I'm not going to shoot people or go to jail for you."

"I'll explain everything when we get to the ranch." He jogs back inside of the bank with their safety deposit box and then returns empty handed.

"You didn't deny robbing the bank, Boone." I lean against my door.

"Don't worry. I didn't rob the bank."

Driving back to the ranch, Boone checks his mirrors repeatedly.

I spend the trip thinking about the collection of objects Jim left for me.

Newspaper clipping. ID card. Photos. Weird material.

"Holy shit!" I yell so loudly Boone swerves onto the shoulder of the road. "Is this what I think it is?"

He flicks his gaze to me before taking the turn that will lead us to the ranch and the sinkhole. "What do you think it is?"

"It's proof the crash happened." My eyes are bugging out

of my head and my body buzzes with excitement. "The Roswell Incident is real."

"That's what Jim wants you to believe."

"I bet those pictures are proof. Do you think they're of the alien autopsy?" I'm practically bouncing as I freak out.

"The truth?" he asks, pulling to a stop in front of the ranch's gate.

"It's not out there, it's right here." I pat the top of the toolbox sitting on the seat between us.

"That's not the truth, Lucy. It's a lie you're supposed to believe."

Wrinkling my forehead, I try to make sense of what he's saying. "Why would Jim lie to me from beyond the grave?"

"Because he knows the truth. The contents of his box is his way of forcing our hand." We pull through the gate and drive up the hill.

"Huh?" I mumble.

Once he parks and gets out of the truck, he waits for me to climb down.

"Let's go inside." He scans the hill above us and the drive behind us.

"You're kind of freaking me out, Boone."

"I'm sorry. I didn't want you to find out until you were ready."

"What? That aliens did crash on your land?" I trail behind him through the front door. "Hold on, do you have the spaceship in one of your outbuildings? Tiny alien graves hidden somewhere on the property?" I'm half joking as I anxiously scan the outbuildings.

I'm rambling because I'm nervous, and I'm nervous because I'm freaking out.

AFTER LEADING THE way to the open living area, he sits on

one side of the huge sectional, and I curl up in the corner so I can face him.

He won't look at me, resting his elbows on his knees with his hands knotted in his hair.

"Boone?"

"I hate to crush your hopes, but what you believe to be the truth about aliens and the UFO crash is a cover up."

"For a military weather balloon? Is that what the material is from?" I ask, hopeful that there's a simple explanation.

"No, although the Defense Department happily spread that story as their own after the fact."

A million thoughts swirl in my head. "Instead of me asking you questions, can you just tell me the whole story? I'll sign an NDA or whatever you need."

He reaches out his hand for me to take. "I trust you. You don't need to sign anything."

I squeeze his fingers. "Then spill it, Santos."

"The official crash site and debris field from '47 are fake, but it's not a government cover up. My great-grandfather planted it."

"Go on," I tell him, curiosity sending my pulse racing.

"If he could convince some people to believe in little green men and flying saucers, the ensuing debate would keep the population focused on the wrong information. So he created a crash site with the wreckage of an old ship and added some dummies my great-grandmother made from wax and paint. You'll notice the first headline said captured, not recovered. The military was a little slow to react and start their own cover up, but the secret spy weather balloon story eventually stuck."

My questions now have questions of their own. "What kind of ship? Old wreckage? Why would he do that? Wrong information? What's the right info?"

"Slow down and I'll try to explain." He squeezes my hand,

sending a small shock of static across my skin.

I jerk away and stand, pacing. "Why would your great-grand-father do that?"

"Distraction," he says, thankfully remaining seated while I stalk the room like a nervous lion.

"From?" I ask.

"Us."

"You and me? We weren't even born yet." My brain is running a lap behind him.

"No, us as in my family." He gives me an intense look. "Protecting the truth."

"Why?" I'm down to using single syllables.

"Lucy." He uses the tone that sends sparks of desire through my body. "Think about the timeline."

"I hate that you're asking me to do math right now." Inhaling, I stop my pacing and sit on the arm of the sectional. "Your grandfather moved here in the early 1940s, bought a bunch of land. Then faked an alien crash and little green men in 1947. As a distraction."

"Facts," he confirms.

"But why? Future tourism?"

"No, that was an unfortunate outcome he never could've predicted. The little green men were supposed to be horrifying. Not an adorable little space friend to be used on every possible product."

"Other than the *E.T.* phenomenon, I'm not getting it. What am I missing?" My forehead aches from how hard I'm furrowing my brows in thought. "Why did we have to leave the bank so fast?"

"Because Zed isn't paranoid. People are listening and watching. Imagine if the ufologists found out you inherited proof of the little green men? You'd be all over the international media in hours. Do you want that?"

"Hell no," I blurt out.

He studies me, waiting for me to figure out the bigger picture.

"You said the wreckage of a ship. Not a fake prop like the supposed alien corpses." Speaking slowly, I hear the blood whooshing in my ears from how hard my heart is pumping right now. My voice shakes when I say, "Boone?"

"Yes, Lucy."

"This is going to sound crazy, really crazy. So far beyond my usual weird rambling."

"Ask me anything." He stands and walks closer to my edge of the couch, leaving a comfortable perimeter of personal and safety space.

"Are you human?" I can't believe the words coming out of my mouth, but something tells me it's the right question. "You once asked me to consider the fact I'm not asking the right questions because I'm working off of incorrect information. Is . . . is this what you meant?"

I want to high five myself for asking without passing out, or running out of here screaming. Or doing the former then the latter. Where would I go? Suddenly this house feels extremely isolated.

"Breathe, Lucy." He's smart to remind me.

"You brought me out here to your lair where no one can hear me scream."

He closes the distance between us faster than expected. One second he's a few feet away, the next he's cupping my face.

"Answer my question. Please," I whisper because he's *right there* and there's no need to shout. Especially not if he has super fancy alien hearing.

"Yes, I'm human." He gives me a sheepish half-smile. "At least part of me is."

"You can't say stuff like that. I don't know if I can believe you."

He sits back against the cushions. "You can trust me. I'm part human. My great-grandmother was human, so Shari and I are hybrids."

"And your great-grandfather?"

"Panaeon, or in the most simplistic terms, an alien. Although with this country's laws, I'm not sure if he'd qualify as an illegal alien or legal. He was undocumented for sure."

He's making jokes. About being an immigrant from outer space.

"So your great-grandmother had sex with an intergalactic traveler? A lover from another galaxy?"

"They met and fell in love like anyone else."

"Like us," I add. "Did she know? That he was from . . . Mars?" I take a wild guess.

"Panaeon."

"Pan-e-on. Panaeon." I repeat his pronunciation. "Right. And that's where?"

"Very far away." He chuckles. "I'll show you the constellation later."

"You're family is from a different galaxy? My brain hurts from thinking about the physics involved if you came from the moon. How is that even possible?"

"It's not important. No one's going to quiz you later." He touches my hand, sending warmth up my arm.

"But you look human. You have all the regular parts and bits." I'm churning out random observations at this point.

"Bits?" he asks.

"Male genitals."

"We're ninety-nine percent genetically identical, so it makes sense the bits are, too."

"Same as chimps." Great, now I'm thinking about monkey sex. I think my head is two seconds from exploding.

"Are you calling me a primate?" He looks insulted and that makes me laugh.

"Simply pointing out the similarity. What about your freakishly fast reflexes?"

"Hereditary. We have both human and Panaeon genetics. Speed is one of our traits. Empathy is another. Shari obliviously got more of that characteristic." His smile is shy, almost apologetic.

"And your eyes changing? They're not just hazel, are they?"

"No, they reflect our emotions. We suck at poker."

"Is being ridiculously handsome part of your other genes?" I have questions shoving each other out of the way in my brain.

His lips curl into a sexy smile. "Our features tend to be more symmetrical, which is apparently the current standard of beauty."

"You have incredible stamina. In bed." I add the last part like I'm reading a Chinese fortune cookie and trying to make it dirty.

"We can tap into deep energy sources more easily than—"

"Humans," I finish for him. "Me."

"Non-hybrids," he quips.

A horrible idea hits me. "Are you going to want to do butt stuff to me?"

His eyes bug out of his face. "Now is when you want to talk about anal sex?"

"Everyone knows aliens are into anal probing." Waiting, I give him a pointed look.

He closes his eyes and inhales deeply. "More lies. I wish people wouldn't blame their kinks on others."

I poke his arm to get him to open his eyes. "So if not to probe human butts, why did the Panaeons come here? Panaeonites? Panaeonians?"

"Panaeons works. The same reason any group colonizes an area: resources."

"Green chiles from New Mexico?"

This makes him laugh. "No, gypsum. White Sands is the largest dune field in the world, conveniently visible from space. The surrounding area is filled with layers of it. For decades, gypsum was mined in the area, and then small ships transported it to the staging area on the moon."

"Our moon?" I ask, thinking of my dad's saying.

"Our moon. Then the moon landing took place and we had to abandon it."

"Are you saying you're stranded here?"

"I'm from here. Roswell is home." He smiles. "But to answer your question, as NASA and other space agencies expanded their technology, it has complicated Panaeon missions to Earth. There hasn't been a return in almost twenty years."

"The sinkholes?" I ask.

"The result of greed and mining too heavily in one area. Same as the salt caverns, just a different mineral."

"Interesting." Talking about mining and transports makes this conversation feel normal. Like we're discussing silver mining in Colorado.

"You're handling this surprisingly well."

"You should see the word soup in my brain." I bobble my head on my neck to demonstrate the internal chaos.

"Ask me anything." He runs a finger down my arm, leaving a wake of goosebumps.

"Zed? What role does he play in this?" No idea why I'm thinking about him right now.

"He knows our secret. When you showed up, he remembered your father's story from his research as soon as he heard your name. And that's when he let me know you were finally here."

"Finally?" My eyes widen.

"This is a lot to process. How about we save the rest for tomorrow?" He's completely sincere.

And delusional if he thinks I'll be sleeping at all tonight.

"No?" he answers for me.

I shake my head.

"Can we at least make dinner while we talk? I'm starved."

Food is the last thing I want, but I join my alien boyfriend in the kitchen. Jumping up to sit on the island, I continue my questioning. "Do you know what happened to my father?"

"Yes, and no. I know the why, but not the where."

"The time for being cryptic has passed, don't you think?" I say, a sharp edge to my tone.

He exhales and fills a pot with water before answering me. "I want to give you a definitive answer, but I can't."

"Please tell me what you know. Anything is better than the nothing I've lived with for years." I blink away a fresh batch of tears, confusion and anger mix with hope.

"Your grandfather on your dad's side worked as a ranch manager for us for a few years early on. He learned about my great-grandfather, but kept our secret. When your dad was little, his father died protecting us when the government got to close to the truth."

My heart aches for the kid version of my dad losing his own father.

"My family took care of your grandmother and dad financially until he went off to college."

"Where he met my mom."

Boone meets my eyes. "Yes."

"You know my whole life story?" My voice shakes.

He glances away for a second. "Yes."

"This is a whole other level of creepy stalker, you know?" I try to laugh but it comes out like fake "ha ha ha" villain laughter.

Pressing his lips together, he ducks his chin. "I hope when you know the full truth, you'll think I'm worth it."

"I love you," I say. Because I do.

"And I love you. I'll be the luckiest man in the world if I'm the one who gets to be loved by you."

His words melt my heart, but don't lessen my need for answers.

"Tell me what you know," I demand.

"You chose aliens over not knowing, remember that. Do you want the short or long version tonight?" He looks nervous and that gives me anxiety.

"Short, so I can interrupt and ask a million questions." I give him a weak smile, which he kisses away. When our lips part, I whisper, "I just kissed an alien."

"Hybrid," he corrects me.

"Alien boyfriend has a better ring to it. If I tell people my boyfriend is a hybrid, they'll think you're part Prius."

He laughs and tries to kiss me at the same time. He fails.

"You know this part. Your parents met and fell in love in Albuquerque."

"Whirlwind romance that resulted in marriage and me within six months," I explain although I suspect he already knows everything. "Then they moved back to Pine Bluff."

"To protect you and your mom."

"I always wondered why they left New Mexico."

"According to my family, the Defense Department started funding their UFO threat and protection department in the early nineties. This means they were searching for aliens. We think your dad saw something, maybe told the wrong person some sensitive information. Then your parents left and cut off all communication with us."

"Did my mom know?" I wish she were here to fill in all the gaps in Boone's story.

"We don't think so. If she did, she never revealed it to us or anyone else. I'm sorry she died."

"I'm sorry, too." No tears fill my eyes. I think I'm dehydrated at this point. Or numb. Because, you know, my boyfriend is half alien.

"When she died, we thought you might come west. Hoped you would. My family feels responsible for what happened to your dad and your mom having to hide away."

"She left me a note telling me to go west. I thought it was a metaphor."

"Maybe she knew more than we suspected," he mumbles.

"What about the symbol? I drew it in my dad's book when I was little. What does it really mean? Besides a random sinkhole that probably isn't random at all."

"It's a combination of symbols. The astrological sign for Earth is a cross inside a circle. It also references a four dimensional graph for Minkowski's spacetime."

"Hold on, Shari once joked that if you were a twin, you'd break the space time continuum. I didn't know what she meant."

"She thinks she's funny. It's a physics joke."

I could have him try to explain the humor behind spacetime jokes, or I can ask the question that led me here.

"What happened to my dad? Did he leave on a transport ship?" This is the moment I've waited for since I was nine.

"In the late nineties there was an increase of UFO sightings in New York and along the East Coast. Drew a lot of attention," he explains.

"I discovered that in my research. It supported the alien abduction theory even without a sighting the night he disappeared."

"I'm just going to say this like ripping off a Band-Aid. Okay?" He holds both my hands in his.

"Okay." I bite my bottom lip as I wait.

"He wasn't abducted. He left voluntarily. That's all we know." The words leave Boone's mouth in a calm, logical order.

The revelation slices through my heart. "He chose to leave?"

"As far as we can tell, it wasn't supposed to be permanent. While on this planet, we can't communicate with our ships or Panaeon. The last transport left that summer and we haven't had contact with the fleet since."

"How are you sure he didn't wander away and fall into a sink-hole, or get eaten by a bear?"

"It's possible, but you chose aliens as the explanation you want-ed to believe. This is all I know. And I'm so sorry I can't give you more. If I could bring him back for you, I would." Tears brighten his green eyes.

"If you don't know for sure, why did you tell me the truth about being a hybrid? I could expose you." That's a lie. I never would.

"But you won't," he says, confidently staring into my eyes.

"How do you know?" Challenging him, I lift my eyebrow. My inner skeptic hasn't completely gone silent.

"I love you, and loving means trusting the other person with our true self." His soul shines in his eyes.

I was wrong about being too dehydrated to make more tears.

"Why are you crying?" He kisses away the salty streaks on my face.

"Because I didn't find what I was looking for," I say, softly.

"I'm sorry, Lucy," he whispers, his lips brushing mine.

"Don't be. They're happy tears. I found something better." I smile through my tears.

Leaning away, he meets my eyes again. "What's that?"

"Love."

Acknowledgements

My heart and gratitude belong to my husband, who listened to the early germs of this story while we were in Roswell in 2015. It may have taken three years to get from there to here, but this book would never have happened if it weren't for your love and encouragement. Someday we'll go back for more green chile cheeseburgers.

To my dad, I wish you were still here to read this one. Thanks for passing on your love of good stories and road trips.

Thank you to my family and their friends in New Mexico, who shared personal stories about what happened out in the desert in 1947. Those conversations sparked the idea for Lucy and Boone. Maybe it was a super spy weather balloon. Maybe it wasn't.

I am blessed to work with amazing, magical women who turn my manuscripts into a books. To my beta readers, MJ and Dianne, thank you for letting me know this wasn't as weird and crazy as I first thought. Thank you for your early feedback. MJ, we'll always have Monday. Thank you for cleaning up my messes, Melissa Ringsted at There for You Editing and Elli Reed. Thank you to Hang Le for the perfect cover for this story. I'm still blown away by it. Thanks as always to Christine Borgford for making the interior of the book as beautiful as the cover.

Big thanks to the amazing Jennifer Beach for the beautiful teasers and keeping me organized. Thank you to Jessica Estep and KP Simmon at Inkslinger PR; and Jeananna and Kylie at Give Me Books for your help spreading the word about my books and for your continuing support. To Meire Dias at Bookcase Literary Agency, thank you for all you do behind the scenes.

To the RC, your enthusiasm and support keep me going. To Christina, I don't know what I'd do without you. To the members of Daisyland, thank you for spending part of your days with me in our little virtual treehouse. Thank you for being my readers and my cheerleaders.

To the members of the Nerdy Little Book Herd, thanks for welcoming into the group and being a happy, fun place to hang out. Autumn and Laurie, thanks for listening. Becca, you're the best. To Benita and Tina, you are bright, shiny stars. Thanks to all of my fellow authors who continue to inspire me with their dedication to writing and this business. Special thanks to Julia, Tina, Katherine, M.E., Heather, Andrea, Tijan, Debra, Helena, Erika, Penny, Elizabeth, Shannon, Nic, CC, Julie, and Rachel. Thank you for your friendship and checking on me while I wrote this book that felt like it would never be finished. Thank you all for lifting me up and encouraging me on a daily basis.

To the Indie book community and Romancelandia at large, thank you for the support, kindness, and generosity that goes far beyond writing and publishing. To every single blogger who reads, reviews, shares and promotes the authors and books you love, thank you. Your hard work and dedication to books is a gift to readers. Thank you for supporting me and my writing.

Most of all, dear reader, thank you for reading this book. Thank you for taking the chance on something different.

I appreciate every review, message, and email from you.

Come find me on social media and say hi, or email me at *daisy@daisyprescott.com*.

xo
Daisy

About Daisy

Daisy Prescott is a USA Today bestselling author of contemporary romantic comedies, including Modern Love Stories, the Wingmen series, and the Love with Altitude series. She also dabbles in magical realism in her Bewitched serial.

Daisy currently lives in a real life Stars Hollow in the Boston suburbs with her husband, their rescue dog Mr. Fox Mulder, and an indeterminate number of imaginary house goats in pajamas. When not writing, she can be found in the garden or kitchen, lost in a good book, or on social media, usually talking about books and sloths.

www.daisyprescott.com

www.twitter.com/Daisy_Prescott

www.facebook.com/daisyprescottauthorpage

www.instagram.com/daisyprescott

Note to the Reader

To keep up with me, sign up for my mailing list. Lots of exciting news, a newsletter exclusive serial, and tons of new books coming your way in 2018. Let's keep in touch!

As a reader myself, I know how important other readers' recommendations are when it comes to choosing my next book. I'd be honored and so grateful if you will take the time to write a short review of Tinfoil Heart. Please post your review on Goodreads or on your favorite retailer. Thanks in advance!

Made in the USA
Columbia, SC
09 September 2018